Karin Baine lives in North[...]
her husband, two sons and [...]
notebook collection. Her mother and her
grandmother's vast collection of books inspired
her love of reading and her dream of becoming a
Mills & Boon author. Now she can tell people she
has a *proper* job! You can follow Karin on Twitter,
@karinbaine1, or visit her website for the latest
news—karinbaine.com.

Three-times Golden Heart® finalist **Tina Beckett**
learned to pack her suitcases almost before she
learned to read. Born to a military family, she has
lived in the United States, Puerto Rico, Portugal
and Brazil. In addition to travelling, Tina loves to
cuddle with her pug, Alex, spend time with her
family, and hit the trails on her horse. Learn more
about Tina from her website, or 'friend' her on
Facebook.

NURSE'S RISK WITH THE REBEL

KARIN BAINE

RESISTING THE BROODING HEART SURGEON

TINA BECKETT

MILLS & BOON

First published in Great Britain 2023
by Mills & Boon, an imprint of HarperCollins*Publishers* Ltd,
1 London Bridge Street, London, SE1 9GF

www.harpercollins.co.uk

HarperCollins*Publishers* Macken House, 39/40 Mayor Street Upper,
Dublin 1, D01 C9W8, Ireland

Nurse's Risk with the Rebel © 2023 Karin Baine

Resisting the Brooding Heart Surgeon © 2023 Tina Beckett

ISBN: 978-0-263-30618-7

09/23

This book is produced from independently certified FSC™ paper to ensure responsible forest management.
For more information visit: www.harpercollins.co.uk/green.

Printed and Bound in the UK using 100% Renewable Electricity at CPI Group (UK) Ltd, Croydon, CR0 4YY

NURSE'S RISK
WITH THE REBEL

KARIN BAINE

MILLS & BOON

This is Jennie's fault!

CHAPTER ONE

HEAT BURNED JAY'S eyes as he watched his new life go up in flames.

'I guess you didn't need to get here in such a hurry after all, huh?' Marko, the taxi driver who'd given him a ride from the landing strip, stood beside him watching the fire service battle the inferno engulfing the house he hadn't even got to set foot in.

'I guess not.'

'If I'd known you were having a barbie I would've grabbed a few snags.'

Although he'd been working in Australia for over two years now, Jay wasn't sure he'd ever get used to that dry sense of humour.

'Now what do I do?' he said to no one in particular. His move to the Outback in Victoria was supposed to be an adventure, but he had hoped to just climb into bed tonight and sleep. Not look on, helpless, as the accommodation he'd been provided with as part of the package for his new flight doctor position went up in smoke. The red and gold tongues of the fire illuminating the dark night sky would've been pretty if it didn't represent more loss.

'There are no more scheduled flights out of Dream Gulley and goodness knows when the Royal Flying Doctor Service will get alternative accommodation sorted out for you. You know anyone else out this way, mate?'

'No.' He hadn't seen much sign of civilisation flying in, but he supposed that was why he was here. The flying doctor service was to give the rural community medical services they couldn't easily access because of the location. Unfortunately, until he got to know anyone out here there was no one he could ask for a sofa for the night.

Marko shrugged. 'You could try the pub. They have rooms there.'

'Okay, thanks.' There didn't seem to be any other option, especially since the only person he'd met since getting off that plane was now high-tailing it back to his pick-up truck before he could ask him for a bed.

Jay spotted a police car pull up and went over to speak to the officer who got out. 'Hi. Er…can you tell me what happened?'

'That's not a local accent.' The cop eyed him with some suspicion.

'No, I'm from London, England. Jay Brooke. I was supposed to be moving in here tonight.'

The furrowed brow soon morphed into something friendlier.

'Ah, you're the new doc? Didn't know you were a pom.' He shook hands with Jay.

'Nice to meet you.' He didn't take offence at the affectionate nickname—he'd heard it a lot in the time he'd been in the country.

'Sorry it isn't in better circumstances. Too early to tell what caused the fire, but it's been hotter than hell lately and it doesn't take much to start a fire out here when everything is dry as dirt. It's a tinderbox and one spark could set the whole town on fire. On top of that, we don't have the emergency services on tap out this way, but I guess you know all about that.'

'I guess so. Do you need me for anything, or can I go and find somewhere else to stay the night? Marko said the pub might have a room?' He was too tired to get upset about the fact he was standing here in the middle of nowhere with all his worldly possessions in a couple of bags, watching the life he was supposed to share with Sharyn go up in flames.

It was probably fitting when this had been her dream. She'd been the one who'd talked him into coming out here with that stupid tick list, and without her he was struggling to complete it. They'd moved to Melbourne to start a new life together, never in a million years expecting she would be dead just over a year later from a heart condition she didn't even know about.

Those three years they'd spent saving and planning for their epic adventure seemed so long ago now. That sense of excitement he'd uncharacteristically felt as they'd made their list of things they wanted to experience was now replaced with an unending feeling of loss. This was supposed to be his freedom from the troubled childhood that had leaked into his adulthood, leaving him tied to his job and his home, afraid to venture too far from the places he felt safe. Sharyn had rescued him from that life, forced him out of his comfort zone on their crazy dates taking pottery classes, visiting animal shelters to volunteer, or just jumping on a train and seeing where they ended up. She'd shown him how to have fun, how to live life without being afraid of what was coming next.

Coming to Australia to explore more of those crazy

adventures had been her idea and he'd been happy to
go along with it because he loved her and wanted to be
with her.

It had been great in those early days, visiting new
places, doing things he could only have dreamed about
when he was that frightened little boy locked in the closet,
waiting for his father to take out his drunken temper on
him.

Then one morning he'd found Sharyn dead in their
bed and his whole new world had shattered, leaving him
stranded without a purpose or anyone to lean on for support. They'd been planning on working for the RFDS,
training in Melbourne so they could make the transition,
anticipating so many more adventures in Victoria. Sharyn
was going to be the flight nurse, with him as the flight
doctor, so they'd be working and living together. Without her, he didn't know who he was, or what he should
be doing.

He'd finished his training and taken the post out here
because that had been their plan, but he wasn't even sure
if he wanted any of this any more without her.

Perhaps this fire was a sign that he should call it quits
and go back to his old life. Except that life had been without colour before Sharyn came into it, and he was afraid
to go back to that dark place now she was gone. Reason
enough, he supposed, to carry on with the adventures
they'd planned together. At least it gave him a reason to
get up in the morning, a purpose for the foreseeable future, though he didn't know what he'd do once he'd ticked
everything off that worn piece of paper he kept in his
jacket pocket close to his heart.

'We'll probably need to get a few details from you, but

we can do that tomorrow. I'm sure Barb will find you a bed for the night. Probably hers.' The cop gave a hearty laugh and almost winded Jay with a slap on the back. He managed a feeble smile in response.

'So, the pub?' Without wanting to seem rude, he wished someone would simply point him in the right direction before he was forced to spend the night sleeping under the stars, along with whatever dangerous beasts lived out here in the Aussie wilds.

'Yeah, it's back there. Can't miss it, mate, just follow the noise.' The officer tipped his head back in the opposite direction to the burning wreckage that was supposed to be Jay's new life.

'Thanks for your help,' he muttered, hoping this wasn't a sign of things to come. The community hadn't exactly been falling over themselves to make him feel at home so far.

'No problem. Just don't leave town.'

'As if I have a choice.' Jay lifted his bags and turned his back on the fierce heat, walking towards the town lights, and the aforementioned racket echoing through the night.

The Buchanan Arms was an imposing brown brick building standing on the edge of town. Jay imagined it was a leftover from the gold-mining days of the early nineteen-hundreds, when towns built up around nearby goldfields during the boom period. Each floor was punctuated with white trimmed arches which reminded him of those Mark Twain era ornate paddle steamers. He couldn't help but wonder if the interior had been updated at any stage in the last hundred years or so.

Jay opened the doors. All eyes turned on him, and the room went silent.

He stood there like a roo in the headlights. Pub-goers froze mid-drink, watching him suspiciously over their glasses. He hovered, deciding whether to stay or flee, contemplating taking his chance sleeping al fresco after all.

'Yes, love, what can I get you?' Thankfully, the brunette behind the bar shouted over at him, her acceptance apparently enough for the patrons to lose interest in him and return to their conversations and beer.

'Lager, please.' Whilst he didn't particularly feel like drinking, his throat was dry from the smoky atmosphere outside, and he thought he should attempt a conversation at least if he was going to make friends around here.

He perched on a barstool at the counter and set his bags on the floor, facing the mirrored backdrop displaying the large selection of spirit optics available. The barmaid set his pint in front of him, the condensation sliding down the glass making him lick his lips in anticipation of the cold brew slaking his thirst.

'I'm looking for Barb. Can you tell me where I might find her?'

'You've found her.'

'Great. I need somewhere to stay tonight and Marko said you might have a room available.'

'Oh, he did, did he? I don't let rooms any more, more trouble than it's worth. He knows that. Then again, Marko doesn't usually heed anything a woman has to say around here.' She glanced over at the corner, forcing a curious Jay to swivel around to see what was going on behind him.

Marko, who must have come here when Jay was talking to the police officer, was standing with a beer in his hand, pressing himself up against a blonde bending over the pool table trying to take a shot. Jay thought he was the woman's boyfriend until she batted him away.

'Knock it off, Marko. I'm not interested.' She stood up, brushed down her thigh-skimming skirt and walked around to the other side of the table.

Jay took a swig of his beer, still watching the interaction now it had become clear they weren't a couple. Although he'd only spent a car ride in the man's presence, it was sufficient to know the sweaty, dirt-smeared taxi driver wasn't exactly a prize catch. Especially for a woman who looked like that.

'I was good enough for you last month,' Marko boasted, proving Jay wrong.

He went back to his beer, realising there probably weren't a lot of options for single, attractive women out here in a town of not much more than two hundred people. It wasn't like the city, where dating was available at the swipe of a screen and people could pick and choose a partner based on their outward appearance. Not that he had any experience of dating out here, when he and Sharyn had been an established couple when they'd arrived. Together five years, she'd been his world, and he'd planned on proposing to her once they'd settled. When he'd been with her, no other woman had even been on his radar, and now he was grieving her loss too much to even contemplate meeting someone else.

'Yeah, well, I must've been desperate. I'm not interested, Marko.'

Jay was trying to block out the conversation. It shouldn't have been hard with the cacophony of sounds carrying on around him. Even Barb had lost interest, leaving him to go and serve someone else, conversation about possible accommodation seemingly over too. At this rate he might as well get on the first flight back to Melbourne and try to get his old job back at the hospital in the emergency department.

'Aw, come on, Meadow. You know you want me really.'

Out of the corner of his eye, Jay saw the man who'd brought him to town trap the pretty pool player in the corner of the bar whilst the rest of the patrons appeared oblivious to what was going on.

'I think the lady said she wasn't interested,' he said, loud enough to be heard above the general chatter, setting his beer back down on the counter. Jay wasn't the sort to get into fights or drama, but neither was he the kind of man to sit back and let a woman be publicly harassed without doing anything. It was that culture of being passive through fear of making a scene which let men like Marko think they could get away with that disgusting behaviour.

He felt all eyes on him, the atmosphere thick with tension, everyone apparently waiting for someone else to make the next move. Marko slowly turned around to face Jay, finally giving his prey some space to breathe.

'Who the hell do you think you are, telling me what to do? You've only been in town five minutes.'

'Long enough to realise what a piece of work you are, and that this lady doesn't want to know you.'

'This is none of your business, mate. The *lady* is capable of making her own decisions.'

'I think she already made it, but you appear to be hard of hearing, *mate*.' Jay slowly rose from his barstool, sick of this place already, and the stench of Marko's body odour problem still fresh in his nostrils.

'What, do you think you're in with a shot, big guy? You think you can sweet-talk my girl with that fake British accent and find yourself a bed for the night? I don't think so.' Marko fronted up to him and, after the day he'd had, Jay was ready to knock him out just to shut him up.

'Hey, you two, I'm still here, and very capable of defending myself as well as making decisions! Marko, rack off, and you, whoever you are, I'm not into macho morons either.' The woman who'd been fending off Marko's advances wedged herself between them, clearly not afraid to make her opinions known.

Close up, Jay could see why Marko had become territorial. She was beautiful, and feisty. He could see by the tension in her body and the fire burning in her blue eyes that she'd been holding back, and Marko was lucky she hadn't shoved that pool cue somewhere very personal. It was clear to Jay she could fight her own battles if she chose to, so he backed off. Marko clicked his tongue against his teeth before he stood down.

'I'm sorry. I didn't mean to—' Jay attempted an apology but the petite firecracker grabbed her coat and bag and shoulder charged them both on her way out of the door.

'Making friends already?' Barb set another beer in front of Jay before he could refuse it.

'Looks like it.' He drained the first bottle and set to work on the second.

'Don't mind our Meadow, she's got her daddy's temper. As for Marko, he's harmless, if a bit too handsy.'

The source of the evening's unpleasantness was sitting in the corner nursing his beer, glaring daggers at Jay. He was sorry he'd given him a tip now.

'I was only trying to help.'

'I know, don't take it personally. We wouldn't have let it go too far, but we know from experience not to offer Meadow any help unless she asks for it. She's a spitfire, that one. But it is nice to have a real gentleman here and I think we could find you a bed for the night at least.'

'Thank you. You have no idea how grateful I am after the night I've had. I just watched my new home burn to the ground.' As soon as he finished his beer, he'd say goodnight and disappear upstairs. Hopefully, tomorrow would be a better start.

'You're the new flight doc?'

He supposed he'd have to get used to everyone knowing his business now in a town this small, a world away from the anonymity of the city, where he'd been able to grieve Sharyn without getting dragged into other people's drama. Tonight had taught him one lesson and that was to think before he acted. The opposite of everything Sharyn had taught him.

When they'd met in London, he'd been working all the time, his life completely devoted to helping others, leaving no time for himself. Relationships up until that point had been brief physical affairs because he hadn't been in the right head space to share his life with anyone. Sharyn had shown him how to have fun, how to live, and persuaded him that moving to Australia would be a great adventure, leaving behind the trauma of his childhood to embrace the endless possibilities available in a new country.

Although it had given him a few sleepless nights, he'd been excited for the move. Melbourne was supposed to have been the start of their new life, the base for everything they wanted to do, all the adventures they were going to experience. Neither of them could have known that all of their plans were going to come to a premature end.

Now, moving to the Outback without Sharyn, he was just going through the motions. It no longer felt like an adventure, just something that was expected of him. Instead of more big plans for working together and exploring the countryside, he was here alone, grieving for the woman he loved and the future they would never get to have. Getting himself into trouble in the meantime.

'Yeah,' he conceded eventually, resigned to the fact that everyone would know who he was and why he was here soon enough.

Barb tipped her head back and gave a chesty laugh, the kind that came from years of hard smoking and living.

'What's so funny about that?' He'd had a good reputation back home, a steady job, and he'd given it all up to gamble on a better life out here. So far, it had been a nightmare. He had hoped this would be his new start, but now it seemed he was simply making enemies. Neither Marko nor the lovely Meadow were likely to buy him a beer any time soon. That left him another one hundred and ninety-eight residents to try and befriend or risk complete alienation.

'Meadow is the flight nurse you'll be working alongside. Good luck with that.' Barb bit back another laugh as she walked away, apparently to share the news with the rest of the bar, a raucous chorus of laughs sounding soon after she spoke. With that final humiliation Jay decided to call it a night. It sounded as though tomorrow wasn't going to prove any more successful than today if he'd just ticked off his new colleague.

Maybe he'd get lucky and she wouldn't recognise him once he'd had a shower and a shave...

Meadow stomped into the flight base, ready for her shift. Hopefully, she'd be kept busy enough to get out of this funk she'd been in since last night.

'What have we got?' she asked Kate, the base manager who co-ordinated the calls providing healthcare for communities which didn't have a local medical facility to call on. As well as emergency aeromedical retrieval they provided patient transfers, primary healthcare and fly-in, fly-out general practitioner clinics in rural areas.

'We've got that vaccination clinic for the kids out in Whitley today. Other than that, it's pretty quiet so far. Touch wood.' The older woman, who'd been here long before Meadow came to work, rapped her knuckles on her head so as not to tempt fate. Although if there was one person whose head was certainly not wooden, it was Kate. She was the hub of the service, if not the building. Sometimes Meadow wondered if she ever left work at all when she always seemed to be here, organising everything and everybody.

'As much as I don't wish anyone ill, I could do with a distraction today, before I go and give that bogan Marko a piece of my mind.' She dropped the file Kate had just given her with a thump on the desk, wishing it was Marko's head.

'Oh? What's he done now?'

'Just Marko being his usual obnoxious self. I was very restrained, if I do say so myself. He didn't go home with a pool cue embedded in his skull.' She shouldn't have encouraged him last month and given in to his attentions. Now he had false hopes for something more between them.

In her defence, she'd been feeling particularly low when he'd asked her to dance and bought her a couple of beers. It had been a while since her last relationship, and there weren't a lot of viable options out this way. She'd grown up with most of the men her age out here and none of them were the reliable type, including Marko. No one stayed for long in Dream Gulley and those who'd been born here left as soon as they could because there were no prospects in the old Outback mining town. She was only here because it was the place her father had last settled and he was the only family she had left, bar her mother, who had remarried and started a new life in Queensland.

Meadow didn't worry so much about her, she had a job and a partner. It was her father's life that still lacked stability—her father's and hers.

Kate reached across the desk to pat her hand. 'It's about time you found a nice man to settle down with.'

Meadow's laugh was completely devoid of mirth. 'Don't you think I've tried? All I want is someone with a good job who wants to get married and have kids. That's all. It's not such a big ask, is it?'

Kate tilted her head to one side and gave her that sympathetic look everyone had when they found out Meadow was single and over thirty. Meadow had known plenty of girls who'd married young and whose partners cheated on them, or ran off because they were too immature to deal with having a family. So she'd taken her time, and apparently been left with the dregs, but she still wasn't going to settle. If she was expected to make compromises she'd rather stay single. She was used to doing everything on her own anyway.

'Don't take this the wrong way, but maybe you're being too picky?'

She snatched her hand from under Kate's. It was all right for her; she'd found her nice guy with the steady job and they'd been together for ever. And yes, she was jealous, but that didn't mean she was going to lumber herself with the first sweaty ape who showed an interest in her. Not again, anyway.

'I most definitely am. I'm not going to be my mother.'

'Your mother's lovely.'

'I'm not denying that, but she waited until we left Dad before she made any sort of life for herself. We were so unsettled, with Dad chasing his fortune all over the country. Gold-hunting isn't as glamorous as everyone thinks it is. It's an obsession, an addiction, which cost him his family, and does he have anything to show for it after all this time? No.' It was a touchy subject for her. Although she looked out for her father, they didn't have much of a relationship. His choice. After years of traipsing around the country with him on a whim, all their money ploughed into whatever sure thing he'd found, it wasn't surprising her mother had eventually had enough and issued him an ultimatum.

He'd chosen the gold, or rather, the pursuit of it, rather than settling down in a nice house in town. But he had made an attempt at compromise, buying land and finally putting down roots. It had come too late for her mother, who'd left him anyway. Meadow still held some resentment over that. Her father had tried, her mother hadn't. She'd moved out anyway and rented a place for her and

Meadow in the town. It had seemed cruel to her to live so close but give up on their family as a whole and she'd tried to keep a relationship with her father over the years because he had no one else, but it wasn't easy.

A few years later, when her mother had met someone else and planned a new life in Queensland, she'd tried to get Meadow to go with her, but she hadn't been ready to give up on her dad. At eighteen, she'd been old enough to make the decision to stay, to train as a nurse and have a life of her own. Staying close by for her father if he ever needed her.

Once in a while they saw each other in the pub, or she called in to make sure he was doing all right. It felt like a one-sided relationship when she was the one making all the effort, but she was fighting a losing battle against the one true love in his life. Gold. Meadow didn't think it was about making his fortune any more, it was the buzz he got from it that kept him going. Like a gambling addict always chasing the win, even when he made any money he put it back in, hoping for a bigger pay-out at the end.

'Not everyone's like your dad, hon.'

'You reckon? I've dated a few feckless wasters in my time, unwittingly, I might add. They always start out attentive and reliable but it's not long before you find out they're still using multiple profiles on every dating app that exists, or they're living at home with their mother because they've gambled every last cent they ever had.' That last one had come as a shock. Shawn had seemed perfect for her, but she wasn't prepared to be around another man who lied to her or who had the potential to sacrifice her for his vices, as her father had done. She was going to have to be more vigilant than ever when it came to her love life or she'd end up with someone like Marko and convince herself he would change. Like her mother must have done a hundred times before she'd plucked up the courage to walk away from her father.

'You've just been unlucky.'

'I'm beginning to think I'll have to move to the city if I'm ever going to meet someone.'

'I don't know… That new doc is here and he's a bit of a hunk. He's already been in this morning. I sent him over to the hangar to meet the engineering crew. I hear he's single too.' Kate gave her a wink and Meadow knew she'd been giving him the third degree already.

'Yeah, well, looks aren't everything,' she grumbled, her mood not improved by Kate's mooning over the new doctor's arrival. After her disastrous dating life so far, she was tempted to just surround herself with stray cats and dogs for company instead of burdening herself with another disappointing man. Even handsome strangers thought they could wade in and she'd fall at their feet, grateful for the attention.

She thought back to last night and the man at the bar who'd made a show of her. As if she couldn't handle Marko on her own and needed someone who looked like an action figure to save her. Perhaps he'd thought playing her white knight would've earned him a place in her bed instead of Marko, unaware it took a lot more than a pretty face and smouldering grey eyes to impress her. Like every other new face around town, he'd probably only been passing through anyway. They got a lot of strangers stopping off for a drink or supplies on their way to more exotic locations. No one came here on purpose and it wasn't easy to attract staff. That was why the

RFDS offered incentives like accommodation and attractive salaries with the positions.

After the fire last night, she assumed the new doc had spent the night in a fancy city hotel, counting himself lucky. With nowhere to live, he wasn't likely to stick around anyway, so there was no point in getting doe-eyed over him like Kate. Meadow was more concerned with having someone here long-term to pick up the slack and ease her workload.

'Oh, yeah? See for yourself,' Kate whispered before sitting up in her chair and plastering a great big smile on her face. 'Morning, Dr Brooke.'

'Just call me Jay.'

Upon hearing the English accent, Meadow pivoted to see who had come in. It seemed to happen in slow motion—the sun creating a halo effect around his head, illuminating that buzzcut she recognised from the man who'd annoyed her even in her dreams last night. He offered a bright white smile in response to Kate's as he removed his mirrored sunglasses, and a pair of familiar grey eyes homed in on her.

'Oh, for goodness' sake…' It was just her luck to get some macho moron as her new workmate, who'd be bossing her around in no time. He'd already made it clear he didn't trust her to do things without his help.

'Hello again, Meadow.' He acknowledged her with a tip of his head. 'And you, of course, Kate.'

The manager's coy giggle did nothing to alleviate Meadow's irritation. Neither did the way Dr Jay Brooke said her name, as though he was mocking it, mocking her.

She told herself it wouldn't be for long. His house had just burned down, there was nothing left for him here.

It was only that thought that would get her through a day spent in close quarters with him.

CHAPTER TWO

'I KNOW WE got off on the wrong foot last night...' Jay's voice was tinny over the headset, distorting that English accent that she already found jarring. Mostly because it reminded her of the scene in the pub last night and some behaviour she'd rather forget.

'Greg, can you isolate our headsets please?' If Jay was going to talk about private matters, she preferred their pilot not to overhear. At least this way the conversation would remain between the two of them. Greg wasn't known for tact or discretion when it came to other people's personal lives, or his own.

'Are you two having a lovers' tiff already? You work fast, man.'

'I'm not... We're not...' Jay looked flustered.

'Ignore him. He thinks he's funny. Greg, headsets, please.' She was not in the mood for another smartass man.

'I was just saying I know I was out of line last night.'

Meadow might have been tempted to ignore Jay altogether, but since there were only the two of them seated in the rear of the small craft it would've been petty. The inside of the shiny new plane was sleek, modern and well equipped for medical emergencies. However, that meant there wasn't much room to avoid people, their seats facing one another to leave space for injured patients and gurneys.

She settled for flashing him a sarcastic smile. 'Just a bit.'

'I was only trying to help.'

'I understand that, but, for future reference, I can look after myself.' She wasn't going to pretend to be grateful and reinforce his delusional saviour complex.

'I heard, and duly noted. The next time one of your exes tries to take liberties with you, it's none of my business.' He held his hands up in surrender and she had an irrational urge to slap him.

'You're right, it's not, but, for the record, Marko is not an ex.' Damn, now she wanted to know who had been talking to him and what exactly they'd said about her. She hadn't realised she had a reputation for being trouble. If anything, she went out of her way to avoid it, which was why she wasn't happy about being with old grey eyes here every day. He was trouble in rolled-up shirtsleeves and butt-hugging slacks. Hopefully, by tomorrow he'd be in regulation uniform and look like everyone else in the crew.

'Okay, one-night stand, or whatever he is…' He seemed to lose interest in the conversation, looking out of the window rather than at her when he was making her fit to be tied.

She supposed the vista was stunning, but she'd become accustomed to the vast desert planes, taking the warm red and gold lands stretched out before them for granted. Still, she thought the English were supposed to be famed for their manners.

'I have not had, and never will have, a one-night stand

with Marko, or anyone else.' This was not an appropriate conversation to be having during working hours, but she'd be damned if she was going to let him think she was the kind of woman who slept around. She had high standards and, for reasons she currently didn't understand, it was important for this new doctor to know that.

'It was just that he said—'

'We had one kiss. I was drunk and lonely, we all make mistakes, but that was it. Now, can we drop the subject?' She wasn't proud of herself and would be content to erase the whole ordeal from her memory if everyone would let her.

Jay shrugged, as if it didn't matter to him if she slept around or was a virtual nun. 'So what's the score today? I mean, what will I be doing out here?'

His turn of phrase, along with the accent, was new to her. It wasn't the cut-glass, posh tone of the upper-class gentleman she'd heard on TV and in films, but something grittier, earthier. Something she associated more with English gangster films, or Victorian street urchins. If he called anyone *guvnor*, she'd lose it. Although he was probably expecting her to say *fair dinkum* every two minutes if stereotypes were to be believed.

'Getting to know some of the locals. It's primarily a vaccination clinic for the pre-schoolers, but we'll have walk-in patients who've been waiting to see a doctor.'

'That doesn't sound very organised.'

'You'd better not let Kate hear you say that. It's as organised as we can get out here. People take medical advice where they can get it and it's our responsibility to make sure they get it, wherever and whenever we can. It's a bit like a GP practice, only more...informal.' She didn't know how to prepare him for the long chats about family and the personal questions, of which there would be plenty for an out-of-towner like him. For some people their visit was the only chance to socialise outside of their own little community and they liked to make the most of it. Usually, it turned into some sort of impromptu party, with food and drink provided by their attending patients. She just hoped Jay showed his appreciation and accepted whatever happened in the spirit in which it was offered. Or that it was so far out of his comfort zone it would make him yearn for a more formal arena, away from her.

It wasn't just that they'd had a run-in last night, or that he was devilishly attractive, which unnerved her about her new colleague. Years of living on a knife-edge, her home life dictated by her father's obsession, had built up a defence mechanism which she very rarely disengaged. Even less so since she'd been lied to and let down repeatedly by men who'd sworn they loved her. All she wanted was a stable relationship and it had eluded her since birth.

There was something dangerous about Jay which set alarm bells ringing in her head. A warning that he was someone she should stay away from. Whether it turned out he was on the run from a life of crime in the UK or he was just another man who wouldn't last five minutes out here, she didn't think it was a good idea to get close to him. Not that she had any intention of getting to know him outside of work.

He arched an eyebrow in query. 'You mean I won't be limited to ten minutes per patient in between phone triage and home visits? How will I ever cope?'

The sarcasm didn't do anything to endear him to her. Neither did knowing he wasn't a regimented English doc who apparently wouldn't be put off by the lack of structure in the job after all.

'Why did you take this job?' She hadn't meant to say it out loud but curiosity had got the better of her. For someone to travel halfway across the world and take a position in what must be completely alien territory to him, there must have been a strong motivation. It wasn't as though they weren't looking for doctors in Melbourne or on the Gold Coast, where life seemed much more glamorous and touristy. Where they had sun, sea and probably sex, on tap. All this place offered was dry heat, dirt, and despair.

She only stayed here because it was the one place she'd ever felt really at home. The place her father had finally settled down and they'd lived in long enough for her to get to know people. She'd been fifteen when her parents had split, eighteen when her mother had met someone else and decided to move away to Queensland. Old enough to decide she didn't want to uproot her life again. The three years she'd had living in Dream Gulley with her mother had given her a sense of security, even if their family had been broken. Leaving her life there to start somewhere new again simply hadn't appealed to her.

Her father had been working on the same claim for fifteen years now and, to her knowledge, had never found anything more than a few nuggets of gold which barely kept him afloat. She checked in on him from time to time but it was more of a welfare visit to a vulnerable man than anything. He'd let her down too many times for her to ever fully trust him again.

Jay adjusted the belt around his waist and couldn't seem to meet her eye. 'I like a challenge.'

'Oh? So you get bored easily?' This sounded promising. Not that she wanted to be stuck with the majority of the workload again, but if he tired of life out here pretty quickly he'd be moving on elsewhere and out of harm's way. Next time she might get lucky with a married, elderly female doctor who posed no threat to her peace of mind.

'Not exactly. Life should be an adventure, shouldn't it? What is it if we aren't always seeking that thrill of discovering something new?'

She gave a triumphant 'hmph', knowing she'd pinned him exactly right. Jay Brooke was just a younger, more attractive version of her father. Never happy with what he had and always looking for something better. It was all about the chase for him and she was glad she'd found that out straight away instead of when it was too late and she'd actually begun to expect anything from him. At least now she could cling on to that fact to prevent herself from liking Dr Brooke.

'Er...it's safe. Just how I like it.' Even as she said it she knew it made her sound boring, but she'd rather be that than carry on the family's unreliability gene.

'Meadow, you need to learn how to love life.' He shook his head and clicked his tongue like someone who had all the answers instead of the new fish in this backwater pond.

'Ladies and gentlemen, please put your trays up, make sure your seats are in the upright position and hold onto your butts. This is gonna get bumpy.' Greg interrupted their conversation to tell them in his own unique way that they had arrived, giving her the perfect excuse not to have to explain herself. Or listen to Jay telling her how she should behave when he knew nothing about her.

The plane landed with a bump, kicking up a dust cloud of dirt and debris in lieu of a proper runway.

'Looks like we're here. I hope you put your sunscreen on.' She unbuckled her belt and got out of the plane as fast as she could, inhaling a lungful of the warm air when she stepped outside. Born and raised here in the Outback, she was used to the oppressive heat and seemingly relentless sun. For those who'd grown up with more inclement weather, she hoped the novelty would wear off. Especially when there wasn't much in the way of air conditioning in these parts.

She looked across at Jay now, opening his top button and fanning himself with a patient file. Sweat was already beading on his forehead.

'Are you going to be okay? I know you're probably not used to the temperatures.'

'I'll be fine. I've already worked out here for a couple of years.' He headed towards the farmhouse, set his bag and files on the porch steps and walked around the side.

Meadow watched as he ran the outside tap, cupped his hands under the water and splashed it on his face. He scooped another handful over his head and the back of his neck, the water soaking through the thin fabric of his white shirt to leave it translucent and clinging to his torso. She could see the outline of his chest and the ripple of muscles below. All she needed now was some sexy music and a stripper pole to enjoy the floor show even more.

'Aren't you coming in? Everyone's waiting out back for you.' Noelle, one half of the couple who owned the farm, called her from inside the main house.

Meadow hadn't realised she'd been staring until Jay looked up and smirked. This was not good at all. The last thing she needed was to encourage another meathead into thinking she was interested just because he looked good. She was usually more professional than this, more sensible, and she totally blamed Jay Brooke for the distraction.

Jay could have sworn he saw a flicker of something more than irritation in Meadow's pale blue eyes before she flounced off into the house. Wishful thinking, he supposed, when she'd shown nothing but contempt towards him. Oh, so far, she'd been professional and efficient around him, but he hadn't exactly made a good impression on their initial meeting.

He'd had a slight advantage this morning, coming in knowing they were going to be working together. It had obviously come as an unpleasant surprise to her. In the short time he'd been with her, it was clear she wasn't someone who hid her emotions well. If only he hadn't got involved last night, they might have managed to get along. As it was, he was always going to be trying to make it up to her. He'd read the situation wrong, but he couldn't be sure he would do things any differently now, even knowing Meadow was not the helpless damsel he'd mistaken her for.

He followed her into the house, seeking shade from the punishing sun, if not a reprieve from the heat. It was an old-fashioned farmstead, a world away from the modern city life he'd been enjoying until recently. He walked through the hallway, lined with family photos on the walls, to the kitchen, which seemed to be the hub of activity. Meadow was already laying out the medical supplies on the large wooden dining table.

'We're doing this here?'

Meadow looked up at him with that frown she only seemed to wear for him. 'Yes. It's where we've always done it. The Bright family very generously let us use their house so we can see everyone at once.'

There was something in her tone that said, *Be gracious, just shut up and get on with it.* So he did, not wanting to offend their hosts, or anyone else if he could help it.

'Do we have appointments, or a list?' Surely they needed something to work from.

'Well, I know everyone and, as far as I can tell, they're all here. Just work your way through the queue.'

He hesitated for a moment, until Meadow sighed and waved him away. 'They're all waiting for you on the porch.'

True enough, there was a queue of people snaked around the corner and out into the garden, with the Bright family supplying chairs and drinks to those waiting. It was an unusual set-up but obviously one that worked well for the people in the area and he wasn't about to rock the boat.

'Who's next to see the doctor?' he asked the assembled crowd as he hung his stethoscope around his neck and prepared to run his first Outback clinic. Sharyn would've been proud.

Jay had been working flat-out in his makeshift office in the Brights' front room, whilst Meadow took care of the vaccination clinic in the kitchen. Once he'd got over his initial surprise it had pretty much been like any other day in a practice managing minor ailments. The notable difference being the time he got to spend with his patients. He'd already been invited to dinner with at least five families, provided marriage counselling, and had several offers to set him up on dates. Despite the distance separating most of the people he'd seen today, there was a real sense of community and he was sure that was because of the service the RFDS and the Bright family provided.

He'd heard a fair share of gossip among the attempts at matchmaking on his behalf. Most had already heard about his run-in with Meadow and dispensed their own advice in accordance. It was obvious she was well respected and liked by the locals, most of whom had known her for years. The consensus seemed to be that she'd had a rough time growing up and it had made her...spiky. Also, that he should definitely apologise because he would need her onside. Something he'd already decided, but he thanked everyone for their advice regardless.

'Would you like a glass of lemonade, Dr Brooke?' Mrs Bright knocked on the door in between patients and he jumped at the chance for a cool drink. Although he'd brought his own water bottle with him, he'd drunk most of it and the little left was now warm.

'That would be lovely, thank you.'

'There's some food here too if you want to take a break?' Meadow appeared at the door too, munching a sandwich. Jay's stomach rumbled before he could respond.

'I'll take that as a yes,' she said with a grin, holding out a plate of sandwiches for him to choose from.

'Why not?' He helped himself to a tuna mayo and stepped out of his makeshift office to join everyone else outside. Several trestle tables had been set up in the grounds and were groaning with food, no doubt provided not only by the Brights but the people who'd come to see them today. He already had more plastic tubs of casserole and lasagne he'd been gifted than he could hope to use. Especially since he didn't even know if he had a bed tonight, never mind a fridge or an oven.

'They like to make a day of it.' Meadow smiled at him from the other side of the table and handed him a paper plate.

'It is a lot of food.'

'Everyone wants to do their bit and show their appreciation. Besides, what use is a doctor who faints from hunger or dehydration?' She poured him a glass of water, looking very at home amongst everyone here. Despite the fact she was working, she seemed more relaxed than he'd seen so far.

Last night he'd been too absorbed with his own problems to really pay attention, but standing here, with the sunshine gilding the dark blonde waves of her hair and bringing out the freckles on her button nose, he could see she was a real *beaut*, as the locals said.

'This is the happiest I've seen you,' he said, when he realised he'd been staring too long.

Meadow popped a cherry tomato in her mouth and bit down. 'I love it out here. It's very family orientated.'

'Do you have family out this way?' It occurred to him he knew nothing about his new colleague, other than she had a temper and played a mean game of pool.

'My mum moved to Queensland over ten years ago. Her and my dad split up and she remarried, but I stayed here. It's all I've ever known.' She shrugged as though that was the beginning and the end of the tale, but Jay was sure there was a lot more she wasn't saying.

'And your dad?'

He could sense the shift in her demeanour immediately.

'He's not too far from here, but we're not close.'

Jay decided not to probe any further. He got it, and wasn't in the mood to share details of his messed-up relationship with his father either.

'Well, everyone I've met today only has lovely things to say about you.'

'Really? I've had every one of your patients come out and tell me to be nicer to you.' She laughed and Jay was sure it was the sweetest sound he'd heard in days. A real salve for his spirits after all the upheaval he'd been through since his arrival, and more welcome than another scolding.

'I didn't say anything, I swear.'

'I know, they just seem to really like you. Goodness knows why.'

He knew she was teasing and he was relieved she was comfortable enough around him now to do so, even if it had come from other people's opinions rather than her own.

'I'm sorry about last night—'

'I'm sorry—'

They stumbled over their apologies, only to end up grinning at each other like loons. Jay stuffed half of a chicken salad sandwich in his mouth before he said anything stupid enough to ruin their truce.

'You just caught me at a bad time. I'm getting over a break-up and Marko was being his usual drongo self...'

He swallowed down his food and took a sip of water, almost choking at her admission. 'I shouldn't have got involved. I'd had my fair share of the *drongo* too, having just endured a ride over from the plane with him. You really kissed him?'

She laughed again. 'Don't. I wish I could erase it from my memory. I hear your place burned down too, so I guess you weren't having a great night either?'

'You could say that.'

'I take it you found alternative accommodation? You don't look as though you've slept in a ditch.'

'Thanks... I think. Barb let me stay at the pub last night. I think she took pity on me after you publicly humiliated me.'

Meadow winced.

'Don't worry, you did me a favour, but you might have to come back and do it again if I can't persuade her to let me stay another night.'

'They haven't offered you somewhere else?'

'Nowhere local. There isn't an abundance of free housing here, as I'm sure you can appreciate.'

'I'm sure you could bag yourself a room for the night with some of your patients,' she said with a glint in her eye.

'I have been offered a few numbers, and I don't think it's just for phone consultations, but obviously, as a professional, I had to decline.'

'Obviously...'

'Hopefully, the service will find something for me or I don't know what I'm going to do.' Not only did he want more time to get to know the people here better, but he hadn't planned his next challenge beyond this one yet. There were only a few things left to complete and without Sharyn's list guiding him he would be a rudderless ship. At least they'd planned this step of their journey together, and he didn't want to fail her memory now.

Meadow opened her mouth to speak, then closed it

again, as if she'd been about to say something and changed her mind. Given their short history, he imagined it was probably a suggestion to relocate somewhere far away from her. He hoped she'd decided against another sly dig because they seemed to be making progress in their working relationship today. This relaxed atmosphere was certainly more conducive to a happy work life than being stuck inside four walls.

His background had already made him more than a tad claustrophobic, and though he'd enjoyed the short stint in general practice he'd done as part of his training, he'd struggled with the conditions. Being cooped up all day in a small room reminded him too much of those traumatic days when he'd barely got to see sunlight, often locked in his bedroom by his father in one of his frequent alcohol-fuelled rages.

For some reason, Jay's father had blamed Jay for his mother leaving, when it had certainly been his own abusive behaviour which had seen her off. Jay could hardly remember what she looked like when he hadn't been more than four or five at the time, but he did recall the tears and rows. Not an environment anyone would've wanted to remain in, yet he couldn't forgive her for not taking him with her. For leaving him there to endure years of physical and mental torture until he was old enough to make his escape too.

Jay's nightmarish journey back into the past was punctuated by screams. He thought he'd imagined them, that they were remnants of that life come back to haunt him, crying out with every lash of his father's belt across his body. Then he saw all of the adults around him running towards the group of children who'd been playing nearby.

Even Meadow had joined the concerned party racing across the grounds.

Among the screaming and crying he heard the word 'Snake!'

The children, bar one little boy who was lying on the ground, were running and emitting ear-piercing shrieks as the mothers tried to guide them back to the house.

'What happened?' he asked Meadow, joining the melee. She was already kneeling down beside the boy, who was shaking, his face deathly pale.

'Snakebite. Did anyone see what kind of snake it was?' she yelled to those who'd been present.

'King brown, I think,' a father carrying his toddler out of harm's way shouted back.

'Can someone get my medical bag, please?' Meadow shouted to the crowd and Mrs Bright came running back a short time later with her kit.

'Is Brodie going to be okay?' a woman holding the boy's hand asked, tears welling in her eyes.

'He needs to get to the hospital as it's the best place to keep an eye on that bite, but we're going to stabilise him first. I'm going to use a pressure bandage around the bite site to prevent the venom from getting any further into the bloodstream. We need to immobilise the limb but I want to get him into the house out of danger first. What do you say, Dr Brooke?' Meadow pulled out a bandage and wrapped it around the child's leg as she spoke, deferring to him for the last word, but he knew she had more experience in this area than he did.

'Whatever you think, Nurse Williams. I'll radio through to base and tell Greg to stand by for hospital

transfer.' He relayed the situation and requested antivenom and tetanus to administer on the plane.

'Brodie, mate, you're going to be okay,' he reassured
the boy, who was clutching onto his mother's hand with
all of his might.

Jay had done enough training to know this was a highly
venomous snake they were dealing with and although it
might not be as potent as other snakes, there were still
dangerous side-effects from a bite. It could cause paraly-
sis from muscle damage and affect blood clotting, along
with extreme pain and swelling. Although they could
administer some antivenom en route, they needed to get
the child to hospital in case he needed more. As long as
they moved quickly, he should be all right.

'We should get him into the house,' Meadow added.

Jay scooped the child into his arms and hurried into
the house. Meadow rushed ahead and was clearing the
table when he arrived so he was able to lay the child out
to take a better look. He checked their patient's pulse and
breathing and, once he was satisfied that he was out of the
woods, began looking for a makeshift weapon.

'Did anyone see where the snake went?' Jay didn't want
Meadow, or anyone else, to suffer too.

A couple of the kids pointed towards a pile of brush
and branches.

'What are you doing?' Meadow asked.

'Get him ready for transfer to hospital for observation.
I'm going to make sure no one else gets hurt.'

'What? Jay, don't be crazy.'

Ignoring her pleas, he grabbed an old potato sack lying
by the back door and a rake he found lying out front. He
ran over to the wood pile and poked the debris until a

small brown head hissed back at him. Although he wasn't a snake wrangler, he'd seen it done before. All he had to do was get the creature into the bag without getting himself killed, then they could call someone to get rid of it. He held the bag open with one hand, and with the other he tried to hook the rake prongs under the snake. It lunged at him, forked tongue flicking, trying to reach its prey.

Despite wearing long trousers, Jay wasn't confident that covered legs would prevent him suffering injury. The snake flicked its tongue, its beady eyes locked onto Jay. A couple of metres long, it could cover the distance between it and Jay in a split second if it chose to attack. If it launched itself and managed to clamp its fangs into Jay's leg, he'd have a job trying to unclamp it again. King browns were known to bite repeatedly to envenomate their prey. If Jay lost focus and gave it a chance to strike, he was facing considerable pain and swelling at the very least.

He took a step back as the snake slithered across the ground, agitated now and coming for him. Holding the rake at arm's length, he tried again, scooping the beast up into the air. It was caught between the prongs, trying to wrap itself around the shaft, as Jay carefully placed the opened sack beneath it. He placed his captive inside, using the rake to close the bag over until he was able to pull the drawstring tight around it.

'I've got it. Someone call the snake catcher, and for goodness' sake keep away from this area.' He wiped the sweat from his brow and took deep breaths as the snake in the bag writhed and hissed its irritation at being trapped. It was quite a feat for a non-native of the country and he was feeling quite proud of himself when Meadow came running out shouting.

'Are you out of your mind? You could have been bitten too. It's the number one rule to stay away from a snake if you see it, not chase after it.'

'I… I just wanted to make sure no one else got hurt.'

'There are people who do that for a living. People who know what they're doing.' She was standing with her arms crossed, lips drawn into a tight line, a deep frown across her forehead, looking every bit as angry as the snake.

'I didn't think.' He'd acted on pure instinct, wanting to protect her and the children.

'Clearly.' There was almost steam coming out of Meadow's ears and Jay lamented the fact he'd upset her again when they'd been making progress.

'Well, there's no harm done and I'll know for next time not to try and impress you with my snake charming skills.'

'You're an idiot.' Despite her unrelenting hard stare, Jay was sure there'd been a slight tilt to her mouth.

'Why do you care anyway? I would've thought you'd be glad to see the back of me if I got bitten and died.' It was an improvement in relations that she didn't apparently want to see him expire, after last night when he was certain she would've killed him with that death stare if she could.

'Too much paperwork,' she said and turned on her heel. 'Now we need to get Brodie to the hospital. We can come back again tomorrow and finish the clinic. They'll understand.'

Jay followed her lead. It was going to take him a while to learn the ropes and Meadow had more experience of the best working practice out here, even if she was a reluctant teacher.

Although her concern for his safety, demonstrated via that infamous temper, only made him want to get to know her a bit better.

CHAPTER THREE

MEADOW'S STOMACH WAS still roiling and it wasn't anything to do with the bumpy take-off as they headed towards the nearest hospital. Brodie seemed fine, thanks to the antivenom and the quick actions of everyone involved, and snakebites were common enough in their line of work out here. It was Jay's reckless actions which had left her shaken.

The last thing she'd expected him to do was chase after a venomous snake. It hadn't been bravado or a need to show off, he was one of that particular breed that terrified her—the reckless kind. Her father had been selfish in his actions, seeking his gold without thought for his family. Although Jay had acted in everyone else's interests, disregarding his own safety, the two men had one thing in common. They didn't give a thought for the worry and distress their actions might have caused those around them. Jay was much like her father in that way, acting without thinking. Doing what he wanted and disregarding anyone else who didn't agree. Exactly the type of man she tried to avoid. Except she had no choice now they were working together.

Up until the moment he'd scared the life out of her, and come close to losing his own in the process, they'd been doing well. He'd been attentive and supportive to the patients, and to her when she'd needed any advice for her junior attendees. The families had certainly taken to him and he was definitely easy on the eye. He'd taken a good-natured ribbing about his accent from some of the locals and earned respect in return. People liked him and that was half of the battle working in some of the more remote areas. Gaining everyone's trust wasn't always an easy task for outsiders but he'd worked hard today, gaining acceptance. She'd even mellowed, and had briefly considered putting him in touch with her father, who often rented out the old shearers' quarters on his land for extra income.

In the end she'd held back, uncertain if she wanted to offer a solution to his accommodation problem and keep him around. His action hero behaviour, taking on a snake without any regard for health and safety, had further deterred her from mentioning anything. She had one hare-brained male wreaking havoc in her life and she didn't need a second one.

'Well, I guess I can add snake wrangling to my CV,' Jay eventually said to break the silence, with Brodie sleeping soundly on the trolley between them.

She refused to laugh at his feeble attempt at humour when the thought of what could have happened was still making her feel sick. What if he'd been bitten and had an adverse reaction? He was the one who was supposed to be treating the patients, not leaving her to deal with everything because he'd acted thoughtlessly.

'You were lucky,' she said in the end, not wishing him to know how worried she'd been about his welfare when he'd only gloat about it. It wouldn't do any good to let him think she cared; it would only encourage him to be more reckless in future.

'That was one thing we should've had on our list. Sharyn would've got a kick out of that one.' The wistful smile on his lips and the mention of another woman awakened something ugly inside her that felt almost territorial, like a feral cat wanting to attack anyone who dared encroach on her space. If she'd been at home she'd have gone for a cool shower to wash away these inappropriate, and frankly baffling, feelings.

'Sharyn? Is that your wife?' she ventured, though she didn't see a ring on his finger or understand how a marriage would work with one half working out here on his own.

He shook his head. 'My girlfriend. She…um…she died last year, not long after we moved out. Sudden Arrhythmic Death Syndrome.'

Meadow immediately regretted the jealousy which had prompted her to ask, when he was clearly a man still grieving his loss. She knew the term was used for heart conditions which had no recognised cause and that the death must have been unexpected and traumatic in someone so young.

'I'm so sorry, Jay.'

Now she felt bad about the hard time she had given him from the moment they'd met, when he must have been going through hell. She might not know how it felt to have a loved one die but she knew a thing or two about loss. Her family had disintegrated long ago, her father merely another elderly member of the community she kept an eye on, and her mother too far away to have a proper relationship with. She could only imagine the void left in Jay's heart, losing someone he'd planned to start a new life in Australia with.

'It's okay, but you should know she's the one who encouraged me to act first and think later.' He laughed and she could tell he was lost in good memories of times they'd spent together, long before Meadow had known he even existed.

'Oh? You mean she would be happy with you risking your life to catch a snake?' She didn't think she'd ever get over that one.

'Yeah, probably,' he chuckled. 'She was the adrenaline junkie. Believe it or not, I was the cautious one, but she showed me excitement and spontaneity, and how to really live.'

All the things Meadow fought against when it reminded her too much of her unreliable father and the uncertainty of the life her mother had endured for far too long.

'She sounds like a wonderful person. You must miss her.'

'I do. It was her idea to come out here, to spread my wings. We had this tick list of all the things we were going to do. I had no idea it would literally kill her. Ironically, she had the cardiac arrest in her sleep, not during one of our crazy stunts, but I'm sure it was those adrenaline-rushing events that triggered it. It's silly, given the circumstances, but I still want to keep on with the list. It gives me something to focus on.' He pulled out a tatty piece of paper with a list of adventures written on it, most of which had tick marks beside them.

To-Do List:
  Take a cooking class
  Stroke a koala
  Surf on Bondi Beach

Sky dive
Pan for gold
Swim with sharks
Dive on the Great Barrier Reef
Work with the RFDS
Eat some Bush tucker
Bungee jump off the Sydney Harbour Bridge

'That's a lovely way to honour her memory. Do you have many still to complete?' Meadow could only imagine the tragic circumstances of finding his girlfriend dead like that and understood his need to continue with the journey they'd started together. Though she was itching to know what was on it, she also didn't want to intrude on such a personal memento.

'There are still a few—bungee jumping off the Sydney Harbour Bridge, swimming with sharks, diving on the Great Barrier Reef... Although I reckon snake wrestling tops a few of those.'

'Is there anything a bit safer on there? Even thinking about doing any of those is making me shudder.' If someone paid her a million bucks she couldn't imagine wanting to do anything on that list, never mind doing it for fun.

'Panning for gold, stroking a koala, going to Bondi Beach—they were things Sharyn just wanted to do because she'd seen them on TV when she was younger.' He tried to flatten the crumpled piece of paper on his leg and Meadow could see the handwriting on it had already started to fade. She wondered how many hundreds of times he'd read it or lovingly stroked the words of the only link he probably had left to his girlfriend.

Although he was obviously broken-hearted over his

loss, at least he'd had a great love. Her relationships had all ended in disaster, with no one meeting her expectations. It was difficult for her to trust anyone when the people in her life had always let her down.

That lack of security early on in her childhood, moving from one plot of land to the next according to her father's whim, had been followed by her mother's decision to end their marriage when they had eventually settled somewhere. She was always afraid that everyone was going to leave, or do something to ruin any feeling of security. It didn't make relationships easy when she couldn't let herself fully trust her partner. Not helped when her instincts had been proven right thus far, and past boyfriends had validated that need to protect herself first. She couldn't imagine any of them carrying out her wishes once she was gone, when they hadn't managed during her lifetime. Jay must have loved his Sharyn very much and she felt bad that he had to do the rest of this on his own.

Meadow yawned as she poured herself a cup of coffee. The early night she'd planned last night had eluded her, her mind and conscience keeping her awake long into the night. Neither she nor Jay had left the hospital until Brodie's parents arrived to be with him. Since there was no room on the plane and they had their other children to see to, they'd had to arrange childcare and make the drive to the hospital themselves. It had begun to get dark by the time Meadow and Jay had returned to the base.

With Greg and Kate both having plans, Kate's date night with her husband, and Greg hooking up with whoever would have him, it had been left to her to drop Jay back at the pub. She'd stopped in long enough to plead his case for another overnight stay, but the noise and hub-bub of the place had guaranteed he wouldn't have had any better night's sleep than she'd had. After the day they'd had, she reckoned they'd both needed it too.

She took her coffee into the living room and tried to distract herself with a magazine, but she was flicking through the pages without really taking anything in. Her mind was still locked on yesterday, and the personal in-formation Jay had shared with her. He'd had a bad run since moving from England and it was in her nature to try and make him feel better. As someone who'd grown up never fully comfortable in her surroundings, always waiting for the rug to be pulled from under her, she em-pathised with other people's struggles. She didn't like watching anyone go through a bad time, remembering how it was to feel so alone and wanting someone to no-tice, to do something about it. If she could help people in need, she did. Whether it was checking in on her father, donating to foodbanks or giving someone a lift when they needed one, she did it to try and make people feel better.

Jay had left her with a moral dilemma. He was clearly someone who was suffering, who needed help, and she could offer a solution to one of his problems at least. There was nothing she could do about his grief, or the list he wanted to complete in Sharyn's name, but she did know somewhere he might be able to stay after his home had burned down before he'd set foot in it: the shearers' quarters on her father's land. The trouble with that sce-nario was two-fold. Firstly, she would have to speak to her father and he wasn't answering his phone. Part of the reason she'd gone into the pub was to see if he was there before she said anything to Jay. The second problem was that inviting Jay to stay on her dad's land would mean moving him further into her life when every instinct was telling her to keep him at a distance.

In the end she knew she would have to do the right thing, if only so she could sleep soundly in her bed at night without her conscience bothering her.

Jay might have scared her half to death with his snake antics but everyone else seemed to love him. It was clear he'd been through a lot and she didn't want him to feel unwelcome, even though they'd got off on the wrong foot. His house burning down on top of his grief might explain him losing his temper with Marko that night, though it didn't excuse hers. She'd taken her bad mood out on him at a time when he'd needed some understanding. There was one way she could try to make amends, even if it would make her life a little more complicated than it already was.

Jay was mourning his girlfriend, clearly not in the market for another relationship, so she had no reason to worry that he was somehow going to hurt her. Romance wasn't on the cards at all. He was a work colleague, one that infuriated her at times, but she would get used to him the way she had with Greg, the party animal. Greg often regaled her with tales of his debauched nights out and, though she didn't agree with his lifestyle, he was good at his job so they muddled along. It certainly didn't keep her awake at night, anxious about getting involved with him and the repercussions if it did happen, when she was the one single woman in town who hadn't been out with him. She didn't know what made Jay Brooke special, but she was hoping that if she did this one thing for him she could stop him from invading her thoughts.

* * *

It took her all day to pluck up the courage to broach the subject, and only then because she knew it would be dark again soon and Jay was worried about asking Barb for another night at the pub. Although he'd been professional and courteous to the patients they'd transferred to the hospital today, she'd seen him yawning when he thought no one could see. It was clear his current accommodation wasn't ideal and it wouldn't do for the flight doctor to be deprived of sleep when he had such an important job to do for the people of Dream Gulley. Therefore, she had no choice.

Meadow cleared her throat, the words seeming to stick in her throat as though her body was trying to stop her from saying them. 'I think I know a place where you can stay. Until you get something else sorted out at least.'

'Oh?' The hope in his eyes told her she was doing the right thing, though it went against her desire to keep him at a distance. A man who had a tick list of adrenaline-fuelled activities to work through and clearly thought nothing of launching himself at a venomous snake was not someone she needed around her. That was pain just waiting to happen for both of them.

'My dad has a place, a gold claim called Rainbow's Walk. There's an old shack there that used to be for shearers. He sometimes rents it out to other gold hunters.' There were a few who still passed by this way and tried their luck in the old mines. Ironically, though this was the place her mother had finally decided she'd had enough and left him, Meadow's dad had settled here after having some success. He'd bought the land, convinced this would be his big pay-off. Fifteen years later he was still waiting, so he had to raise money to pay the bills somehow.

'Are you serious?' Jay looked delighted. 'That would be great and maybe I can tick that gold panning thing off my list too.'

'Don't hold your breath. I can't promise gold or a happy home. If I could, I might still have a family,' she muttered, drawing a quizzical glance from her colleague.

'Anything is better than what I currently have, which is nothing. When can you speak to him?'

'I…er… I suppose I can take you out to see him after work.' She should check in on her dad, she thought. It had been a while since they'd last spoken, and then there was this business with him not answering his phone. Not that he was great about staying in touch at the best of times. He only had a mobile phone because Meadow had insisted on it when he was often working in extreme temperatures and dangerous conditions. She fired off a text to let him know she'd be stopping by, but there was no guarantee he'd read the message or even had the phone turned on. Still, Jay was in urgent need of a place to stay and after everything he'd been through he deserved a break.

She would simply have to set aside any awkwardness on her part and accept that Jay was going to be in her life from now on.

Jay leaned so his head was partially out of the car window, trying to take in some fresh air. Easier said than done with the dust cloud the wheels of Meadow's Jeep was kicking up. He hadn't realised he got travel sick until he'd been bouncing over this dirt track in the heat. Neither he nor Sharyn had accounted for the lack of air con in these more remote places. He'd had to sleep in the buff at the pub last night, very aware there was no lock on his door and that there had been a full house. It hadn't been the most relaxing sleep he'd ever had, sweating his bits off and keeping one eye on the door in case an inebriated customer mistook his room for the toilets.

Although Barb might have been persuaded to let him stay another night, he was glad Meadow had come up with an alternative solution. And surprised. Up until then he was sure she'd have done anything to get rid of him. Especially after the snake debacle. He'd acted without thinking, he knew that, but Meadow had really freaked out about it. It was possible she'd thawed towards him after he'd opened up a little bit about Sharyn, something he didn't usually do but he'd been trying to explain his behaviour. Sharyn was the one who'd dragged him out of his shell and made him want to experience all life had to offer instead of living as though he was still trapped inside his childhood home. Although even she would have drawn the line at something so dangerous.

It had taken Meadow some time to tell him her father might have somewhere he could stay. Waiting until they'd finished their shift and he was getting ready to go cap in hand to Barb again because it seemed his only option. Meadow had said her relationship with her father was strained, and it did make him wonder more about her private life. She hadn't shared much with him other than her parents' separation, and after the other night's events he assumed she was single—but that was all he really knew.

'Thank you for doing this,' he said, fighting to be heard over the noise of the engine as Meadow floored it across the scorched earth, taking any bumps in the road at full speed.

'I said I would make enquiries. I'm not promising anything. I told you I haven't been able to get hold of him. It's not unusual, he doesn't always have his phone on him, but we'll go and see if he's about.'

'So…your dad is a gold hunter? That must have made for an interesting childhood.'

'You could say that,' Meadow muttered through gritted teeth and forced the car into the next gear. All signs that he should leave the subject alone but he wanted to get to know her better, even if just to make their working relationship a little easier.

'Are you sure he'll be all right with me staying?' Despite his dire need for somewhere to stay, he didn't want to be the cause of any family drama, or indeed end up in the middle of it either.

'Well, he hasn't answered my text, but if you've got cash I'm sure he can be persuaded to take in a lodger.'

It wasn't the effusive invitation he would've hoped for, and now he was imagining some dirty, curmudgeonly, stooped figure snatching his wallet off him before sending him to stay in the dunny.

'Hopefully, it won't be for too long and the service will be able to rehouse me somewhere close to work.' It was becoming clear that there wasn't going to be public transport to get him from A to B near her father's land and he'd have to rely on other people, namely his workmates, to get him to work. Less than ideal, but at least it should be quieter than the pub.

'Maybe you should see the place first before you commit,' she said ominously as they drove past several *No*

Trespassers signs and pulled up outside what looked as though it had started life as a static caravan but over the years had had a lean-to and porch added on at some point. Jay wasn't sure it would still be standing after a strong gust of wind and it made him wonder where the hell he'd be staying. This place certainly wouldn't be in the tourist information offered by the service when trying to entice doctors from abroad.

'Dad? Are you in there?' Meadow knocked on the screen door before letting herself inside. It appeared security wasn't a big factor here, which was concerning for someone who made his living from finding gold. Either he didn't get many people trying to steal off him or he never found anything worth anyone coming out all this way for in the first place. Given what sparse information Meadow had shared with him, he suspected the latter to be true.

Jay hovered on the porch, waiting for a signal that he should set foot inside, but instead Meadow came back out with her phone to her ear. 'He's not here. Must be out digging in the dirt. That's how he got his nickname. No one calls him Derek, it's always Digger.'

She hopped down off the porch and Jay followed her out onto the property. It was a vast, sparce area, the dusty red vista occasionally broken by spiky scrub. It put him in mind of an old Western and he half expected to see an old saloon with swinging doors and grizzled old gunslingers the further they walked out onto the land away from the main house.

'It seems quite a lonely existence,' he noted, thinking he wouldn't want to live out here on his own. At least not permanently, and not if he had to work here too, with no chance to speak to anyone. Although he'd had a brief period after Sharyn died of not wanting to see or speak to anyone, generally he enjoyed being with people. It hadn't been easy at first, after years of seclusion, but the foster family who'd taken him in, after his father's abuse had been discovered, had supported him and encouraged him to join all sorts of clubs to socialise. He'd been behind in his education because he'd missed so much school, but caught up thanks to their dedication. If it wasn't for them, he wouldn't have found the courage to go on to medical school, even though he'd spent more time studying than indulging in the full student experience of pubbing and clubbing.

It was meeting Sharyn that had forced him out of his comfort zone and gave him a life worth living. Being around people was a good tonic and he'd come to need it since Sharyn had gone and life had become all too quiet.

'I guess that's how he likes it.' Meadow shrugged, yet again giving off the vibe that their relationship was strained.

'It's not healthy though.'

'Don't you think I don't know that?' Meadow snapped, throwing him a deathly glare over her shoulder. 'None of this is healthy. It's an obsession which has completely taken over his life, but does he listen? No.'

She stomped away and though he knew she'd probably prefer it if he disappeared, Jay had no choice but to follow her. It was a mystery to him how anyone ever found their way out here with no landmarks to navigate by and he knew he'd never find his way back to the house without a guide. He took his medical bag just in case.

'Dad? Are you out here?' Meadow called out every few

steps to try and elicit a response, but not even the sound of digging could be heard anywhere.

'Mr Williams? Can you hear us?' Wanting to be of some use but not venturing too far from his companion, Jay called out too.

They walked for some distance, calling out and searching behind every piece of brush to no avail. He could see the panic begin to set in with Meadow, who seemed more worried than annoyed about her father's disappearance now.

'His truck's outside the house so he's here somewhere…'

'We'll find him,' he assured her, determined to stay out here looking for as long as they had enough light. At some point, though, they might have to consider calling in extra help if Meadow was absolutely certain he was out here and in trouble. He'd gone through a traumatic loss and he wouldn't wish that on anyone. Especially not someone who was going against her instincts and trying to help him rebuild his life.

Meadow inhaled deep breaths to keep her heart regulated in her effort to keep the rising panic at bay. It wasn't going to do anyone any good for her to lose it, though she was worried her father was lying out here somewhere, unnoticed perhaps for days. He wasn't the only one who wasn't great at staying in touch. They mightn't have much of an emotional relationship these days but he was still her father and she didn't wish any harm to come to him.

She was glad she had Jay with her in case something had happened. It was clear he was a good doctor with excellent people skills when he'd even managed to win her over after she'd blasted him in the pub that first night. More than those things, she suspected he was a good hugger and that might be something she'd need before the end of the day.

Perhaps it was the fact that he was mourning his girl-friend, added to spending more time with him, that made her lower her defences. As though she didn't have to be on her guard so much around him, that he wasn't a threat to her peace of mind. An attractive man with an apparent death wish could have tested her when they were going to be in such close proximity all the time. If she'd been drawn to him his reckless attitude would have been very difficult for her to reconcile with, but now she knew she was safe, that he wasn't interested in her or anyone else whilst he was lost in grief. It might not be so bad after all to have someone around who could do their job and be the sort of man she might be able to rely on in the midst of a crisis without worrying there would be a price to pay later. She'd be sure to keep some distance, though, when he had a list of risky escapades still to work his way through.

'Wait.' She put a hand out to stop Jay where he was, thinking she heard a noise somewhere nearby. They stood still and she tried to block out the sound of the wind and the birds overhead. She even held her breath so as not to contribute any sound.

Eventually she was sure she heard a faint cry coming from over beyond the ridge, where the land dipped down towards the boundary.

'I can hear something,' Jay confirmed.

They both ran to where she was sure there'd been a low moan. Sure enough, they found her father rolled into the ditch on the other side, dirty, bloody and scorched by the sun.

'Dad!' She dropped to her knees and felt for his pulse. It was weak, but he was breathing.

'I'll phone it in.' Jay got straight onto the phone to relay their co-ordinates, though their colleagues knew where her father's place was located, before going to aid Meadow's father too. After a preliminary exam, there didn't seem to be any major trauma, the cut on his head likely occurring as he'd fallen into the ditch. Although he might have suffered a concussion too.

'I think he's dehydrated.' Meadow took the water bottle which was attached to her belt and lifted her father's head to pour a little onto his dry, cracked lips.

'How long have you been out here, Mr Williams?' Jay fished around in his bag for an ice pack, broke it to activate the cooling ingredients, wrapped it in a cloth and placed it around his neck.

'Don't…know…' he mumbled, seeming confused and disoriented.

'Dad, it's me. You're going to be all right,' Meadow reassured him as she lifted her father's legs up to rest them on her knees to lower the risk of him going into shock. Even though she was afraid he'd been out here since last night at least when he hadn't answered his phone. If he didn't recover from this, the guilt of not coming out here sooner, of worrying about her own petty fears instead, would haunt her for ever.

'It looks a lot like heat exhaustion, though it looks as though he's hit his head too.' The man's skin was clammy, his pulse racing, and when Jay put a thermometer under his tongue he found he was running a temperature. All signs that he'd been exposed to the punishing sun for too long, although it was difficult to tell if the heat or the fall had overwhelmed him first. Either way, they had to get his temperature down or there was a possibility of damage to his internal organs. Meadow was already taking off his socks and shoes and Jay swiped the water bottle to pour some on a cloth. He laid it across her father's forehead.

'What have I told you about coming out here without your phone? It's got to be forty degrees and no water bottle I can see.' Even in Meadow's scolding, Jay could hear the concern in her voice for the father with whom she apparently didn't have a relationship worth talking about.

He knew what it was like to be estranged from a parent, not having seen either of his in nearly twenty years and with no desire to rectify that situation. Despite Meadow's protestations, he thought there was still love there, but he could understand her not wanting to get hurt. With a little time, and some repentance from her father, he was sure this parent/child relationship might be salvaged after all. They just had to make sure he was okay first.

'Sorry,' her dad mouthed, as a tear dripped down Meadow's face.

She swiped it away and gave him a watery smile. 'You will be if you do this again, you silly old coot.'

'Is he on any medication?' Jay asked, in case it should exacerbate the problem.

Meadow shook her head.

'I think we should get an IV set up. We don't know how long they'll take to get out here.' He pulled out a saline drip from the emergency supplies, to replenish the fluids lost before the organs began to shut down, and inserted a canula into her father's arm.

'No...hospital...' he gasped, apparently as stubborn as his daughter.

'You have to get proper treatment. We don't know how long you've been out here exposed to the elements, or how long you were unconscious. They'll need to do blood tests at the hospital to make sure your organs are functioning properly, check that head injury and get that temperature down before they'll even think about letting you go home.' Meadow helped him sit up for another sip of water and wetted the cloth for his forehead again.

'I...need...to...work...'

'You need to rest.'

'Bills...'

'They can wait. It could take days or weeks before you're ready to go back to work and even then you're going to have to be more careful, Dad.'

Her father made an attempt to sit up. 'Can't afford... to...sit...around...'

'You could get some help in.'

'Yes, Mr Williams, we'd actually come to see if I could rent a room from you. Maybe I could help out somehow with your work?' Jay was willing to give his assistance in return for the lodging and it might even earn him some Brownie points with Meadow.

Or not. She shot him an unimpressed look. 'You'd get yourself killed. You don't know the first thing about working this land and I don't need another fool out here who won't listen to me.'

'You do,' her father croaked out to draw back her attention.

'I do what?'

'Know the work, Meadow. I'll agree to go to hospital if you help out on the land until I get out.'

'That's blackmail, Dad,' she sighed.

The old man gave a croaky laugh and Meadow knew her fate had been sealed.

CHAPTER FOUR

'THANKS FOR THIS,' Jay said for the hundredth time as he set his bags inside the old weatherboard cottage.

'Well, it's too late for either of us to go anywhere else tonight. Besides, it looks like I'll be moonlighting as a gold hunter in whatever spare time I have.' Meadow was leaning in the doorway, still wearing her uniform, which was more red than blue now, covered with dirt and blood from their earlier drama.

'Surely he doesn't expect you to actually dig?' If it was the kind of work which could render an experienced man almost to the point of death, it was inconceivable to Jay that Meadow's father would expect his own daughter to do it. Especially when she was already working in such a demanding role.

She arched an eyebrow at him. 'Clearly you don't know my father. Gold comes before everything. You saw how he was willing to put his life on the line today and all he came up with were a few tiny nuggets to show for it. He claims he's found a patch, and that's why he didn't want to leave.'

'A patch?'

'It's a small area with a concentration of gold deposits. The reason he bought this land was because he was convinced there was still gold to find. It was thought there was an ancient dried-up riverbed on site, a prime source for undiscovered gold deposits. This has only spurred him on more, thinking there's more to be found, and he doesn't trust anyone else to work it for him. Except for me.' She let out a sigh which seemed to come from the very depths of her soul, as though she was used to dealing with his idiosyncrasies and was bone-weary from it. Jay couldn't blame her if she didn't get any form of love or thanks in return.

'You know I'll help if I can.'

She shook her head. 'No. If he thought there was a stranger digging his patch he'd discharge himself from hospital and run us both off his property. Besides, I'll be quicker doing it myself than trying to stop you from killing yourself again.'

'Whatever you say.' It was in Jay's nature to protest and offer to help rather than stand by and expect her to do such hard manual labour herself, but he left it alone for tonight. They'd been through a lot over the course of these past twenty-four hours and there was no point in starting another argument. If he annoyed her any more there was a very real chance he'd end up with nowhere to stay tonight.

'Give me half an hour to shower and find something to wear, then you can come up to the house for something to eat.'

'You don't have to—'

'It's been a long day. We're both tired and hungry. You'll be lucky if there's hot water in this shack, never mind food in the cupboard. Call it an act of mercy.' She turned and walked out into the falling darkness before he could stop her, or thank her.

Despite their differences, and though she might have done so begrudgingly, Meadow had been the only one who'd helped him since he'd arrived. For someone who claimed to want a quiet life, she seemed to be smack in the middle of other people's dramas and Jay couldn't help but admire her plucky spirit and kindness. Meadow was unlike anyone he'd ever met and he was looking forward to getting to know her better.

This was one of those times Meadow wished her father had a proper house, with a real bath so she could relax instead of hopping under a slow trickle of cold water trying to shower. They'd never had any luxuries when she was young, but since earning her own money she'd become accustomed to simple pleasures such as a functional bathroom, mains electricity and air conditioning.

At least her father should be comfortable in hospital with a decent bed and nutritious meals until he felt better. He'd put up a bit of a fight when the plane had arrived to airlift him away but he'd soon conceded, which was all the confirmation she needed that he wasn't himself. She and Jay had gone with him and once he was settled and reassured that she wouldn't let trespassers raid his patch, they'd bagged a lift back. It had been easier for her to stay the night than to come back first thing to pick up where he'd left off, and Jay needed someone to show him around. She couldn't very well dump him out here and expect him to fend for himself. That was tomorrow's plan.

Tonight, she'd be a polite host and rustle up something to eat to thank him for his assistance with her father. Although she could have managed on her own it was nice to have that backup and someone to share the responsibility for once. Since her mother had gone it had been solely down to her to keep an eye on her dad, even though they weren't close. Today proved why she could never completely sever all ties. Despite everything he'd done, or how he'd treated them, she'd never forgive herself if something happened to him and she could have prevented it. She didn't even want to think about what could have happened if they hadn't called by today.

A shiver crawled over her skin and she didn't think it was from the tepid water trickling over her.

She shut off the shower and grabbed a threadbare towel to dry herself. Her uniform and underwear were in the wash so she could wear them tomorrow, so she had no choice but to use her father's robe, hanging on the back of the door, to preserve her modesty in the meantime.

She padded down the hallway towards the kitchen and leapt a couple of feet into the air when she saw a figure standing in front of her.

'Sorry, I called out but you must not have heard me.' Jay was standing at the cooker frying something which smelt good enough to make her stomach rumble.

'I was in the shower. You didn't have to do this.' She gestured towards the table, which had been laid with plates and cutlery and the evidence of his cooking was strewn around the tiny kitchen.

'It's just a stir fry. There was chicken and veg in the fridge so I hope that's okay? I just wanted to say thank you.'

'You didn't have to, but I'm glad you did. I'm starving.' She was too tired and hungry to fight him, especially when he'd made such a lovely gesture. It made a change to have someone cook for her, and to even have someone to share dinner with. Most nights it was a rushed affair and cooking for one seemed so depressing that when she did make something from scratch she made a batch to freeze too. A fresh, nutritious meal prepared by a handsome doctor was a treat indeed.

'I could only find beer in the fridge. I hope your father won't think I've been raiding his supplies. I'll pick some up tomorrow when I'm in town.' Jay added some sweet chilli and garlic sauce along with some noodles before serving, by which time Meadow's mouth was watering in anticipation.

'It's fine. I think he'll be in hospital for a couple of days at least. That gives us plenty of time to restock.' She smiled as she took her plate to sit over at the table on one of the mismatched chairs her father had gathered from the roadside hard rubbish over the years.

Jay came to join her and she noticed him glance at her a little closer. When she looked down she realised that her father's robe was gaping, giving him a clear view down her cleavage. Meadow quickly pulled the sides of the dressing gown closer and tied the belt tighter around her waist.

'Sorry, I don't have a change of clothes with me. I haven't stayed here since I was a teenager.'

'It's fine. I don't think there's a strict dress code for whenever someone breaks into your house and cooks themselves a meal,' Jay joked but Meadow could swear he blushed before he looked away. As though he'd been caught red-handed doing something he shouldn't.

Strangely, the thought of Jay trying to cop a look didn't make her want to throw her beer over him, as she might have done with someone like Marko. She reckoned it was payback for her staring at his backside all day in those tight trousers. They obviously found each other attractive, but it didn't have to make things awkward. It was clear they both had too much emotional baggage to even think about getting romantically involved. No, it was better to think of him as a colleague and forget all about his cute butt, and how thoughtful he'd been to her today, for both of their sakes.

'This is so tasty.' She turned her thoughts and attention back to dinner, which was a much safer topic for tonight.

'I took a cookery class last year. Sharyn thought I should expand my repertoire from spaghetti bolognese or beans on toast to something a bit more adventurous.'

'Was this part of the tick list?'

'Yeah. I started with a nice easy one. It's a shame she won't be around to see me swim with sharks. She was looking forward to that one.' His smile this time was dimmed by the sadness in his eyes which always appeared when he talked about his past with Sharyn. They'd clearly had something special and Meadow was sorry that it had ended so tragically.

'She sounds really special.' Someone full of fun and daring, everything Meadow wasn't.

'She was. She brought out the best in me.' He raised his bottle of beer in a toast and they fell into a companionable silence as they finished their meal together.

'So…what's your long-term plan? I mean, are you planning on staying in town indefinitely?'

'I haven't thought that far ahead. I guess maybe when I've ticked a few more things off my list, or when something else comes up that I think will challenge me.'

The idea of him moving on was already something that

didn't sit well with her when she was just getting used to having him around. Suddenly she was hoping this list would take a while to get through.

'You don't have to complete it though. If you find somewhere you're happy, surely Sharyn would want that for you too?' She couldn't imagine that kind of transient life again at their age, never knowing what was coming next. One childhood of that was enough for a lifetime.

'I guess…but right now I don't see any future beyond that list. Thank you, by the way, for letting me stay.'

'Well, it's not my house and my dad probably doesn't remember the conversation we had about you staying so your gratitude might be premature.' She popped the last piece of chicken into her mouth nonchalantly, whilst making Jay almost choke on his dinner he was laughing so much.

He had to take a swig of beer to wash his food down before he was able to speak again. 'I'm sure I'll find out what he thinks about squatters once he gets out of hospital.'

'I'd sleep with one eye open if I were you,' she teased.

'I'm not sure I'll sleep at all. It's so dark out there you can't see your hand in front of your face.'

'You were expecting floodlights? I'm sure there's a torch in the drawer so you can find your way back.' She kind of liked the absolute darkness away from the town lights, the stars shining so brightly it was as if someone had spilled diamonds over the black velvet sky. It gave her a sense of peace, a familiarity, when the sky was the one constant she'd ever had on their travels with her father.

Jay winced. 'The lights don't work. I think the bulbs need replacing.'

'Oh. Sorry. It must have been a while since anyone stayed there. I'll pick some up tomorrow when I'm at the shops.'

Jay stood, collecting the plates to take them over to the sink to wash. 'Do you think there might be some spares in the cupboard? I don't really want to wait until tomorrow.'

There was an edgy air to him she hadn't encountered before, he was usually so assured in his actions, and she wondered what had caused the shift in him.

'It'll be fine. I told you I'll find you a torch. What, are you afraid of the dark?'

He dropped his gaze to his feet, embarrassment radiating across the kitchen to where she sat, and she knew she'd hit a nerve.

'I'm not afraid of it…uncomfortable would be a more accurate description.'

'Sorry, I didn't realise.' This land, as much as she resented it when it represented everything that had gone wrong in her life, was familiar to her. She forgot that not everyone treated a remote, desolate spot like home. This would all be alien to someone who'd grown up in the big city without an inch of space around him unoccupied or lit by fluorescent lights.

'I just had some bad experiences when I was younger.'

'I'm sorry to hear that. There are just some things you never get over, I suppose.' Although she was curious to know what had happened to make this strapping bloke 'uncomfortable' in the dark, Meadow wasn't going to ask him to relive his trauma. It wasn't going to solve anything other than her curiosity and that would be selfish. She had her hang-ups and didn't share them with anyone either. Jay had a right to his privacy and his pride, even if she did bear ill will towards whoever or whatever had caused him such obvious distress.

'Some things. Others you have to try and work your way through before they can stunt your growth.' He could easily have been talking about her, when her past still dictated how she lived her life—cautiously, with order and structure so no one could hurt her again.

It hadn't been completely foolproof, when her disastrous love life had still left a mark on her. Though none of her relationships had been serious enough to be devastating when they'd ended, each breakup had left her thinking that she couldn't trust anyone except herself. If anything, it had made her more wary about inviting anyone else into her life.

She wondered if things would've been better if she had ever thrown caution to the wind and lived the same nomadic existence as her father, even for a short time. Simply stopped worrying about the consequences of her actions to live in the moment. Although the thought of doing something spontaneous or potentially dangerous brought her out in a rash. She couldn't understand why certain people seemed to get a kick out of it. Jay included.

'That's what the tick list is about? Do you think it has enhanced your life in any way, or is it just something you've committed to doing and now you have to see it through?' She was genuinely curious and hoped this line of questioning wasn't impinging on his grief or past traumas when it seemed such a big part of his life.

He was silent for a moment, contemplating his answer, but thankfully didn't appear upset by her interest in the matter. 'It definitely broadened my horizons and pushed me so far out of my comfort zone at times I think it has made me stronger as a person. Now… I don't know. I guess I'll just keep going with it until my life has a new direction.'

Meadow pitied his aimless existence but only because he seemed so forlorn and lost at present. If he'd been happy alone doing whatever thrilling adventures they'd planned she might have envied him. Now it just seemed as though it was a chore he had to carry out because he had nothing else to do with his life. She was happy in her job, settled in her own home, but sometimes she had a sense that she might be missing out. Certainly she'd never experienced the rush her father got from gold hunting, or that Jay and his girlfriend had once enjoyed from chasing the next thrill.

'What did you do before you lost Sharyn? Anything you really enjoyed?' Meadow wondered why there'd ever been a need for him to have such a list. Perhaps his childhood trauma had been so great it had affected all aspects of his life, much like hers. If that was the case, perhaps she should get some tips on how to move past it. Scary though that idea was, she didn't want to stay angry at her father her whole life and end up some bitter, twisted old spinster who never left her house.

Jay smiled and she noticed a dimple peeking out at the corner of his mouth. 'I did enjoy the skydive, even though I had to be pushed out of the plane.'

'Oh, my goodness! I know we're up in the air all the time, but actually jumping out of a plane for fun is beyond my comprehension.'

He laughed at her horror. 'I was strapped to my instructor, and I don't think I'd be in a hurry to do it again, but it was a real buzz.'

'So is sticking your finger in an electric socket, but I don't think I'd be in a hurry to do that either,' Meadow mused, a little in awe of the bravery it must have taken to go through with such a feat.

'You have to try these things,' he said with a shrug.

'Er, no, I don't.'

'I thought that way too, before Sharyn.'

'I don't mean to sound rude, but was this really for your benefit, or was she simply an adrenaline junkie?' Meadow knew she was treading on perilous ground saying something like that about the woman Jay loved, but if she'd ever had a boyfriend who'd forced her to put her life in danger like that, she was pretty sure someone would've staged an intervention on her behalf. That kind of coercive control was part of the reason none of her relationships had ever worked. The moment they tried to persuade her to do something she wasn't happy about was when she got the hell out of there. She knew her own mind, what she was comfortable with, and spontaneity to her was simply a way of trying to force her to do something she didn't want to.

Like the time Shawn had sprung a surprise white-water rafting trip on her for her birthday, trying to make out it was for her when he was the one who wanted to do it. She hadn't been prepared to drop everything and travel halfway across the country to drown herself in the name of fun, so that had been the end of that.

'A bit of both, I suppose. She enjoyed her extreme sports and I needed to live a little. I wasn't just some lovesick puppy trailing around doing everything she said, in case that's what you think.'

'No, I didn't mean—' She tried to back-pedal but Jay clearly wanted to put the record straight.

'I loved her and I was willing to try different things but I had my limits too. I drew the line at base jumping. Despite any previous evidence to the contrary, I do not in fact have a death wish.' He leaned across the table and held her gaze, his dark eyes reminding her that he was very much his own man, strong and independent, and captivating.

'So…your turn.' Eventually he shifted back into his seat, leaving her blinking as though she'd just come out of a hypnotic trance.

'What…what do you want to know?' There was a knot in her stomach tightening by the second, waiting for him to extract information from her. She had no desire to be pitted against the ghost of a woman whose idea of a good time had only been when there was a risk of death or serious injury involved, because she would be found sorely lacking. The most adventure she ever had was letting the fuel in her car go lower than the halfway mark before filling up. There was nothing to write home about when it came to relationships either. She was beginning to regret quizzing him on his if she was about to be subjected to the humiliation of sharing the details of her boring love life.

'Meadow's a curious name. Especially out here.'

The breath she let out was one of relief. 'Mum was originally from Brisbane. My dad met her out there when he was working in construction. They moved here to the gold fields so he could pursue his dream.'

'Are they hippies? It's a lovely name, but very unusual.'

Meadow's relief was short-lived, knowing she was going to have to share at least one piece of embarrassing information. 'You know how some celebrities like to name their children after the cities they were conceived in… Well…'

She let the silence fill in the blanks, Jay's raucous laughter signalling the very second the penny dropped.

'I'll never look at you the same way again. That's priceless.' He dissolved into fits of laughter again and she was glad they'd brought some levity back into the situation, though it had come at her expense.

'I suppose I should be thankful it wasn't in the dunny or somewhere equally glamorous. At least Meadow sounds pretty.'

'It suits you. A floral oasis in the midst of the desert.' He clinked his bottle to hers and it was her turn to blush. It was the nicest compliment anyone had ever paid her. After a lifetime of teasing at every school she'd ever briefly attended, she thought she might actually start to like the name her parents had inappropriately explained during the awkward enough teen years.

'I think it reminded Mum of home.'

'Do you get to see much of her?'

'Not as much as I should because she lives so far away, but we stay in touch.'

'You could take a trip some time. It does the soul good to blow away the cobwebs once in a while.'

'I'm good here. Not really one for travelling.'

'Meadow, you're in a plane every day. Everyone needs a holiday every once in a while, is all I'm saying. You could go see your mum and kill two birds with one trip.'

'What about your family? Aren't they missing you?' She turned the question back on him, the best way she knew to get herself off the hook and stop him asking any more questions about her background. After everything he'd told her about his life with Sharyn it would've sounded tragic to him that she never left town because she needed that safety of the familiar. This dirt town was the equivalent of a tatty old security blanket that she couldn't let go of, even at thirty years of age.

'I doubt it.' Jay's expression changed at the mere mention of his family, his thunderous frown a clear indication that he did have a chequered history there too. At his reaction she would hazard a guess that his parents had something to do with the issues he was still dealing with. Unlike her, he'd chosen to escape the place which had caused him pain, and she had to wonder if emigrating was a more extreme reaction to the trauma than never leaving town. If they found a happy medium there might be a chance of real progress for both of them.

'Mum left when I was about five, so I don't remember much about her, and haven't heard from her since. Dad was an abusive drunk who should never have been allowed to raise a child, but I guess that's why she left in the first place. To cut a long story short, I was taken into care when I was fourteen. I had one foster family who were really good to me, but they have their hands full with all the other kids they've taken in since. I check in with them every now and then but I don't have any of my own family to go back and visit. None who I have a wish to ever see again, at least.' There was a hardness to him whenever he spoke about his parents that Meadow was sure came from a place of pain. It hadn't gone unnoticed that he'd skipped over the details, the brief synopsis of his life enough for her to realise he'd had a difficult time growing up too. The fact that he'd become a doctor, helping others, and in a different country, was to be commended.

'I suppose this is a clean slate for you. I mean, I know it's not the one you'd planned, but you can build a whole new life for yourself.' It would be nice to leave the past far behind, but it was clear time and distance hadn't managed to erase Jay's troubling memories either. The most either of them could hope for was to eventually move on and not let the past encroach on their present or future any more than it already had.

'Our move out to Melbourne was so full of hope for the future. As though the world was ours for the taking. Coming out here, no offence, felt more like a chore. Something I had to do because it was on the list. Don't get me wrong, I know I have to create a new life for myself. It's just knowing where to start.'

'I don't know about the future, but for now you've got a room at least.'

Jay drained his bottle and tossed it into the overflowing recycling bin. 'I think that's my cue to leave. Early start in the morning.'

He started towards the door and Meadow rushed to catch up with him, grabbing a bulb from the lamp sitting in the lounge area, and a torch from the drawer in the kitchen.

'Here, take this with you. I want you to be comfortable. Although I can't guarantee what the mattress on the bed is like. It's probably been there since the first gold rush.'

'It's fine. Everything seems new enough and there were clean sheets in the cupboard. Thanks for the bulb.'

Meadow was surprised that her father appeared to have been taking care of the place when he couldn't seem to do the same for himself. Every time he cleared a new plot to work on, he had to hire earthmovers and some locals to do the heavier lifting for him. She supposed he had people staying more than she'd thought. Perhaps he realised he was making more from renting out the room than his prospecting.

'If there's anything you need just let me know and I'll see if I can sort it for you.' It was the least she could do until her father was back to keep an eye on things here. Jay had been great helping her get him to hospital, brushing off any insults or resistance from her father, who'd fought against the idea at every turn, often physically, but Jay had managed to get him onto the stretcher and talk him down from the various threats he'd made during his disoriented episode. Being dehydrated and concussed, along with his prolonged exposure, had made him more belligerent than usual.

The interaction between the two had made her wonder more about Jay's childhood. It was sure to have brought back memories, none of them pleasant, when he'd had a combative parent of his own. More than that, he'd called him abusive. Her father might have been neglectful, emotionally distant, but he'd never raised a hand to her when she was a child. When she put the information he'd shared about his father along with his fear of the dark she was sure there was a tragic tale behind it all that was even more unbearable than her own.

He'd been so sweet today with the patients at the clinic, and cooking for her tonight, and he didn't deserve to have had someone treat him so badly. The calm, reasoned way he'd spoken to her father made her think he'd had experience of dealing with someone who was out of control.

It hurt to imagine what situations he'd been in for that kind of survival instinct to kick in, that need to placate someone so irate before they caused damage. Although it sounded as though it was too late for Jay, who was already scarred by whatever his father had done.

If this was his new life, his new start, Meadow wanted to help make it better for him. Even if it was only by giving him a lightbulb for now.

'Thanks. You made today a better day, Meadow.' His sad expression made her heart break all over again.

Careful to make sure her robe was tightly fastened first, she stood up on her tiptoes to kiss him on the cheek. 'Thanks for a lovely night, Jay.'

She didn't know what happened in that moment, but she delayed moving back from that slight contact when her lips touched his cheek. Their eyes met, their hot breath filling the space and silence between them as they both seemed to contemplate their next move. She felt his arms move around her, resting on her hips briefly before he pulled away from her again.

'Any time,' he said, his voice deeper and gruffer than she'd heard before now. Regret probably—she was feeling it too for almost acting on that growing attraction.

She had never been one to jump into a fling, or act on impulse simply because she liked the look of someone, or related to them more than anyone she'd ever met. A lot of factors came into play before she even thought about getting involved with someone. Usually. Especially with a man who represented everything she was afraid of in the world. He lived his life on a whim, thriving on change and a challenge. Jay Brooke was not the one who could offer her the stability she'd been craving her whole life.

So why did it feel so good to have her blood pumping this hard around her body?

She put her feet back down on solid ground, doing her best to come to her senses.

'Don't say that. I'll be expecting you to cook for me every night.' She forced out a shaky laugh in an attempt to cover her awkward goodbye.

'Any time,' he repeated with a grin on his face before he walked out into the night.

Meadow watched the light from the torch bobbing across the darkness until he reached the shack. Once she saw the light in the bedroom go on she smiled to herself, happy he was safe. She closed the door and leaned against it, the blood in her veins fizzing with adrenaline, and she wondered if it was this kind of excitement which caused her father's addiction. And if it was hereditary.

CHAPTER FIVE

'HOW'S YOUR DAD TODAY?' Making small talk on the plane flying into a medical emergency was necessary to keep him sane. Jay needed something to take his mind off the scene of the traffic accident awaiting them at the end of the flight and it was better than sitting here with Meadow in silence after last night. After the way they'd left things, that almost-kiss on the doorstep, he needed to prevent things from becoming weird between them.

They'd shared a moment on her doorstep. Likely one born out of tiredness and loneliness, perhaps with a dash of chemistry upping the ante. It had been a nice way to wind down the evening, sharing a meal in good company. Though he'd overshared, talking about his childhood, something he'd hardly ever talked about with Sharyn, never mind someone he'd only known for a matter of days. He put it down to the situation, working closely together and dealing with her own difficult parent. Plus he'd been feeling vulnerable opening up to her the way he had, and having to admit his fear of the dark, even if he'd omitted his reasons.

Giving him a bulb so he would feel safe and comfortable in his new, strange environment, without any hint of ridicule, had lowered his defences. Meadow had understood his need for the simple gesture and done it without asking any questions.

As much as he'd loved Sharyn, she had always pushed him to tell her more, to delve deeper into those memories and share his pain. He knew the abuse he'd suffered was something he needed to get off his chest, but once he'd told her what had happened he hadn't seen the need to revisit it. She'd been something of an amateur psychologist, always seeking the reasons for people's behaviour, perhaps to better understand her own desire to take risks and live on the edge. Whilst speaking about what his father had done to him as a boy had given him the freedom to move on with his life, talking about it opened up old wounds that never got a chance to fully heal. Meadow seemed to understand his boundaries, his need for personal space, even without knowing the circumstances. That was a connection he didn't want to throw away with one stupid act of recklessness.

Of course there was an attraction. She was a beautiful woman, but they were colleagues and anything more than that would be a complication neither of them needed. He certainly wasn't ready to get into another relationship, and Meadow was the kind of woman who needed something more than he could ever give her. It was clear that her father's lifestyle had been the cause of their conflict in the past and staying here long-term was not in Jay's plans for the future. He would only be in town until he could figure out the new path he wanted to take. Although he was a little lost at the minute, he was sure it wasn't one on a red dirt track leading to nowhere.

'He seems to be getting back to his old self. I spoke to him on the phone this morning and he was bending my

ear about getting out in the field to do some digging.'
Meadow rolled her eyes, seeming more eager to attend
this accident scene than have to do her father's bidding.

'He really couldn't leave it for a few days? It doesn't
seem fair to expect you to do that kind of manual work
on top of the day job, as well as entertain his new lodger.'
The reference to last night made him think of those few
seconds on the doorstep when he'd forgotten about his
parents, Sharyn, the fire, even the list. His entire being
had been focused on Meadow and the feel of her lips on
his skin, the fresh smell of her hair and the need to hold
her in his arms. He'd been tempted to do just that before
common sense had kicked in to remind him who she was
and what they were doing. Today he hoped to get back on
track as co-workers who occasionally rubbed each other
up the wrong way, figuratively speaking.

'Every cent counts, or nugget in my dad's case. He
won't be able to settle if he thinks there's gold sitting
out there, waiting for someone other than him to find it.
I suppose I'm the next best thing since I'd actually give
it to him. It's not totally alien to me. There was a time I
used to enjoy going out with him, using the metal detector and my little trowel. Except I wasn't efficient enough
and once I got older I realised it was mainly a waste of
time, effort and a life.' The bitter tone matched the frown
line blighting her forehead as she spoke about their toxic
relationship.

Jay wondered that she maintained any contact with
the man when he'd clearly caused her so much emotional
damage. He'd chosen to never set eyes on his father again,
to completely remove the source of his pain. Whilst he
admired Meadow for trying to maintain some sort of

connection, he couldn't help but think it came at a huge cost to her wellbeing.

'Hopefully it won't be for long, eh?' If her father's condition was improving it would take some of the pressure from her shoulders, and it might also lessen the chance of temptation. Once her father was ensconced back in his own home Meadow wouldn't feel as though she had to stick around and spend time with Jay out of hours.

'I was thinking I'd move into Dad's place for a couple of days, until he gets home at least. I don't want to be driving back and forward all the time.' Perhaps seeing the look of concern on his face that they would actually be spending more time together for the foreseeable future, she added, 'Plus, it means we can car share to work.'

'Great.' Jay forced a smile. It would solve the problem of how he was going to get to work until he sorted out his own transport, but it also entailed being with Meadow most of the working day. He was going to have to keep his wits about him, have the tangible plan of his future close at hand at all times, holding the list close to his heart instead of Meadow.

'We're coming in to land. Brace for impact,' Greg notified them over the intercom. The terrain, as Jay was finding out, didn't always provide a smooth landing. They often had to set down in less than ideal locations, making it a bumpy experience as the wheels met the rocky landscape. It certainly wasn't the flight experience he'd been used to on his journey from the UK to Oz.

He and Meadow both made sure they were buckled in to their seats and prepared to launch into full medical emergency mode once they hit the dirt. Their kit was ready to go in their bags so they could get the patients stabilised as soon as possible before transferring them to hospital.

'You ready for this?' Meadow asked as the plane bumped along the ground.

'I hope so.' This was his first emergency call as a flight doctor, and whilst he'd had plenty of experience dealing with those, he was used to having more facilities at his disposal. At an accident site all of the emergency services would be more readily available, with local hospitals nearby to provide all the latest medical equipment and technology, not to mention the best surgeons, to treat whatever life-changing injuries might occur.

Out here, they were the first responders, the nearest hospital miles away, with probably the most basic facilities to treat the casualties. Responsibility was going to be primarily borne by him and Meadow and they had no real idea what they were walking into.

As soon as the plane stopped moving, they unclipped their belts and grabbed their medical bags. The territory still unfamiliar to him, he followed Meadow as she ran towards the main road, and thanked modern technology for getting them to this exact location when it all looked the same at eye level.

The crash involved an articulated lorry and a heavy loader. With those kinds of large vehicles, and depending on the speeds involved, the impact was huge. He hoped the drivers had been wearing seatbelts at least, to give them a chance. The anticipation of what they would find always gave him that feeling in the pit of his stomach of impending doom, but it was his job to get there as quickly as possible and minimise the severity of potential injuries.

Meadow too was rushing to the scene without a second thought, and he wondered what had prompted her to work in this field when they did have to walk into the unknown like this. She certainly didn't seem to like her father living his life that way. Although there weren't that many options available out here for people who wanted to work in the medical field, so she might not have had a choice if she'd wanted to pursue her nursing career. Even more reason to admire her when she was willing to face whatever fears she had to help others.

'You check the truck driver's vitals. I'll go to the other guy.' Jay moved towards the heavy machinery; the front of the vehicle had obviously taken the brunt of the impact and spun across the road. It was half off the road, the window smashed and arcs from the tyre marks scorched into the road.

He swore when he realised the driver hadn't been belted in. Though he was lucky not to have gone through the windscreen, his head was bleeding profusely from where he'd obviously hit the glass.

'Hello. Can you hear me? You've been in an accident. My name's Jay, I'm with the flying doctor service. Open your eyes if you can hear me.' The man was unconscious, unresponsive and hanging halfway out of the vehicle. He had a pulse but there was a chance the collision could've caused him spinal injuries and they needed to stabilise his neck so as not to exacerbate any damage already done.

'Can you give me a hand?' he called to Greg, who'd brought the stretcher and back board so they could immobilise the patient ready for transit. Between them, they managed to gently manoeuvre him out and lie him flat on the board.

Jay checked his pulse and his breathing to make sure

the move hadn't caused any deterioration in his condition. Once he was satisfied the patient was stable enough to be transferred, they began pushing him back towards the plane.

'Jay? Come here, quick.' An anxious-sounding Meadow beckoned him over to the truck, where the driver was lying on the ground, fitting.

'What happened?'

'He was conscious, and insisted on getting out of the cab, against my advice. Then he just dropped to the ground.' Meadow was already down beside him, loosening the top button on his shirt to help him breathe easier.

'Did he mention being epileptic? Maybe that's what caused the crash.' It was difficult to tell without having a medical history to hand, or diagnostic tools. All they could do was wait out the seizure and get him to the hospital for tests.

'Wait!' Meadow stopped Jay just as he was about to move him into the recovery position. 'His tongue's rolled back.'

With one hand on his forehead and one on his chin, she tilted the driver's head back to open his airway and move the tongue forward again. Although it wasn't physically possible for the man to swallow his tongue, it had blocked his airway, preventing oxygen from getting to his lungs, but with Meadow's vigilance it had been a quick fix.

Jay brushed away the bits of rock and glass littering the ground around them so the patient wouldn't injure himself further. Thankfully, the seizure didn't last long, and they were able to move him into the recovery position, after which he began to regain some consciousness.

'Hi, I'm Meadow from the flying doctor service, remember? You were involved in an accident and have just had a seizure. We're going to have to get you to hospital to check things out, okay?' Meadow talked to him calmly as she held his hand, the man still disoriented and drifting in and out of consciousness.

Once Greg returned with another stretcher, they were able to lift him onto it and all make their way back to the plane. Hopefully, the injuries the men had suffered were superficial and there was no internal bleeding or broken bones to complicate recovery. They would only find out for sure when they reached the hospital, by which point Jay and Meadow would be handing over the responsibility and treatment to the staff there.

They made sure the patients were secure and ready for transporting before securing their own seatbelts. Only then did Jay relax some of the tension from his body with a sigh. He saw Meadow grinning out of the corner of his eye.

'It's full-on, isn't it?' she said.

'I feel like I've just run a marathon. I'm used to the adrenaline rush working in emergency departments, but actually being out in the field, or the desert, brings a whole new dimension to the job.'

'Is that a good or bad thing?' She cocked her head to one side, waiting for his answer as though she genuinely cared whether or not he was enjoying his new role.

'It'll never be boring I suppose. Sharyn would approve.'

'It's definitely challenging at times, but rewarding too. You'll get to know most of the community doing this job. They're like an extended family.'

'It's a surprising career path for someone who professes not to like the unpredictable nature of life out in the sticks.'

'I didn't want to move to the city, this is my home. If anything, life with my dad, on the move, out in the middle of nowhere, gave me some understanding of what people need in the way of medical services out here. I wanted to help, it's as simple as that.'

'I think you're more of an adventurer than you care to admit, Meadow Williams.'

She'd proved to him again today that she was as brave as she was kind-hearted. A dangerous combination, even to someone who didn't think he'd want to share his life with anyone ever again.

'Are you coming round to mine later? I'm having a few birthday drinks and firing the barbie up.' Greg approached Meadow and Jay some time later, back at the base. They'd safely delivered the victims of the accident to the hospital and finished their open clinic for the day. Meadow was hoping to finish up the paperwork and drive her stuff over to her dad's place.

'I don't think so. I have a lot to do tonight.'

Jay gave her a nudge. 'Oh, come on. It'll give me a chance to get to meet some new people. Or would you rather keep me all to yourself?'

Meadow rolled her eyes. He was surprisingly perky after the day they'd had, whilst she was barely managing to stifle a yawn. 'Knock yourself out, Party Boy, but I have work to do if my dad's going to keep a roof over his head.'

'Surely you're not going digging out there tonight? You can do it tomorrow when you're off. I reckon we need to let off some steam and it'll save you from having to make me dinner. I think it's your turn to cook, isn't it?'

'I don't remember saying that.'

She thought about the possible evening ahead, when they probably would end up spending it together, alone, and came to the fast conclusion it wasn't a good idea. They'd come close to doing something stupid last night and another cosy dinner together, getting to know each other even more in a repeat of last night, wasn't going to help her avoid temptation.

'Well, we haven't had time to grocery shop and barely got to eat lunch. We could get something to eat, toast Greg a happy birthday, and leave. No offence, mate.' Jay clapped Greg on the back in apology for the assumption they'd only stay long enough to fill their bellies.

'None taken. Meadow doesn't usually come to any of our shindigs, so it'll be a birthday treat to have you there. Make sure you both bring your swimming togs.'

'No way.'

'Not a chance.'

Meadow's protest was quickly followed by Jay's as Greg walked away from them. The last thing she needed was to see him parading about in his swimwear as if he were participating in a beauty pageant for hot doctors. It would be no contest when he'd surely take the tiara anyway.

'Dinner and one drink. That's it.'

'It's a date.'

'Not a date,' she corrected, knowing full well he was teasing her.

'Dinner, a drink, back to your place… I'd call that a date.'

'I'd call that wishful thinking. Now, do you want a lift home or not?' Meadow wondered how he'd react if she actually said yes to a date. Now, that would give him something to think about. Unfortunately, it also put more thoughts in her head that she definitely shouldn't be having about a co-worker.

'Why don't you socialise with the rest of the crew?' Jay asked as they drove back towards the town.

'I socialise. I'm just choosy about what events I attend.'

'Like playing pool in the pub with people like Marko?'

Oh, he knew how to push her buttons!

'I told you I was having a rough time. I'd just broken up with someone and I was a bit vulnerable and lonely.' She didn't know why she was explaining herself to him, other than to make sure he knew that wasn't her usual behaviour. Every time she thought of Marko and their drunken antics she cringed. She had a similar reaction when she recalled the way she'd been with Jay that first night. In hindsight, he'd only been looking out for her, calling Marko out for being inappropriate, and something she should have appreciated when everyone else let him get away with it. It seemed to have done the trick at least; Marko had kept his distance since Jay had stepped in to protect her.

'Sorry. Your personal life is none of my business, as is who you play pool with, or kiss in a moment of weakness.' The playful tone drew the side eye from Meadow.

'I don't make a habit of it.' In case he got any idea that he was next, especially after last night's near-miss. Hopefully, she'd learned her lesson and wouldn't make another embarrassing mistake she'd live to regret. It was the main reason she'd agreed to attend this party, regardless that she'd rather crawl into bed for an early night. Jay had a point about meeting other people and making new friends. If he managed to do that, they might not spend so much time together. He might find someone else to give him a lift to work, to find a room for him or that he could cook meals for. Then she could get back to her quiet life in her own house, with no distracting Englishman around to annoy her.

'Hey, guys. Grab yourself a few snags before they're all gone.' Greg greeted them wearing a pair of bright yellow board shorts and a white vest that almost blinded Meadow when he opened the door.

'Happy birthday, mate.' Jay leaned in and gave their co-worker a manly hug with lots of back-slapping involved.

'We brought you a case of beer as a present. I hope that's okay?' They'd stopped off on the way for the joint purchase, realising they couldn't turn up empty-handed to a birthday party.

'You can never go wrong with the old grog, can you?' He took the beer from Meadow and tucked it under his arm before leading them out towards the backyard.

Like most of the houses around the area, hers included, it wasn't a vast property but Greg had managed to squeeze a small pool into the backyard where everyone was currently congregated.

He directed them towards the cloud of smoke coming from the barbecue. 'Grub's over on the table, there's a few stubbies in the fridge, and towels on the decking if you fancy a swim.'

'We won't be staying that long, sorry. I'm staying at

my dad's place at the minute so I have to drive back out there.' Meadow made her excuse early so she could duck away as soon as possible without having to go through the rigmarole of saying goodbye and him trying to persuade her to stay. Greg had enough family and friends, not many of whom she was acquainted with, to keep him busy. Given the stories she'd heard of the drunken antics that went on at some of Greg's pool parties, she wasn't tempted to stay until the inebriated masses decided it was a good idea to go skinny-dipping. She tried not to let her mind wander towards Jay getting involved with such abandon in case she was tempted.

'Sorry, mate.' Jay made his apology too, even though he was free to stay on if he wished. Although with Marko the only local taxi driver as his alternative means of transport, perhaps she wasn't giving him any option but to leave with her.

'Wait…' Greg looked at Meadow then back to Jay. 'Are you two together?'

'We're living together,' Jay casually replied, lifting a bottle of beer from the bucket of ice under the table.

'No, we're not.' Meadow huffed out a breath through gritted teeth.

'I mean, you don't seem a likely couple, but fair play to ya.' Greg clinked the bottle of beer he was now holding in his hand to Jay's.

'We're not together, and why would we make an unlikely couple?' It was ridiculous to be outraged by the comment when she was taking pains to make sure Greg knew they weren't a couple, but Meadow knew the comment was sure to be an insult against her. Greg and Jay had hit it off immediately, whereas it had taken her and their pilot some time to build up a good working rapport. He was another man who took risks; sometimes he had to when it came to getting to their patients. By no means was he reckless, but some of the hairy situations they'd found themselves in over the years had caused some friction. They had different ways of doing things, and though they didn't always agree, they both wanted the best for their patients and muddled along. A bit like her and Jay, except they'd never had a cosy dinner for two or nearly pashed on the doorstep.

Greg held his hands up in surrender and she knew it was because he was expecting her to go ape at him after what he was about to say. 'It's just…don't take this the wrong way, but you can be a bit uptight sometimes, Meads. Jay's more laidback, like me.'

Meadow opened and closed her mouth but words refused to come and fight against the character assassination because she knew it was true. She couldn't help being the stickler for rules she was because it was how she protected herself and others around her. Safety was a big issue for someone who'd grown up without it, emotionally and physically.

'Was that the doorbell? I'll have to go and let more bogans in if we're really gonna get this party started. Whoo!' With his beer held aloft, Greg disappeared back into the house, giving her no further chance to defend herself.

'Don't let him upset you. He is like me, sometimes he doesn't think before he speaks. Being cautious isn't a bad thing. It's what I like about you.' Jay's words managed to alleviate some of the pain Greg had clumsily inflicted upon her.

He liked her.

'You like that I'm boring?' Okay, the tail from the sting was still embedded somewhere under her skin.

'I never said you were boring. I said you were cautious. After being with Sharyn, who was always pushing me to do something out of my comfort zone, it's nice to be around someone who'll just let me be.' Jay gave a little chuckle to himself.

She knew he wasn't disrespecting his cherished girl-friend but perhaps now, with a bit of time and space, he realised that he didn't have to be constantly challenging himself.

'Some peace and quiet now and again can be good for the soul.'

'As can doing something exhilarating and breaking out of the norm,' Jay added, giving her pause to think that it didn't have to be one way or another.

Once again, that niggling feeling that she should let loose and do something spontaneous, just to see what happened, was creeping into her thoughts. Although the only reckless thing she'd imagined doing recently was kissing Jay, and the fallout from that would have been a price too high to pay when they'd still have to work to-gether. She knew she'd be in danger of liking him too much, and getting romantically involved meant being invested in his welfare, his safety. Something he didn't appear to value. Falling for Jay proved a risk too far if it entailed having her heart broken when he left her for the next thrill elsewhere.

'I'm here, aren't I?' She took a bottle from the ice bucket, cracked the lid on the edge of the table and chugged back the beer in defiance.

'Yes, you are. Maybe for your next venture you could

go shark swimming with me.' He didn't take his eyes off her as he took a swig of lager, as though watching for her reaction. As much as she wanted to prove a point, she wasn't going to put herself in danger simply to try and get one up on him.

'If I won't even get in the pool here, what makes you think I'd even entertain that idea? I'm thinking more along the lines of stroking a koala. One step at a time, Jay.'

'It's a date,' he replied, walking away.

'Not a date,' she corrected, looking forward to it already.

'Hey, you.' Kate wandered over to her at that moment, or at least Meadow hadn't noticed her until she'd spoken.

'Hey. I didn't think you'd be here.' Meadow pulled her into a one-armed hug, holding her beer with the other.

'Well, Bob thought hanging out with you kids would keep us young at heart.'

'You're not old, Kate.' And she'd a much busier social calendar than Meadow could ever hope to have.

'No? I've only had one glass of wine and I'm ready for my bed. Not that Bob would complain about that.' The usually reserved manager giggled, suggesting it might have been a very large glass she'd had.

'You're lucky to have each other.'

'I guess so. Speaking of romance, you have a glow about you tonight.' She peered closely at Meadow.

'Really? Must be the wine goggles.'

Kate wagged a finger. 'Nope. I've known you a long time, Meadow Williams, and I can tell when something's changed. I haven't seen you this happy since that Shawn left. Is there a new man on the scene I don't know about?'

Meadow inadvertently cast a look at Jay, who was over talking to some of the guys from the base.

'No,' she said, the high-pitched denial unconvincing even to her own ears.

Kate's jaw dropped. 'The doc?'

She whistled, then raised her glass in a toast. 'I'll give it to you, he does have a peachy bum, love.'

Meadow couldn't argue on that point, but she was perturbed by the fact she was so easy to read. 'Why does everyone think there's something going on between me and Jay? We're just colleagues, like you and me, Kate.'

'Uh-huh. Yet you came here together, according to Greg.' Kate narrowed her eyes at Meadow over the rim of her glass.

Meadow huffed out a sigh of frustration. 'He doesn't have a car. I gave him a lift. He's going to be staying at my dad's old place until he gets sorted out with somewhere else so I guess it'll become a regular thing. It's no biggie.'

Kate set down her glass. 'No biggie? I've known you to have entire relationships without introducing your significant other to your father. You've known Jay for a matter of days and he's living out there? Girl, you've got it bad.'

Meadow tutted and rolled her eyes at the insinuation but felt as though she'd just been slapped. It had taken her some time to convince herself that she should do the right thing and offer Jay the place to stay, that there was nothing more to it than doing him a favour. Now Kate was calling her out on it there was nowhere to hide. She was right, Meadow had kept introductions with her dad to a minimum when it came to romantic partners. Not that Jay was anything of the sort, but even her colleagues only got to meet him if they ran into him by accident at the bar.

She didn't like her family business, and the mess it was, to intersect with the life she'd created for herself in Dream Gulley. In case it somehow contaminated everything she had achieved. Back on Rainbow's Walk were the bad memories of her family splitting up, of leaving her dad behind, but her adult life in town was settled and safe. She had friends and colleagues, a sense of belonging in the community, and didn't like to be seen as Digger's daughter. They knew the sort of person he was, unkempt, irascible and unpredictable. At times she was embarrassed to be associated with him, but she already knew Jay wasn't the sort of person to make that judgement. He'd been through a rough childhood too and understood the importance of keeping a personal life private.

That was the only reason she'd let her defences down and agreed to Jay crossing that line from their working relationship. That almost-kiss had just been a blip. Absolutely no reason for her to panic.

She knocked back the rest of her beer.

Jay stopped teasing Meadow long enough to go and fill a plate likely to give him the meat sweats later, with a green salad on the side to salve his conscience. He'd had no more interest in coming here than she had, but he reckoned it was safer for them to be in a crowd after last night.

By the time they'd had a bite to eat and a drink it would be acceptable for him to head on to his accommodation and leave with Meadow to go back to her dad's. They wouldn't feel obliged to spend more time together once it got dark. Basically, he was using Greg as a buffer to prevent him from crossing a line. It wouldn't go down well if he'd called Marko out for making unwanted advances, only to do the same himself. Although, judging by the way she'd been looking at him and the hitch in her breath when their lips had been a whisper away from touching on the doorstep, the idea hadn't been totally abhorrent to her. Making it even more dangerous.

Deciding to come to the party instead brought its own problems. It was one of the rare occasions when he'd seen her out of her uniform, if he didn't count almost naked bar her dressing gown at dinner. She looked relaxed tonight in her rust-coloured gypsy-style skirt and cropped white top that showed off her tanned, flat belly. Her hair was free from the usual ponytail, the golden waves perfectly framing her heart-shaped face. She'd even put on a little make-up tonight, the pink lipstick making her lips look even more delicious than usual.

He swallowed down his lustful thoughts with another mouthful of cold beer, though he wondered if he'd been at the back of her mind at all when she'd got ready tonight. After another cold shower he'd pulled on a clean shirt, even ironed it first, in order to make a good impression on her. He certainly hadn't taken that level of effort for Greg's sake, whose idea of dressing up was to wear a shirt at all.

They hadn't spent the whole night joined at the hip; after all, he'd told her he wanted to make new friends. That didn't mean he hadn't always had her in the corner of his eye when he'd been shooting the breeze with Greg's friends, and taking a ribbing over his accent. In fact, he could see her now, making her way back to him with a plate of food in her hand and stifling a yawn.

'Too much excitement?'

'Sorry. I didn't sleep well last night, too much going on in my mind.'

'Yeah, me too. I mean, I need to find somewhere permanent to stay and I have an extreme to-do list to complete.' He didn't want her to think he'd been replaying that moment between them in his head over and over again and trying to convince himself he didn't regret walking away.

'No word back from the service?'

'They're looking into it, but I guess the way they see it is I'm already here, doing the job, so they're probably not in a rush to rehouse me. Especially when I'm staying at your dad's place.' Something that wasn't going to be ideal long-term when it meant being around Meadow twenty-four-seven whilst actively trying to avoid getting close to her.

'Tell them they need to compensate you if they're not going to give you the agreed accommodation, that should get them moving.'

'I'll do that. I was wondering if I could accompany you tomorrow for a while when you're digging. That's one more thing I could cross off…'

He didn't like the idea of Meadow doing that kind of dangerous task out on her own when her own father had succumbed to the heat and terrain, despite her having experience, and Jay being a total novice. She probably wouldn't need his help but he wanted to be around to make sure she was okay, and could do so under the pretence of completing another of his challenges.

'I'm not sure…' Meadow was trying to formulate a response which wouldn't hurt his feelings too much when there was the sound of a splash and a scream.

Jay had been watching something unfold over her shoulder and he took off in the direction of the pool. Before she knew what was happening, he'd dived into the pool with a crowd peering down into the deep end. It seemed an age before he emerged with a young woman in his arms. He swam on his back, guiding the woman, who was clearly unconscious, to the edge of the pool, where everyone worked together to get her out of the pool and lay her on the ground. Meadow set her plate down and rushed to help.

'She's not breathing.' Jay was kneeling by the woman, his wet clothes clinging to every hard inch of his body like a second skin, which made it hard not to stare.

Meadow tilted the woman's chin up to try and help her breathe as Jay wiped the water from his eyes. 'She has a cut and a bruise on her head too. She must have knocked herself out.'

'I saw her slip just before she went in the water, but it happened so quickly there was nothing I could do,' Jay said worriedly.

'I think you did plenty,' Meadow told him as he started chest compressions, his interlocked hands pushing down on the middle of the woman's chest in an attempt to bring her back to life.

'Someone call an ambulance,' Jay shouted at the assembled crowd. A blanket was thrown over his shoulders but he shrugged it off, his only concern for the woman at the mercy of his ministrations.

Meadow admired his dedication and determination, but saw him begin to tire, the physical exertion taking its toll on him. 'I can take over for a while.'

He nodded his agreement without argument, a sign not

only of his exhaustion but his trust and respect in her capabilities too. In the end they took turns with the chest compressions whilst Greg cleared the rest of the partygoers away from the area, probably to prevent any further distress if they couldn't bring her back round. It was an intimate yet tense scene, with the two of them working together to save a life. As medics, it was something they encountered every day but here, now, Meadow felt the pressure more. They were at a friend's house, on his birthday, with everyone relying on them to perform a miracle.

Meadow glanced up, feeling Jay's eyes on her as she pumped the woman's chest.

'It'll be okay.' That look, that promise, gave her the strength to keep going, and she was rewarded when their patient spluttered, exhaling some of the water which had filled her lungs.

Between them, they moved her onto her side in the recovery position. She coughed up what was left of the pool water and opened her eyes.

'Hey,' Meadow said softly, stroking the wet hair away from her face. 'You slipped and fell into the pool but you're going to be okay. The ambulance is on the way.'

Jay took the blanket which had been offered to him and covered her shivering body just as they heard the sirens approach. The three of them sat in silence until the paramedics came through, led by a happier-looking Greg.

'Am I glad you guys were here for Junie. I'm not sure I'd have been in any fit state to perform CPR.'

'Next time maybe keep the pool covered if you're going to be drinking. Alcohol and swimming don't mix.' Jay's admonishment seemed to take Greg as much by surprise as it did Meadow. Perhaps he wasn't as reckless with others' lives as he seemed to be with his own and it showed a level of maturity which their colleague had yet to reach.

Jay had acted heroically, and though Meadow didn't know if she would've reacted the same way, she was glad he had. They made a good team, their different ways of doing things working together to get the right outcome. She couldn't help but wonder how that would translate into a more personal relationship. There would never be a dull moment, undoubtedly, but that was also what terrified her when she thought about a possible life with Jay.

Once the paramedics took the patient away Greg called everyone to attention. 'Okay, ladies and gentlemen, I've been assured that Junie is going to be all right, so I think we should get this party back on track. Everyone inside for beer pong!'

Slowly, the partygoers began to filter back inside, leaving Meadow, Jay, Kate and Bob standing outside.

'Never one to let the party stop is our Greg,' Meadow said with a laugh, shaking her head.

'I think that's enough excitement for one night. I'll see you two at work tomorrow.' Kate hugged both of her colleagues before taking her husband's hand and walking away.

It always made Meadow yearn for the sort of relationship they had when she saw Kate and Bob together. Being happily married with a family was something she'd aspired to for a long time. Probably because she hadn't had much experience of it herself. But she was beginning to think it wasn't on the cards for her. She hadn't met anyone who fitted the bill, or who she would trust enough to let that close to her. Okay, so she'd let Jay into her private life, but an adrenaline junkie like him would never be satisfied with someone who simply wanted quiet nights in and a partner to hold hands with.

It didn't stop her from wishing for it.

Once she was alone with Jay, she noticed then that he had begun to shiver, still soaked to the skin.

'You need to get out of those wet clothes before you end up with hypothermia.' Her nursing instincts kicked in and she began to unbutton the shirt presenting his body like a gift to the watching world. The almost transparent fabric clung to the ripples of his stomach, the taut muscles of his chest, pinching around his tight nipples to show her just how cold he was, and Meadow lost herself to the unwrapping of Jay's spectacular form.

He made no move to stop her as she peeled away his shirt and let it fall to the floor, but his eyes never left her face. She could feel that grey steel gaze locked onto her as she concentrated on disrobing him, for his own benefit. The fact that she got to see him like this up close and very personal was merely a bonus.

She barely resisted sliding her hands down the smooth lines of his body, glistening in the moonlight. But when she moved to undo his belt, her fingers refused to obey, fumbling over the simplest of tasks.

'Let me,' Jay insisted, working deftly to undo the fastening before slowly, torturously, to unbutton his fly.

Meadow was watching, mesmerised, and when he let his trousers fall, the belt hitting the tiles with a thud, she had to fight to breathe. His boxers were moulded intimately, and impressively, around his hips, and she couldn't look away.

'Hey, eyes up here. I'm not a sex object, you know.' He laughed and tilted her chin up to look at him.

Her cheeks were burning at being caught out ogling under the pretence of regulating his body heat. Yet embarrassment wasn't the main emotion she was currently feeling. Just looking at him, knowing he was letting her, had awakened that deep need inside her for more. She was unbelievably turned on.

'Sorry. I was just wondering if you needed to take everything off in this situation.' She decided it was better to play along with the flirting than admit she was enjoying the view.

'I will if you will. They do say that skin-to-skin contact is better to produce body heat.' He hooked his fingers into the sides of his underwear and she was sure she was about to get the full Monty when Greg came rushing back, carrying towels and clothes.

'I thought you might need a change of clothes...'

He took one look at them and tutted. 'And you're not together? Pull the other one.'

'It's not what it looks like.'

'I was just taking off my wet clothes.'

They protested their innocence in vain as Greg dropped everything and backed away, holding his hands up. 'Whatever you say.'

'Grow up, Greg,' Meadow pouted, though she couldn't figure out if she was more annoyed at the insinuation or the interruption.

CHAPTER SIX

THE SUN WAS high in the sky when Jay eventually woke. It had been a late night after all. Later still when he'd lain awake into the early hours, going over the events at the party in his mind. Not only on a high after saving that woman's life with Meadow, but also because of the sparks between them which were dangerous so close to a body of water.

Even though they'd been out in the open, he'd been freezing cold and wet and the circumstances anything but sexy, those few seconds of Meadow staring at his partially naked body had been the most erotic thing he'd experienced in a long time.

He didn't know what would have happened if Greg hadn't walked in on them, probably nothing since there was a houseful of people still there. However, the interruption had managed to bring them both back down to earth. So much so they'd barely spoken on the journey back. Meadow hadn't even taken the opportunity to tease him about the neon board shorts and cerise vest top Greg had provided him with in place of the wet clothes he'd carried home in a bag.

They'd said their goodbyes and gone their separate ways as soon as they'd pulled up on her father's property. It was clear she regretted whatever had gone on in her mind as he'd performed his impromptu strip tease, but he hadn't missed that flare of desire she'd briefly allowed to burn before it had been extinguished. In those few seconds he'd got to see a more uninhibited Meadow, a woman who knew what she wanted and wasn't afraid to show it. Then those barriers had popped up again, stealing that light from her eyes, and making sure he redressed in double quick time, the intimate moment obviously over.

Then he'd tossed and turned until dawn, wondering if he'd wanted things to go further and not liking the answer. Yes. He'd been tortured by the thought of going over and knocking on her door to see if she wanted to carry on where they'd left off. Then he realised if she had, she would've come to him. Meadow was a woman who knew her own mind, knew what she wanted, and what she didn't. There had obviously been something, other than Greg's untimely arrival, which had caused her to rethink her interest in him as more than a colleague.

He should be relieved her aversion to spontaneity had saved him from betraying Sharyn's memory. Yet it had been that 'what if?' fantasy which had kept him from sleep, not guilt. Since Sharyn's death he hadn't thought about being with another woman, the grief too raw to let him form any sort of emotional attachment to anyone else. He hadn't even wanted a purely physical hook-up because it would've been empty, meaningless, and would have made his mood sink lower, disgusted with himself for doing it.

Sharyn would have wanted him to meet someone else. She would never have expected him to lock himself away from the world again. In fact, she would've been angry at him for waiting so long before even thinking that getting involved with someone could be a possibility.

As he lay there debating the issue, he realised the whole thing was futile anyway when Meadow clearly didn't see him as relationship material. He knew she was still reeling from a breakup, and whatever issue had caused it was perhaps preventing her from moving on too. Or maybe she just wasn't that into him.

And yet… He considered briefly that lustful look in her eyes as he'd let his trousers drop to the floor.

'Nah,' he said aloud to his empty room, pleased with himself at managing to get Meadow to at least recognise she found him attractive.

After another period of convincing himself he could catch forty winks, only to find himself lying staring at the ceiling again, he had to concede it was time to get up. After a quick wash and a bite of toast, he dressed and headed over to see her.

'Meadow? Are you up?' After getting no response he let himself in—security was noticeably absent and he hoped she was more conscious of it in her own house.

There was no sign of her in the living room or kitchen, though there was an empty cereal bowl and a half-finished glass of orange sitting by the sink. She was another one who'd risen early.

Since she hadn't come out of the bedroom to accuse him of breaking and entering, he deduced she'd already gone out to dig without him. To be fair, she hadn't actually agreed to his request to join her; events had overtaken them. But he had registered his interest so it was jarring to find she'd chosen to ignore his suggestion, knowing it was on the list.

He'd made sure to bring some water with him, along with his phone and a hat. It could be she'd decided she didn't want to encourage his company all the time in case it gave him any ideas about the nature of their relationship. He didn't want to be another Marko so he would respect her boundaries there, but he also wanted to make sure she was safe. Surely she wouldn't mind too much if he stopped by to say hello and check in with her?

Jay wandered out towards the spot where they'd found her father a few days ago, ensuring he kept one eye back on the house to maintain his bearings. Of course Meadow wasn't answering her phone because it had been sitting on the kitchen table where she'd left it. He hoped she hadn't done so intentionally, knowing he'd been keen to go out this morning with her. If so, she really wasn't going to be pleased to see him.

'Meadow?' he called out into the vast expanse in case she'd ventured off track to somewhere new. There was no point in him walking aimlessly into the bush with no idea where she was or where he was going. That was just asking for trouble, and a repeat of what had happened to her dad, which was the last thing she'd want, or need. He wouldn't be very popular if she had to waste her day off getting him airlifted to hospital.

'Meadow? Are you out here?'

'Jay? Be careful. I'll come to you. Wait there.'

He heard her but couldn't see her, and ventured towards the edge of the ditch where her father had come unstuck, careful not to lose his footing too. Peering over the drop, he saw her crouched down in the dirt. With her hair tied up under her wide-brimmed hat, showing off her tanned limbs in khaki shorts and camo shirt, dirt smeared on her cheek, she looked even more gorgeous than last night.

'I told you to wait,' she sighed, standing up to brush the dust from her clothes.

'I'm not going to do anything stupid. I'm just standing here.' He didn't want to be a liability or a source of irritation, he only knew he had to come out here this morning to be with her.

Another hefty sigh. 'I'm busy, Jay.'

She was shielding her eyes with her hand, the sun already blazing down on them at this hour. That, combined with the amount of flies he was constantly having to bat away, made Jay wonder what the attraction of this was, apart from the obvious hope of finding a fortune. He could think of easier ways to make money. It began to make sense why she was so risk-averse and in need of stability. Perhaps why she didn't want to contemplate the idea of being with him when he was always talking about that stupid list. Although it had been important at the time for him and Sharyn, a way for him to break out of old habits, he didn't want it to get in the way of the future.

'Any luck so far?' Even though she would probably be more welcoming if she'd uncovered some gold, it was the only question which came to mind for now.

Meadow frowned. 'Nope. So there goes the patch theory. Give me a hand up.'

She reached up and he hauled her, the detector and pickaxe out of the ditch.

'Are you done for the day then?' Maybe they could take a drive out for some lunch, or spend the afternoon together at a wildlife park for that talked about koala experience.

Meadow gave a shrill laugh. 'No. I'm not going to go

back to my father empty-handed if it kills me. If I can find something decent it could keep him going for a while, and hopefully he won't try and kill himself finding money for next month's bills.'

'So how do you find a good prospect? Where do you start?' Whilst Jay admired her determination to provide for her father, it seemed like relentlessly hard work for very little gain. Unless she did something her experienced father hadn't managed, and uncovered a boulder-sized nugget of golden goodness.

'Well, I thought my dad's finds would've been a good place to start. He always maintained there was a motherlode waiting to be found in the ancient dried riverbed that supposedly ran here. Gold deposits are often transported by rivers, but I've scanned the area and there isn't a signal to be found.' She waved the metal detector in the air and he got the impression if it hadn't been worth a small fortune on its own, she would've launched it into the stratosphere.

'How long have you been out here?'

'Since daybreak. I need to find something, Jay. He'll be so disappointed if I don't, and he'll be straight back out here rather than resting.'

'Okay. So do you have any idea where it would be a good spot to start over?'

'I don't have his map grid of places he's searched before, or intends to search. There are some old gold mines around. Although they're largely mined out, they didn't have the same equipment in the eighteen-hundreds as we do now. I guess that's as good an area as any to try.'

'Can I tag along? I won't get in the way, promise.'

'You're happy to stand out here in near forty-degree

heat, plagued by flies, to just watch?' She was standing with one hand on her hip, detector slung over her shoulder, and she'd never looked more Aussie.

It was tempting to front it out and say yes, that was enough, but they both knew it was a lie. He was dying to try it.

'I'd love to have a go on your bleepy stick thing.'

Meadow rolled her eyes and walked off, calling behind her, 'You ever call it that in front of my dad and you'll be homeless again.'

Jay grinned, knowing he'd got her approval to tag along after all.

Meadow should have insisted that he go back to the house out of harm's way, but the truth was she liked the company. She'd thought she could do this on her own but her frustrated attempts in the heat had left her seconds away from a teary breakdown before Jay had arrived. The sight of him had made her glad he'd ignored her obvious decision to leave without him this morning, despite his request to accompany her.

Things last night had got too hot and steamy, too wet and wild, for her to take any more chances of being alone with him. Yet here they were again, and only time would tell if she'd have the strength to resist another wave of sexual tension capable of turning her into a voyeur. The way she'd watched him undress last night, she might as well have tucked dollars into his jocks and asked for a lap dance, and she was sure he would've obliged. It was only Greg, and the knowledge they'd both regret it in the cold light of day, which had stopped her from asking him for a private show when they'd come home.

Even that notion of this place as being home was skewed, when she'd never seen her dad's land as anything other than something she had to bear. It was only Jay who'd made it feel somewhere safe. Ironic, given that thrill-seeking nature and the current threat to her peace of mind.

After spending most of her adult life looking after herself, her parents off exploring their own lives, it was nice to have someone with her. She knew part of the reason Jay was here was to make sure she didn't get into difficulty. If he'd really wanted to cross something off that damn list, he could've used his day off to go and do something more exciting than digging in the dirt. He couldn't fool her. The sort of man who'd dive into a pool fully clothed to save someone was also the kind who wouldn't be content to stand back and let a woman do hard manual labour alone.

If it was anyone else, she might be offended that he thought she couldn't manage on her own, but that wasn't it with Jay. Despite his risky behaviour at times, she got a sense that he wanted to keep her safe, and that was something she hadn't had from anybody in a long time. Certainly not from her parents, and not from any of her past partners who, now she looked back on it, might be considered weak. Men she knew couldn't hurt her because she didn't love them enough, so she wouldn't be too broken-hearted when they invariably let her down.

She'd always thought it was stability she wanted in a relationship, but she knew there was part of her that craved the sort of excitement someone like Jay brought into her life. Except she needed care and kindness with it, not risk. Her father and Shawn had got their kicks at her expense and inviting Jay further into her life was the ultimate gamble. In this case, instead of risking her family and finances, she would be putting her heart on the line in the hope of winning her prize. Only time would tell if that adventurous streak would win out over her desire for self-preservation. But for now she was glad she had someone to talk to other than herself out here in the wilds.

'What's the story with the mines? I mean, why aren't they still in operation if it's thought there's still gold in them thar hills?' Jay's insistence that he wasn't going to get in her way was already in dispute when it seemed he wasn't one for companionable silence for the journey.

'The gold rush in the later eighteen-hundreds and into the nineteen-hundreds meant every man and his dog was out trying to find gold. They stripped whatever they could, then the mines were simply abandoned and they made their way to new promising sites, until the price of gold crashed. People like my father are convinced that there might still be gold waiting to be found that modern-day equipment can help discover. Trust me, if my father had the money, he'd have these back in operation.'

'But you don't believe there's a fortune still to be made?'

She shook her head. 'I don't think those men would've walked away if there was a sliver of gold left. I mean, I know he's found a few nuggets round about, but nothing that justifies the money and effort he's put in to find it.' Nor the family he'd traded for it.

'I take it he can't be persuaded otherwise?'

'No. I think at this stage he's too pig-headed to admit defeat. It's an obsession, the mistress that took him away from us.' Meadow couldn't help but be resentful. It might've been easier for her to reconcile events in her mind if it had been another woman who'd stolen his time and devotion when she'd been younger. Then she would have had someone else to be angry at other than her father. It made their relationship complicated when she still bore a grudge, yet loved him too much to simply walk away. If he'd had another woman, at least there would've been someone else to look after him too. As things stood, she was the only one he had in his life. Not that he was grateful, or had ever felt the need to say sorry.

Perhaps if he'd ever apologised for neglecting her and her mother, admitted he'd made a mistake, she could have let go of some of that resentment and got on with her life, minus the fear that another man could inflict the same damage. But he hadn't, and so she hadn't found the courage to open up her heart and share her life with anyone capable of breaking her again.

'Yet you're out here, keeping your father's mistress happy in his absence.' Jay was teasing her again but she didn't mind the gentle ribbing when she knew it came from a good place.

'Yes, well, it doesn't mean I'm ecstatic about it, but needs must. Okay, do you want to try?' She turned on the detector, deciding it might take his mind off asking questions for a while, and stop him probing too deeply into her past. It wasn't something she talked about usually, but Jay had a way of making her open up that she wasn't particularly comfortable with when it left her feeling exposed. As if talking about it would allow him to break through her brittle shell to the soft, vulnerable girl behind it, and she'd protect that child as much as she could because no one else ever had.

'I thought you'd never ask!' Jay rubbed his hands together like an excited child waiting to open a Christmas present. With all the other stuff he'd done in his life, the thought that this should give him a similar rush was amusing rather than concerning. It was difficult to tell if this was for her benefit or if he really did get a thrill every time he did something different. If that was the case, it was adorable that he became an excited puppy with every new discovery.

'You need to keep it low to the ground and sweep from side to side, like this.' She did a quick demonstration to show him. 'We're listening for a change in pitch, a sign that it's picking up something metallic underfoot.'

Meadow handed over the detector, hoping he didn't break it or her father would lose his mind.

'Like this?' Jay swung the device wildly, making her twitch.

'You need to go slow and steady so you don't miss anything.' She stood behind him and put her arms around him to rest her hands on top of his and control the motion of the detector.

'Like this?' He turned his head to check he was doing it right, and they were so close it took Meadow right back to that moment on the doorstep when they'd almost kissed. As much as she still wanted that, she couldn't be sure she'd be able to put the fire out if they did light that touch paper.

She released her hold and put some space between their warm bodies again. 'Yeah. I think you've got it now.'

He held her gaze for another few seconds before he finally looked away and she got her breath back. Thankfully, as he got more invested in his detecting, Meadow was able to keep her distance and didn't feel the need to continue a conversation. She followed his slow, steady steps, letting the birdsong fill the silence. And when the detector screeched a sudden discovery her heart nearly pounded out of her chest.

'Is that…? Have I…?' Jay's eyes were wide, his body frozen to the spot, and he so clearly thought he'd found his treasure, Meadow didn't want to burst his bubble.

'It just means there's metal content present. You could've found a rusty old nail or a bottle top. We need to dig and keep searching for the source.' She took a small trowel from her pocket and dropped to her haunches where he'd picked up the signal.

With a scoopful of earth in her hands, she waved it over the detector and listened for the indication that she'd lifted the metal and it wasn't still in the ground. She repeated the process several times, discarding some of the earth with every pass. This morning had unearthed nothing but useless debris already and though she'd be delighted for everyone involved if this was something shiny and precious, she had her doubts.

'What's that?' Jay was kneeling down beside her now, pointing at the contents of her hand. She poked through the mound of dirt to unearth a small lump of metal. Unfortunately, not the one they were looking for.

'Iron ore. Sorry. But it's often thought that where you find a concentration of iron ore, gold could follow.' Meadow vaguely remembered being told that the deposits were often formed in the earth at the same time, but Jay already seemed to have lost interest. He handed the metal detector back over to her and got to his feet.

'I think I'll let the expert take over. Whilst I can definitely see the attraction, I can only imagine the toll it would take on a person, being disappointed time and again to come away empty-handed. And this is how your father makes his living?'

Meadow nodded. 'That's why he needs the extra income.'

It hadn't taken long for Jay to realise what she was up against with the emotional roller coaster of gold hunting. The precarious nature of the work took a certain type of person to want to do it full-time. Clearly that wasn't her and, surprisingly, not Jay either. She supposed he was someone who needed instant gratification in his adventures and he wouldn't find that here unless he was extremely lucky.

'It's not really suited to family life, is it?'

Meadow tossed away the dirt and stood up. 'Tell me about it. I don't know how my mum coped as long as she did, moving from one place to another. Money was tight, schooling wasn't easy, and it's lonely out here in the Outback if you don't have a good support system of friends. But she made the choice to embark on this life with my dad and there's a big part of me that wishes she would've tried harder to make things work. To give Dad credit, he stopped drifting, bought Rainbow's Walk and made an attempt to settle down. Perhaps it was too little, too late for my mother by then, but I can't help thinking if they'd communicated better they could have salvaged their relationship. That we all could have benefitted from a more stable life if she'd stuck it out a little longer.'

As much as she loved her mother, Meadow believed she should shoulder some of the blame for the breakup of their family too. Her father had made an effort, invested the money he'd made in a plot of land to give them that security, only for her mother to walk away anyway. At fifteen years old, Meadow hadn't been given a choice. If she had, she would've stayed and tried to create a family of sorts with just her and her dad. She hadn't even managed a proper relationship with her mother. They'd only had a couple of years of normality before she'd met someone else and decided to move to Queensland. Her father wasn't the only one with a wanderlust and Meadow had been trying to make up for her mother's actions ever since. Instead of welcoming her back into his life with open arms, he'd seemed to retreat further. As though he was afraid she would leave him eventually too. It was a vicious circle they couldn't break free from.

'I probably would've loved life out here. The open space, the freedom, the fresh air...'

'I know I shouldn't ask, but—'

'When my father wasn't beating me in a drunken rage, he'd lock me in the house so I wouldn't leave him, like my mum.' He anticipated her question and answered it before she asked. It didn't make the moment any easier.

Meadow thought of the young Jay, the boy cowed by his father's temper and rules, abandoned by his mother, and there was only one reasonable reaction. She dropped the metal detector, stood up on her tiptoes, threw her arms around his neck and hugged him as tight as she could.

'I'm so sorry.' She screwed her eyes shut, trying to force away the terrible images pushing their way into her mind, and tried not to let the tears fall.

'It's okay.'

She could feel him smile against her cheek, trying to put her at ease when he was reliving the horror that had been his childhood. It made her want to squeeze him tighter. To discover her prison was his freedom was a difficult thought to process. Both had suffered in different ways at the hands of their parents. Jay had clearly suffered physical and emotional abuse, and knowing that he'd gone on to become a doctor, healing others, made him all the more remarkable. Not least because he'd worked through his personal trauma and pushed himself every day to be someone else instead of that frightened child who'd been caged like an animal, his spirit broken. While she remained trapped in her past, too afraid to break out. Perhaps she should take a leaf out of his book if going against the familiar made for a stronger character.

'I wish I had your bravery,' she sighed.

Jay pulled out from her embrace, the expression on his face making her aware he wasn't comfortable with her choice of words.

'I'm not brave. I'm a survivor, that's all. If it wasn't for Sharyn's encouragement I'd still be cocooned in my own safe little world, having swapped my father's imprisonment for one of my own creation. I spent my time going from the hospital and back to my house, with little else in between. It was Sharyn who pushed me out of my comfort zone and encouraged me to explore life around me.'

'It's not surprising after what you went through. Being in your own home, in familiar surroundings, was your security blanket. Don't be so hard on yourself. I still think you're brave to be here. I've never even left the country.'

At times, Meadow found herself envying Sharyn, who'd got to share so much with Jay and had claimed a huge part of his heart, but she was also thankful to her. If not for Sharyn, Jay might never have left the confines of his home and travelled all this way to become an important part of her life. She couldn't imagine not seeing his face at work, or having him accompany her on trips like this, or to parties she didn't really want to attend. He was becoming her link to the world she'd been avoiding for too long, pushing her to do more, the way Sharyn had done for him. Albeit in a less death-defying manner, which she was thankful for.

'Well, you've enough to do here, haven't you? Bravery doesn't have to come in the form of travel or hair-raising stunts. You go to work in a plane every day, flying into the unknown, and it takes courage to maintain a relationship with a parent who didn't always have your best interests at heart.'

Meadow screwed her nose up at that. 'I'm not sure if that's courageous or stupid. I just couldn't make the break. I think I'm still clinging on to that hope of having some sort of family life.'

'And that's okay.' Jay rested his hands on her shoulders. 'Perhaps you can still salvage your relationship and that's amazing if you want that. I just couldn't.'

That familiar darkness clouded his eyes again when talking about his relationship with his father, and despite opening up to her about some of what had happened, Meadow suspected there was more to the harrowing story. It was up to Jay if he wanted to tell her what that was and she hoped some day he would trust her enough to share so she could understand him better.

Even that insight into his home life, and the part that Sharyn had played, explained the importance of that list more than ever. It had been her way of freeing him from the confines of those memories. The security of home had been too tempting to leave, and she knew something about that. At least Jay had been willing to tackle that list when presented with it. Meadow would've laughed in the face of anyone who'd suggested it to her before lighting the barbecue with it.

She offered him a lopsided smile. 'There are different levels of forgiveness and I think your father was beyond it.'

'If he'd even want it. He never showed any remorse, or expressed any regret.'

'I can't say mine ever has either, but I suppose I still have a flicker of hope he will some day, to validate my reluctance to walk away.'

'It might come quicker if I stop blathering and let you find his gold. I promised I wouldn't get in your way.' Jay held his hands up and backed away.

Meadow would've stopped him and insisted he wasn't bothering her, that she appreciated he was able to share the details of his life with her. Except she thought he needed a time out to compose himself and gather his thoughts after unloading that emotional baggage. She knew it wasn't easy and talking about it brought those memories and feelings back. That was why she needed a quiet moment too.

'Don't wander too far,' was all the advice she could dispense for now, because her head was too full of thoughts about what it had taken for that abused child to become the man who stood before her now. About how much she admired him, and how much trouble she was in...

CHAPTER SEVEN

JAY NEEDED A bit of space to regroup. He hadn't intended to visit that dark time with Meadow, she just had that way of making him feel comfortable enough to share. She never forced anything, or advised, she simply listened. Perhaps that was all he'd ever needed.

He'd always felt a certain guilt about finally admitting what his father had done to him. It was a teacher he'd confided in on one of the days his father had let him go to school. Unlike most children, he looked forward to school. It was where he got a hot meal and he didn't have to be afraid that anyone was going to hurt him. That morning he'd been allowed to attend because his father was entertaining someone he'd met at the pub the night before and he'd wanted him out of the house.

His teacher had seen the bruises on his arms, and where he'd usually explained them away, he'd been too tired and broken to hide what was happening any more. Things had happened quickly then—social services, police, the foster home. He'd blamed himself when his father had been arrested, as though he'd been the one in the wrong for setting events in motion. There'd been limited contact since, until he'd eventually realised he had to sever all ties if he ever hoped to move on.

Jay hoped Meadow could get the apology she was owed

and save her relationship. Then perhaps she could let go of some of that hurt and drop her guard a fraction more.

In sharing some of his issues, she'd been able to do the same, and he'd like to be able to help her break free of those memories, the way Sharyn had done for him. Maybe then she would consider him as more than an inconvenience.

She'd made it clear she hadn't wanted him with her today, but that was in stark contrast to the way she'd looked at him last night. Although he never thought he'd find anyone after Sharyn, he was beginning to wonder if he and Meadow could have a chance of a future together. They clearly enjoyed each other's company and had a lot in common. He didn't know where exploring the chemistry they had would lead, only that he wanted to try. That was enough to tell him he was moving on from Sharyn and it took someone pretty special to even make him think about doing that.

Jay had been so busy contemplating the past and the future he'd wandered away from the spot where Meadow had been detecting. Although he could still see her, she was little more than a dot in the distance. He wasn't going to go any further, but then he spotted the entrance to the old mine.

Although the wooden framework to the opening had rotted in places and had partially collapsed, there was still enough room for him to go inside. Curiosity and his sense of adventure overtook regard for his own safety and he ducked inside.

It was dank and dusty but the tunnel and the old tools lying around spoke so much of the past he couldn't resist venturing in for a closer look. He felt along the stony walls, imagining the sound of the men who'd come here before him, hammering and digging, all hoping to discover their fortune. He'd seen something of those who'd failed and how it had affected the quality of their lives and those around them. Sadness and disappointment permeated the rock all around him, echoes of the past continuing to haunt this place.

Wooden runners lined his path, where miners had ferried out loads of rubble during their excavations. Darker and deeper, Jay continued his exploration into the cavernous unknown, using the light from his phone to guide him. The air began to thin and he knew he'd have to turn around soon, before he became another casualty.

Eventually he found his path blocked, a mound of rubble preventing him from venturing any further. By the way the rocks were piled high, he thought there'd been some sort of cave-in rather than it being the natural end to the tunnel. Jay attempted to dislodge some of the debris so he could take a look further back and climbed the pile. That was when the glint of something high in the walls caught his eye, a layer of glitter sandwiched in the rock.

He held his phone up for a better look and traced his fingers over the sparkle. A long, steady ribbon of gold threaded through the red walls like a pretty Christmas party dress. Gold. He had no idea why it had been left untouched, or how to get it out, but he was sure this was what they were looking for. He took a couple of pictures for reference before heading back out.

'Meadow!' he yelled, forgetting how far away she was in that precise moment. It was only the echo calling back to him which reminded him where he was, and it wasn't with her. Against everything she'd told him not to do, he'd wandered off. Though he was sure another scolding would be put on the back burner if he managed to line her father's pockets after all.

He scrambled back outside, having to defend his eyes from the blinding sun as he emerged from the dark depths of the earth.

'Meadow!' he called again, running back to where he'd left her, keen to share his discovery as soon as possible and be hero for the day.

'Jay? Where the hell did you go?' Meadow stomped towards him, metal detector over her shoulder, pick in her hand, face like thunder, and he knew he was in for it.

'I know, I know, I'm an idiot for wandering off, but come and see this.'

'What?' Her exasperation was palpable, no doubt because she'd wasted valuable digging time trying to locate him. Jay hoped she'd be appeased once he showed her the wonders waiting in the mine for her.

'I've found something.' He was bursting to tell her but he wanted to see her face when she saw it for herself. To be the one who put a smile on her face was his reward.

'Just tell me what it is so I can get back to work.'

It was clear he'd really ticked her off but, risking her wrath, he pulled her towards the mine. 'You need to see it for yourself.'

'I'm not going in there. Are you crazy? That's condemned.'

'Trust me,' he said, fixing her with a determined stare until she huffed out a breath and stopped resisting.

'Fine.' She dropped her tools and prepared to follow him in, even if it was begrudgingly.

'Did your father ever excavate in here?'

'I'm not sure if he had more than a cursory look because it had already been mined out and it's not fit for purpose any more.' She emphasised the last point loudly so he was in no doubt that she thought this a fool's errand. He was willing to let her think that until he proved otherwise. It was still possible he hadn't found the riches he hoped, and remembered there was something about fool's gold which could still apply.

'It's fine. I've already been inside.' From the outside it looked precarious, the wooden slats had rotted but the walls still seemed sound to him.

Meadow tutted. 'Of course you have. Show me what it is you think you've found, then I can get out of here and do some real work.'

Jay ignored the scepticism, looking forward to the forthcoming apology. Though he was sure there was much more real work to be done before they had any gold in their hands.

'It's down this way.' He led her further in with the light of his phone, though it seemed a longer walk in this time around.

'Jay, it's really not safe in here. The timbers are rotten and the walls need shoring up properly again. We don't even have hard hats. Just tell me what it is, we can take proper safety measures, then come back out when we know there's no risk of a cave-in.' Meadow wasn't keeping pace with him, holding back enough to let him see she was worried, that cautious nature blazing bright, despite current appearances. He loved the adventurer look on her, that image of her looking up at him from the ditch, dirt smeared on her face, a world away from the smartly turned-out nurse he was used to seeing.

'It's not far, I promise. I just want you to see it for your-self, then we can get out again.' They'd come this far now, it seemed a pity not to let her see the gold in situ too. He kept the photographs to himself for now.

'It had better be worth it,' she grumbled, picking up the pace again.

Jay was bursting to tell her. He was the sort of person who got equally excited at giving a gift as the recipient, often blabbing the contents before they got to open it. His joyful enthusiasm was the result of not experiencing the whole gift culture for himself growing up. The first year his foster family had bought him Christmas presents he'd burst into tears, not used to such a display of kind-ness. Then he'd spent the next year saving to return the favour. Although this wasn't something he'd saved for, or picked out specially, he figured this was still a gift. His present to her, and something he was sure she'd ap-preciate. Doing this for her might also help her see him as more than an inconvenience. Jay wanted her to think of him as a potential partner.

He mightn't always be the safest bet, but he wanted what was best for her and would do everything in his power to show her that. Some day she might decide he was worth taking a chance on and they could venture into this next unknown chapter together.

Eventually they came to the section he recognised where the trail narrowed and evidence of previous min-ing wasn't so abundant, as though they'd given up before reaching this point. He kicked away some of the loose rubble from Meadow's path.

'It's just up here.' He held up the light and waited for her to stand beside him.

'Is that…?' Standing up on tiptoe, she reached up and trailed her fingers along the wall as he'd done.

He nodded, grinning as he saw the realisation dawn in her eyes and the smile spread across her face as though she'd swallowed the gold and its glittery beams were shooting straight out of her mouth.

'Gold.' Jay kept his voice low, as though afraid that by saying it too loudly it would attract would-be thieves who'd loot the place before Meadow and her father saw the benefit of the find.

'Okay.' Meadow was trembling but he could see her fighting the urge to scream and shout like he wanted to. 'We need to take a note of the exact location and board up the entrance so no one can get in until we can secure the structure. Dad will need a lot of equipment to extract that seam of fine gold.'

'But we found it.' Nothing was going to take away from his pride and excitement at having found the gold her father had spent most of his life searching for, all because he'd taken a risk.

'Yeah. We did it.' She could no longer hold back her excitement, it seemed, as she high-fived him.

'Come here,' he growled, wanting to celebrate properly. He grabbed her up and swung her around. Meadow was laughing, her hands wrapped around his neck as they spun.

As they slowly came to a stop his head was still spinning, with thoughts only of Meadow and how much he wanted to kiss her. He couldn't take his eyes off her lips, and when she kept her arms around his neck even when her feet were back on the ground, Jay knew this time they were both ready.

Her lips were soft and welcoming against his and when she leaned her body closer into him, he was completely undone.

Meadow was still floating on air even though Jay had stopped whirling her around as though she weighed nothing more than a feather. The gold was undoubtedly the treasure they'd been looking for, but kissing Jay was the ultimate prize. Waiting all this time, fighting against her feelings and all the untimely interruptions, made it all the sweeter. This was what she wanted. His hands on her waist, fingers brushing the bare skin at the bottom of her back, was almost as erotic as watching him strip by the pool. She'd cursed herself for not following up on that moment last night and denying herself the chance to taste the excitement for herself. Now she'd braved the unknown she was content that the reality of the fantasy hadn't disappointed.

Jay was confident and assured in his touch, his mouth demanding on hers, and she was happy on this occasion she'd taken a risk when it had given her such rich rewards. She didn't want to think about future consequences and potential heartbreak and for once simply enjoy some spontaneity. This wasn't planned, probably wasn't a good idea in the long run, but it was the most passionate encounter she'd had in for ever, and they hadn't even taken their clothes off. She gave a little shiver at the thought of taking that next step. If Jay could make her feel this reckless, provide so much excitement in one kiss, she knew there were further riches still waiting to be discovered.

Jay was sliding his hands up her bare back now, pulling her ever tighter to his body as though he couldn't get close enough. That skin-to-skin contact sent ripples of pleasure rushing to every erogenous zone, and puckering her nipples into tight peaks. She knew it was turning him on too when she could feel the hard evidence pressing into her belly. It was insanity and she knew they'd have to put a stop to things soon, but she didn't want to in case that cautious, vulnerable side of her stepped in again with a wagging finger.

She was distracted by a small thud, followed by several more. Jay pulled away from her to check out the disturbance. That was when she felt something drop onto her head. It took her a moment to realise what it was and in that short space of time pieces of the roof were raining down on them both.

'We need to get out of here now, Jay.' She grabbed his hand and started towards the exit.

There was a loud rumble and the earth seemed to rise up to meet them. She felt the full force of Jay's body slam into her and the air was forced from her lungs.

'Meadow? Can you hear me? Squeeze my hand.'

The darkness was drawing close but the sound of Jay's voice was the greater pull.

'Speak to me. Please tell me you're all right. I'm so sorry I brought you in here. I'm so stupid.'

She heard the desperation in his voice and wanted to reassure him she was okay but she couldn't find the strength to say the words or open her eyes.

'I should have listened to you. I'm so sorry I put you in danger.'

She felt something on her cheek, a tender caress which

was much more pleasant than the pounding going on in her head.

'Jay?' she eventually managed to croak, her lips dry with dust.

'Oh, thank goodness.' He gathered her up and the warmth of his body encompassed her. It was tempting to fall back into that deep sleep when she was in his arms, safe and secure, but she had a nagging feeling there was a reason she shouldn't.

'What happened?' she asked, struggling to sit up unassisted, trying to process what was going on.

'A cave-in. I can't see any way to get out. The exit's blocked. Here, take a sip of water. You took a nasty hit.' He held a bottle of water to her lips and poured enough just to wet them.

'I think that was you tackling me to the ground,' she tried to joke, knowing that he'd put himself between her and the roof of the mine. He must've taken the brunt of the hit, trying to protect her.

'Sorry. I acted without thinking, as usual.'

'It's not your fault. I think we both got carried away.' She tried to smile but the pain from her throbbing temple prevented her. When she reached up to touch the spot her fingers were coated in sticky red blood.

'You hit your head when you fell, but it's stopped bleeding. Let me clean it up for you.' He moved to pour more water on her, but she put out a hand to stop him.

'Save it. We might need it if we can't get out of here.' Her head was a bit fuzzy but she knew she'd need her wits about her if they were going to make it back out of here alive.

She looked around as she wiped her shirtsleeve across

her forehead. They were backed up against the section of the mine which had caused all the trouble, and though the air was thick with dust and debris, she could see they were completely surrounded by rubble and broken timbers blocking the path. It looked as though whatever ancient structure had been keeping the roof supported had finally given way. Whether it had been bad timing on their part or they'd inadvertently caused the rockfall they'd probably never know. The important thing now was to figure a way out of this mess.

'I don't suppose you've got a phone signal?' She was only half joking, praying there was still an easy way to fix their predicament.

'Sorry. I think it's buried somewhere. Even if it wasn't smashed to bits, I'm not sure I'd get a signal. On the positive side, we do seem to be trapped in an air pocket so we won't suffocate just yet.'

'No, we might die a slow death from thirst or starvation first.' Meadow wasn't one to panic but she knew the chances of anyone finding them out here were slim. Her father wouldn't be home for days and wasn't likely to come straight to the mine, and whilst they would be missed at work she doubted they'd ever guess they'd managed to get themselves trapped down an old gold mine. Judging by Greg's comments, they'd probably suspect they'd run off somewhere exotic together. Chance would've been a fine thing.

She steadied herself against the wall as she got up, causing a few more displaced rocks to fall in the process. Then she began tackling the rocky obstruction blocking their way home, removing one stone at a time.

'Don't waste your energy, Meadow. There's no way

we can shift all that by hand. It goes way back. I've already looked.'

Refusing to believe they couldn't dig their way out of
this mess, she removed a few more rocks, only to cause
an avalanche raining down on her from the top of the pile.

'Meadow, for goodness' sake! You're going to get yourself killed.' Jay rushed at her again, pulling her away
from the rockfall and forcing her to toss the one still in
her hand back onto the pile.

'We need to get out.' She was trying to keep her cool
but the fact remained they were trapped in an old mine,
miles from anywhere, with no one likely to come looking for them any time soon.

'I know that. Don't you think I know that? But it's not
going to help if you hurt yourself.'

It was only when she turned her head to look at him
that she could see the panic in his eyes. She was about to
apologise for worrying him when she realised he had his
hand on his chest, seemingly gasping for breath.

'Jay? Are you okay?' Caught up in her own panic, she
hadn't bothered to check and see if he'd been hurt during
the melee. After all, he'd thrown himself at her, using his
body to shield her from the walls collapsing all around
them. He could've suffered blunt force trauma, broken
ribs or internal bleeding, and they'd both been more concerned about her knock on the head.

'Do you have any chest pain?' She checked his pupils
the best she could without any light, and his pulse. His
heart was racing, probably causing his sudden shortness
of breath since there weren't any obvious injuries.

'Can't…breathe…'

It took her a fraction of a second to realise he was having a panic attack. She'd forgotten his fear of the dark, but circumstances appeared to have triggered that response.

'Just look at me, Jay.' She got him to focus on her instead of his fight for breath. 'You're okay, I'm okay, and we'll get through this.'

Meadow took his hands in hers. 'Take a deep breath, in…and out. That's it. In through the nose, and out through the mouth. I'm here and I'm not going to let anything happen to you.' She took long, slow breaths, encouraging him to do the same, until that initial panic subsided and he was no longer gasping.

Jay eventually let go of her hands and rested them on his knees, doubled over, trying to regain his composure.

'It's fine. Is it the dark? I'm here for you, Jay. You're not alone.'

'It's not just the dark.' He swayed a little and Meadow was afraid he was going to pass out on her.

'Why don't you sit down and have a drink of water?' She helped him over to a corner and sat down beside him, waiting until he was ready to talk.

'Sorry for the drama,' he said eventually.

'Admit it, you were just afraid I was getting all the attention.' She bumped his shoulder with hers to make him smile again.

'I wish that's all it was. At least when I thought you were hurt it stopped me from dwelling on other things.'

'Your dad?' she asked quietly, not wanting to spook him any more. His extreme reaction suggested something more traumatic than she'd even imagined, but she resisted swamping him in another hug. For now.

Jay nodded, scuffing the toe of his shoe into the dirt,

focusing on it rather than looking at her. Even though he had nothing to be ashamed about.

'It wasn't just the house he locked me in. Sometimes it was my bedroom, other times in the wardrobe. It depended on his mood or how much he wanted to punish me. Most of the time I hadn't done anything wrong other than ask if I could have something to eat. He'd go off and get drunk, forget I was there for hours, even days on occasion.'

The horror of what he'd experienced brought tears rushing to Meadow's eyes but she willed them away, knowing if he saw she was upset he wouldn't continue and she knew he needed to get this out. Locking a child in a cupboard for days on end was intolerable cruelty and Meadow could only imagine how terrified the young Jay had been, not knowing if he'd ever see daylight again.

She looked around and understood what had triggered his response. They were completely shut off from the rest of the world with no possible escape, light or even food or water. He was effectively reliving that trauma all over again.

'This was an accident, not a punishment, and I'm sure once Greg and the others at work realise we're missing they'll come looking for us.'

He cocked his head to one side. 'You don't believe that any more than I do.'

'We have to believe it. I'm sure there were many times when you thought your dad would never come back and let you out, but he did. I know it's frightening but it's just an obstacle we have to overcome. Like losing a house in a fire.'

He was still staring at her, enough to make her eventually ask, 'What?'

'You're amazing, that's all.'

'Hardly,' she snorted, flicking away the compliment as though it were another annoying fly.

'No, really. The way you deal with things—work, your father, a big galah like me, afraid of the dark—you take it all in your stride.'

'Not always. I have my moments too and I don't make for an easy person to live with. Ask my ex-boyfriends.' She thought of the men who'd called her high maintenance, and hard to please. None of them had thought her 'amazing'.

'Maybe they're "ex" for a reason.' Jay shrugged.

'Well, Shawn lied to me about the kind of person he was, so that's why he's not in my life any more. Though perhaps he felt it necessary to pretend to be someone who had his own home and was financially stable because nothing less would do for me.'

'That doesn't sound like too much to expect in a potential partner. Although not all of us are ready to sign up for a mortgage just yet.' He was teasing her but it was also a reminder that Jay didn't meet all her requirements either. Maybe, just maybe, she'd been too picky in the past. After all, none of those who'd had their own homes and had plans to settle down had held her attention long enough for her to want to do the same.

'That didn't bother me as much as the gambling of all his wages and the bad credit history, which meant he was still living at home with his mother. It was the secrets and lies I couldn't deal with.'

'Understandable. Although it could be argued that the

problem I had was the complete opposite. Until Sharyn, I didn't do long-term relationships because I didn't want anyone to dig too deeply into my personal affairs. She kind of forced the information out of me, wanted the truth so she could help me move past it.'

'Do you think you'd still be with Sharyn if you hadn't lost her like that?'

Jay considered her question for longer than she'd really expected.

'Honestly, I don't know. Not so long ago, I would undoubtedly have said yes, but that was when I was still in mourning. Sometimes when you lose a loved one you only want to remember the good times, like looking back wearing rose-tinted glasses. Don't get me wrong, she's the reason I'm here in Australia, living a life I never thought possible, but now I'm not sure we would've lasted.'

'Oh?' It seemed such a turnaround from the man who'd clearly still been in love with his recently deceased partner and Meadow wondered what had brought about the change, igniting a little spark of hope that it had been her.

'I loved her, I really did, but so much of our relationship was based on that list and going on adventures, I'm not sure it would've lasted for ever. Now, I can't picture what it would've been like for us as we got older. I don't imagine I'd still be wanting to dive off cliffs or go backpacking in the Himalayas, and Sharyn wouldn't have been one for sitting in an armchair with a blanket round her knees playing board games. I appreciate everything she did was to help me move on from the past, but it also made me a different person to the one she met. I'm sure there'll come a time when I just want to put my feet up.'

'There's a lot to be said for playing board games. Same

adrenaline rush without the imminent threat to life.' Meadow was only partly joking. Board games weren't her thing, neither were extreme sports, but she'd take a quiet life over being stuck in here, not knowing if they were going to live or die.

'That's beginning to sound appealing.' Jay's wonky smile made her heart lurch. She knew she was privileged to see this vulnerable side of him when he was such a happy-go-lucky character on the outside. It was likely he only divulged this valuable personal information to people he trusted, and though it seemed they'd known each other longer, they'd only been acquainted for a few days. From what she'd gathered, he'd waited years before opening up about the abuse he'd suffered. Sharing it with her suggested the bond between them wasn't all in her head.

'As soon as we get out of here, I swear we're having a games night so you can see what you've been missing.' And so they could spend more time together if he wasn't sick of her by then. Despite everything she'd expected him to be on their first run-in, Meadow was beginning to think Jay wanted to settle down somewhere. Maybe she could persuade him to do it with her. If their earlier kiss was anything to go by, they certainly had a chemistry that was worth exploring, and if he was planning on sticking around she might be willing to take a risk after all.

'If we get out.' He stood up, his stress manifesting again as he paced the small area that had escaped the rockfall like a caged bear.

She understood now that the claustrophobia of their situation was equally as triggering as the dark. That feeling of being locked in, fear of the unknown, was just as real for him now as it had been then.

'What can I do to help you, Jay?'

'I don't know.' He rubbed his hands over his scalp as he walked, clearly agitated and building up to another panic attack.

'Okay, what's making you uncomfortable? I know we're stuck here, but what would give you peace of mind in the meantime?' It wasn't something he could easily answer when he was visibly uncomfortable, but at least it would give him something to think about other than the past.

He ducked his head. 'It sounds stupid, especially given our current circumstances, but I need to see the outside. At least have the illusion of fresh air coming in so I can breathe properly. What I remember about being locked up was the stale air. The windows in my room were nailed shut. My dad didn't want me climbing out or shouting for help. Of course, when he threw me in the wardrobe and tied the doors shut I couldn't even see out of the window. It was like being buried alive. Ironic, really, when that's exactly what's happening now.'

Meadow could accept that, but there was no point in both of them panicking, at least until they'd been in here a while longer and it was clear rescue wasn't coming. Instead of asking him more about the conditions he'd been in then, Meadow wanted to suggest something to make him feel more positive.

'A lot of that rubble came from the roof. Maybe there's a gap somewhere up there that we can reach?' If not to get out, at least to give them both some fresh air and a view of the outside world.

'It's not safe, Meadow. We could bring the rest of it down on top of us.'

Oh, how the tables had turned, when Jay was the one

advising caution. It just proved how much his past had impacted on him and how far he'd come, trying to shake it off. Meadow didn't want to court disaster, but she also knew they needed to explore all avenues if they had any hope of getting out of here.

'I'll be careful. I can at least look. Now, help me up onto your shoulders so I can get up there.'

Jay huffed out a sigh, unamused by her suggestion, but he did hunker down to enable her to climb on board. She didn't know if it was because he trusted her judgement or that they were out of options, but he was going along with her idea for now. Meadow hooked one leg over his shoulder and used his head to balance her as she brought the second one over, hanging on for dear life as he stood. It was all very ungainly but there was no room for vanity or pride when their lives were at stake.

She was sure they were a comical sight as they moved, with her perched on Jay's very broad shoulders, feeling her way along the top of the roof, trying to find a chink of light in the darkness. Every now and then she accidentally dislodged a loose piece of earth, which bounced off Jay's head. After the third time he let loose with a stream of expletives.

'Sorry,' she said, stifling a laugh, glad that this distraction was preventing him from getting lost in his traumatic childhood memories at least.

'The last thing I need is a brain injury, thanks,' he muttered.

'Hey, I'm the one risking a nosebleed or worse up here.' She was trying not to think about another possible cave-in when she'd be the one to take the brunt this time, or the height of the fall from Jay's shoulders. For a few minutes she was willing to risk her personal safety if she could do something to ease his anxiety in here.

'And I appreciate it.'

She hadn't expected his gratitude, or the softness of his voice, both of which almost toppled her. Meadow had to steady herself again, thankful he had a hard head for her to lean on.

'We must add tunnelling our way out of a collapsed gold mine to that list of yours.'

'Let's hope we actually get to tick that one off and mark it as done.'

With a seemingly renewed determination Jay shifted beneath her and held onto her shins to secure her. Meadow continued her exploration until she found a tiny crevice up behind one of the few timbers still in place.

'I think there's something up here. Do we have anything I can use to try and push through?'

Meadow's head was spinning as Jay turned, looking for a suitable tool for her to use, then he slowly lowered to the ground, careful not to unseat her.

'I think this is the handle off an old pickaxe or something. Try it.' He handed a long wooden shaft up to her and Meadow carefully poked it into the crack in the roof.

She had to stretch up, relying on Jay to keep her supported, but she trusted him with her safety. Something she'd never thought she'd do.

'I think it's giving way,' she said, pushing the blunt object into the recess and watching the loose dirt fall away.

'Just be careful.'

With one more thrust she broke through, piercing the earth's crust just enough to let a beam of light shine down on them. Unfortunately, the movement knocked her off-balance and Jay struggled to stay on his feet. Before she knew it, she was tumbling back down onto the dirt.

'Ouch.' This time it was her backside which hit the floor, which had more padding than her head but still hurt all the same.

'Sorry.' Jay was lying beside her, clutching his back as he sat up.

'It's not your fault. Anyway, we've got light. Ta-da!'

Regardless of her joking, Jay was stony-faced as he reached out to her, cupping her face in his hands and searching for signs of injury.

'I've told you I'm fine, Jay.'

'I said I wouldn't let you get hurt. You wouldn't even have been up there if it wasn't for me.'

She stroked the side of his face, trying to ease the tense set of his jaw. 'We're in this together, remember?'

He turned his face into her hand and kissed her palm, and when he looked at her again she saw the concern and genuine affection he had for her right there. Despite her triumph, she knew there was a possibility they wouldn't get out of this and she couldn't help but feel as though she'd thrown away a chance at happiness. She'd wasted too much time worrying about the future and had neglected the present. Much like her father, she hadn't appreciated what she had until it was too late.

Jay had appeared in town and shattered that cosy world she'd built around herself, making it infinitely better. She'd found someone who understood her. Well, he'd found her, but she'd been stupidly resisting these growing feelings towards him. Now it might be too late to do anything about it.

'Kiss me, Jay.' For once, she wanted to do something

reckless without worrying about the consequences. Especially when they weren't promised tomorrow.

Jay could have questioned why she wanted this now, if it was a knee-jerk reaction to the situation they'd found themselves in or if she simply wanted some comfort. But he only cared that he wanted the same thing.

They rushed at each other like starved lovers, mouths crashing together, hands clinging to one another, desperate for that connection. If they weren't going to get out of here alive, at least they were going to make the most of the time they had left.

He was sorry he'd brought her here, put her in danger, then freaked out on her because the claustrophobic circumstances triggered those awful childhood memories. Most of all, he was sorry that he might have cost them a future together. It seemed so stupid now to have wasted time when they so obviously wanted one another, pulling at each other's clothes and kissing as though their lives depended on it.

Being with Meadow gave him a very different thrill to those he'd had when he and Sharyn had been together. They didn't need to be doing anything life-threatening to enjoy each other's company—today's events notwithstanding—but this hadn't been planned. In fact, he'd prefer it if they were in a nice cosy bed, preferably in a house. Perhaps he'd finally found a home here, the life he'd probably been searching for his whole life, with a woman who brought out the best in him. He could only hope it wasn't too late.

'If anything happens to me, I just want you to know I really enjoy being with you, Meadow.' He wanted their time together to be special, for however long they had left, and didn't want to shuffle off this mortal coil with any regrets. Since the day he'd arrived in town he'd been fighting his feelings for her because of his loyalty to Sharyn's memory, and his fear of getting close to someone again. There was nothing like facing his own mortality to put everything into perspective. Here, now, nothing else mattered except Meadow.

She stopped kissing his neck and sat back, smiling. 'I'm glad to hear it. I'd hate to think this was some sort of chore.'

'Oh, it's definitely not that. It's all pleasure.'

She purred as he gently lowered her to the ground, using their discarded shirts as a makeshift blanket to protect her from the stony ground. Even as the light outside had begun to fade gradually, Jay had stopped being afraid of the dark. If Meadow had been with him in that house, that room, that cupboard, he wouldn't have suffered as much. When he was with her the part of him who was still that lost little boy seemed as though he was finally finding his peace.

Meadow too needed someone to show her how cherished she was, and he was determined to be the man to do it. If this was their last night on earth, they both deserved to know a little love.

She reached behind her back to undo her bra, whipping it away to reveal the small mounds of her breasts. He palmed one firmly in his hand, plucking the rosy tip between his fingers, and captured the gasp on her lips with his mouth. She was every bit as beautiful as he'd known she would be. Her toned, tanned body, so small beneath him, made his heart weak, and every other part of him hard with desire.

Meadow flicked her tongue along his bottom lip, tasting and teasing, and testing his resolve. He wanted to stay in control, to put her pleasure before his own, but she was fighting against his intention, her hands straying to the fly of his trousers.

'Not yet,' he whispered against her neck and felt her buck against him. When he realised how sensitive she was he dotted wet kisses just there behind her ear, and she shivered when he blew on the damp skin to cool the heat.

Meadow pressed her body ever closer to his, her nipples teasing his skin, begging for his attention. Then she slid her hands down and roughly opened his fly, reaching in to stroke his erection. Jay closed his eyes and groaned. This woman was literally going to be the death of him.

'I said not yet.' He grabbed her hands and pinned them above her head.

'But—' She was pleading with him to stem that ache inside her, he could see it in her eyes, feel it in the arch of her body against him. He wasn't completely without mercy.

Still with her hands caged so she couldn't intervene, Jay took his time kissing every inch of her body. She tilted her head back so he could nuzzle her neck, groaned when he gently nipped the skin along her collarbone. He was driving himself insane as well as Meadow by delaying that bliss he knew was waiting for them.

Lower and lower he dipped his head, using his mouth and tongue to map her body whilst his hands were otherwise engaged. The soft swell of her breast yielded under his mouth until he reached the hardened peak and teased it with his tongue.

'Jay, please—'

Though he wasn't ready to bring them to that ultimate release yet, he drew her nipple greedily into his mouth, tugging gently with his teeth until Meadow was gasping and close to the edge.

He moved so he had one hand still holding her captive and used the other to pull away her shorts and underwear. As he'd expected, she was wet when he dipped a finger inside her, filling her where they both wanted him to be soon before they lost their minds. He circled that sensitive nub, pushing and stroking until she cried out and shuddered against him. His smile was one of triumph and relief as he let go of her wrists.

'Look at you, all proud of yourself,' she said as she stretched lazily beneath him, her body fully on display for him to enjoy.

'Shouldn't I be?'

'If I had a trophy I'd give it to you.' Even in the throes of passion and the most dangerous of circumstances she had the ability to make him laugh.

'But you'll get my name engraved on it first, right?'

'Of course.' With her hand on his cheek, she lifted her head to kiss him. It was a tender touch of her lips against his, a softer display of desire overtaking them, and Jay could wait no longer to make love to her.

He stripped off the rest of his clothes and entered her quickly, both of them emitting a contented sigh as they joined together. This was his safe place. Meadow was all he needed to find his peace.

They moved slowly together at first, savouring each

other, getting used to the fit. If they were together a thousand years he didn't think he'd ever tire of this feeling every time he withdrew and plunged back inside, of filling her and being encompassed by her tight, wet heat.

It was Meadow's time for some payback, nibbling at his earlobes, wrapping her legs tightly around his waist and thrusting up to meet his hips. Doing everything she possibly could to demolish his restraint.

'I don't want you to hold back,' she whispered into his ear and snipped that last thread.

Jay thrust his hips against Meadow's, again and again, that increasing pleasure sensation overtaking all thoughts. Every time she gasped or clenched tighter around him drove him harder, faster to bring them both to that much anticipated final destination. Her hot breath and cry of ecstasy in his ear as she voiced her orgasm spurred his own release. His body shuddered and it seemed as though he was pouring his very soul into her as he climaxed.

Jay knew he was falling for her. What he felt for Meadow was so different to anything he'd ever known that he was beginning to think that even the relationship he'd had with Sharyn had been based more on friendship. It had been fun and exciting and she'd taken away his loneliness, but he didn't remember this kind of high, of almost floating on a cloud of happiness when they were together.

'Are you okay? You're very quiet.' Meadow was watching him intently as he lay down beside her.

'I'm just wondering if I've completely shredded my kneecaps on this ground.'

Her laughter at the injuries he might have sustained whilst in the throes of passion echoed around the mine.

'It's okay, you're worth it.' He leaned over and dropped a long, leisurely kiss on her lips.

'Why, thank you. I'm surprised we didn't bring the whole ceiling down—we weren't exactly quiet.' She placed the flat of her hand on his chest as she snuggled against him.

'At least we're going out with a bang.'

Meadow groaned. 'I'm sure we'll be fine. Have faith.'

'Meadow, if you really believed that you wouldn't have slept with me.' He was challenging her to admit that, or at least that she had some feelings for him. Every time they'd come close to a kiss, she'd run a mile. If they did make it out of here, he wanted to know that they might have a future together.

It was early days but he thought they could have something special together. He knew Meadow had been holding back, probably afraid he was a version of her father, who'd always be looking for the next thrill. That might have been true at one time, but if Meadow was willing to give them a shot he could be persuaded to stick around. If he was going to take a chance, he hoped she would too.

She moved away from him, sitting up and hugging her knees. 'I might not have chosen this time or place, but I can't say I haven't thought about it.'

'There's nothing to be afraid of. I mean apart from dehydration and our impending doom.' Jay managed to raise a smile on her otherwise worried-looking face.

'I don't want to get hurt,' she said so softly he wasn't sure if she meant for him to hear.

He scrambled up into a sitting position, put an arm around her shoulders and shuffled closer. 'I would never do anything to upset you. I know this is all new for both of us, and we're both carrying baggage from relationships and our childhoods, but I like being with you, Meadow.'

'For now. We'll see how you feel when the cavalry arrives.'

He wasn't going to argue with her, even though he didn't think his feelings would change, no matter what tomorrow brought. There didn't seem any point in wasting time debating the issue if they really might not see another day.

'Well, we have to make it through the night first. It'll get cold down here soon. I think we'll have to cuddle together for body heat.' Jay lifted one of her arms and hooked it around his neck before lifting her off the ground and onto his lap. If he was going to die, he'd prefer to do it with a smile on his face.

Meadow knew he was trying to distract her and he was doing a stand-up job of it. It was hard to think about anything except his touch. She didn't want to fret about getting rescued, or if he'd still want her if they were. For once in her life, she just wanted to live in the moment and act on her instincts. Right now, they were telling her she needed Jay to satisfy this pulsing ache for him.

She shifted round so she was straddling his strong thighs, his equally substantial erection nestled between her legs. He claimed possession of her with his mouth on hers, and his hands clamped on her backside. Meadow was already slick with need, her body clearly anticipating round two. This was the one chance she had to really throw caution to the wind and she was going to enjoy every single moment. Deep down, she'd been fighting this because she knew making love with Jay would be intoxicating and something not easily forgotten, just as he was.

Using his shoulders to brace herself, she slid down onto his shaft, letting that feeling of being complete blot out all her worries. Jay buried his head between her breasts and groaned, and she knew it was the same for him.

They worked in tandem, their bodies matching each other's rhythm perfectly, stroke for stroke. That desperate need for one another drove their frantic pace until they were both gasping for breath and that final release. Jay rolled them over so he was on top and with one last hard thrust he cried out against her neck. Little tremors seized his body as he continued to rock against her, and she was so close to the edge that when he pushed his thumb inside her, filling her to the brim, she spilled right over.

This hadn't been the way she'd planned things but being with Jay was something special. Even if they did make it out and Jay decided he wasn't suited to a boring life with her, Meadow knew one night with him had changed her life for ever.

CHAPTER EIGHT

MEADOW WOKE WITH a shiver. When she opened her eyes and saw they were still in their rocky prison that sinking feeling in her stomach came back. Closely followed by a rumble of emptiness loud enough to stir Jay behind her. He tightened his arms around her and buried his head in the crook of her neck.

'Morning.' His sleepy greeting, combined with that comforting cage of his body, helped her relax a little.

'We're still here,' she said, hoping as they'd fallen asleep last night that their enthusiastic lovemaking might somehow have magically transported them into the comfort of her bed.

'It's enough for now.' He threw one leg over the top of hers, the shift behind her letting her know his body was wide awake even if he wasn't.

'At least we have some light again.' Her stomach groaned its disapproval again.

'Breakfast?' He stretched over to reach the bag he'd brought with him and produced what was left of the bottle of water inside and the remnants of the cereal bar they'd found tucked away in one of the pockets last night.

'What I wouldn't do for bacon and eggs, pancakes and orange juice. Mmm…' Her mouth was watering at the thought, but she had to make do with a sip of water and

some crumbs. They were trying to ration out their mea-
gre supplies when she would have happily devoured a
steak, she was so hungry. With their exertions last night,
she was sure Jay had the same hunger gnawing away at
his insides in search of more sustenance.

'Soon,' he promised, bit the small piece of the bar in
half and popped the other one in her mouth before she
could stop him.

That small act of kindness—dare she hope, love—
melted the last of her defences. She was in deep. Meadow
cared more about this man than any of her previous partners and it would be a cruel irony if they perished in here
before she was given the chance to carry on the adventure with him.

'Thank you.' She kissed him full on the mouth, trying to lose herself in that sensation of being safe, despite
their current predicament.

Another shiver claimed her body and she had to gather
some of the old hessian sacks they'd found last night to
use as a blanket.

'We should probably get dressed. As much as I'd be
happy to spend my last hours making love to you, we are
running the risk of hypothermia.'

Although the sun had risen, it wasn't warm enough
to justify lying here unclothed. Whilst the sight of Jay's
naked form was pleasing, and detracted attention from
the destruction around them, she didn't want her propen-
sity for ogling him to come at the expense of their health.

'Hopefully, the afternoon sun will warm us up again.'
She was watching Jay as they dressed in yesterday's
clothes, wishing they could simply step into a nice warm

shower to get clean again. Unlike her father, she wasn't one who usually enjoyed scrabbling about in the dirt.

'Meadow Williams, you're insatiable.' Jay pulled on his shirt without undoing the buttons and came to her again.

'Only with you.' She stood up on tiptoe and threw her arms around his neck, kissing him as if there were literally no tomorrow.

Lost in that sweet, all-consuming taste of Jay on her lips, on the tip of her tongue, she managed to block out everything else around them. All the devastation and the uncertainty of the outside world was nothing but a distant memory. Until the earth began to move around them.

'What's that noise?' Jay ended the kiss abruptly, leaving her dizzy and bereft at the loss.

It took her a moment to compose herself again. That was when she heard a dull roar sounding from somewhere outside. 'There's someone there.'

Jay immediately climbed up to the small hole they'd previously made in the ceiling and began yelling. 'Hello! Is there someone there? We're trapped in the mine!'

'Be careful!' she warned as some of the roof began to fall again, and the pile of rocks blocking their exit appeared to tremble, knocking some loose so they bounced at her feet.

'Meadow?' A voice sounded beyond the obstruction and for a moment she thought it sounded like her father, then dismissed it as wishful thinking.

'We're in here!' she shouted in response, hoping the voice at least was a real chance at escape.

Jay too climbed back down to start yelling. If someone was out there, she didn't know what else they could do other than scream and shout and make their presence known.

'Stand back. We're coming in,' the disembodied voice instructed, and since Jay pulled her out of the way she came to the conclusion it hadn't been a figment of her imagination after all.

He hugged her close but his eyes were still firmly on the blocked path towards their exit, only venturing forward to grab his battered phone when it reappeared with the shifting of the earth. Meadow clung to him, afraid to breathe, or hope, in case it somehow caused the apparent rescue mission to fail.

They watched the pile of rubble gradually topple from the top, and stood as far back into the cave as they could as the bucket of a digger ploughed forward towards them before retreating back into the cavern. As soon as they had a clear space ahead, and a view of the path they'd taken yesterday on their journey here, they began to climb over the mound of earth. They followed the reversing digger into the light, having to shield their eyes against the blinding sun.

Meadow was still blinking when she was practically rugby tackled at the entrance. 'Dad?'

'I thought you were a goner, love.'

'What are you doing out of the hospital?'

'I'm no use lying there doing nothing, thought I may as well be working here. It's just as well, isn't it?'

'But how did you know we were here?'

'How did I know? You've left a bloody trail of my equipment out here.'

Meadow threw her arms around her father and hugged

him tightly. She'd never been so glad to see him. When she finally let go, she could see tears in his eyes.

'I was afraid I was too late. I've never felt so helpless, but I knew I couldn't help you on my own and had to call in a few favours to get the heavy equipment out.'

'It's fine. I'm just glad you got here.' She'd never thought she'd be happy that he'd defied everyone's advice to come out here and work again but if he hadn't, she and Jay would be facing another cold, hungry night in there. Or worse.

'So am I. I knew something wasn't right when you didn't phone to check on me last night at the hospital. I missed not speaking to you on the phone.' Her father hugged her back in an uncharacteristic display of affection. 'I know I haven't been the best dad, or showed you enough love, but I wouldn't want to be without you, Meadow.'

The words, though she'd waited a lifetime to hear them, were an instant balm to her soul. 'You were here when it mattered.'

If a childhood of being overlooked in favour of her father's expensive hobby was what it had taken to reach this moment and save her and Jay from their fate trapped in a mine, she would take it. It seemed her possible demise had been sufficient for them all to rethink their priorities.

'I'm sorry if I've been distant all these years when I know you could have left a long time ago. I think that's what I was afraid of, that you'd go and leave me like your mother.' The pain of the past was still there in every groove of his forehead, but Meadow could also see the genuine remorse and worry for her in his teary eyes.

'Never, Dad. I just want us to be a family. That's all

I've ever wanted.' She gave him another hug because she could without fear he would push her away. He'd been hurting all this time, just like her, and perhaps now they could finally put it behind them and move on together.

She reached back and took Jay's hand. He'd made these past hours more than bearable and she had high hopes that they could capitalise on their progress. It would be nice to have some time together with him too, in a normal setting without the constant threat of death hanging over them. She'd surprised herself by taking a chance on him and letting fate take control for once and, going forward, she planned on doing that more if she was promised the same rewards.

The world hadn't ended because she'd risked her heart and enjoyed herself. In fact, she was hoping her life was going to be more enriched now that she had a new relationship with Jay and her father to look forward to. It was apparent to her now how important she was in both their lives, as they were to her, justifying that need to spend time with them, even when her heart told her it was probably a bad idea.

'I don't know if you remember, but this is Jay. He's the doctor who helped me that day when you were ill and he's lodging in the shack.' She pulled him forward to make the introduction.

'Hello. Thank you so much for coming to our rescue. We thought our days were numbered,' Jay said.

'The pom. I remember you. Are you the reason my daughter nearly died?' Meadow's father took a step towards Jay and Meadow intervened, placing her body between the two men.

'I guess I am—'

'There's a good reason though, Dad.' Meadow put her hand on her father's chest before he could advance any further towards Jay, who she knew could knock him flat on his backside if he chose to. In a way she was touched her father was so riled about the threat to her welfare, but she also wanted the two men to get along. After all, she was hoping they would all be seeing a lot more of each other, especially if Jay was staying on at the shack for a while.

If they had a chance at a future together, and if she had a chance to share her life with a man as exciting as Jay, she was going to defend him, regardless of his occasional irresponsible sense of adventure. Without that, they might never have been brave enough to act on that chemistry they had, or express the feelings she was still too afraid to admit.

'Thanks for your help, guys. If you want to go up to the house, I'll get everyone some drinks and snacks.' Meadow was aware there were still a few local men who'd come to assist her father hanging around and, whilst she and Jay would be eternally grateful to them, she knew her father wouldn't want strangers to hear what she was about to tell him.

He was already looking at her as though she'd lost her marbles, offering to host the gang when she'd just suffered a near-death experience. Not least because he wasn't one for entertaining on the premises.

'Are you sure you're up to that? I think you'd be better having a shower and getting forty winks. Your English friend can do the same. Over at the shack.' Ironically, he was eyeing Jay with the suspicion of an overprotective father who didn't trust him with his daughter's honour.

Well, it was too late for that, but the news Meadow had to share would probably redeem him, and save him from immediate eviction from the property.

'That's exactly what I think we should do, sir, but I think you'll want to hear what your daughter has to say,' Jay said quietly.

The tense stand-off between the two men in her life made Meadow antsy enough that she just had to say it. 'Jay found gold in the mine.'

'What?' Her father's eyes lit up and she could almost see the dollar signs shining on the surface.

'It's true. There's a seam running along the roof of the cave. I made a mistake dragging Meadow in without making the site safe first, but you can take our word for it that it would be worth your while excavating in there again.'

'How? I mean, I've been in there many times over the years and I haven't seen a speck of gold. I wouldn't have missed a whole bloody seam.'

'It's at the very end of the tunnels and there's evidence of previous cave-ins. Perhaps it was uncovered when a chunk of the wall was dislodged during an earthquake or something.' Jay shrugged.

He'd done the hard part and found the gold when Meadow's dad had spent years of hard work and money with limited success. It was a lucky break, despite an uncomfortable night for them both, and maybe it would not only see her father set up for a while longer, it might also endear Jay to him a little more. That was if he didn't resent him for finding it instead of him.

'I'm going to need to get earthmovers and extra hands and equipment in. We'll need to blast it and set up a wash plant to extract the fine gold from the rock.'

Meadow could see her father's mind working over-time, and though it would be an expensive initial outlay she had a feeling it would be worth it. 'It should keep you busy for a while, at least.'

'It's really true?' Her father hugged her again, clearly struggling to process everything that had just happened.

'Yes, it's true, and it's all yours, Dad. Isn't that right, Jay?' Meadow wasn't staking any claim on what had been discovered and she doubted Jay would, but they both looked to him for confirmation.

Thankfully, he nodded. 'Of course. I merely stumbled on it and, strictly speaking, I wasn't even supposed to be here.'

His generous offer to back her prompted her father to shake his hand and would hopefully put an end to hostilities between them.

'Right, well, I need to make a few calls. I suggest you two go back to the house and get cleaned up and get some food on the go for the guys. I'll have to secure this place as best I can in the meantime.' Her father rolled up his sleeves and began clearing some of the debris away from the entrance.

'Don't do too much, Dad. You're only just out of hospital and I don't want to have to book you a return flight.'

'Listen, I'll go back, get washed and have a bite to eat and then I'll come back and help your dad get this boarded up.' It was Jay who was able to give her peace of mind about leaving her dad out here all alone again so soon after his own accident. At least with Jay he'd not only have an extra pair of hands and get the work done in half the time, but he was someone with medical experience who would intervene if her father showed signs of a relapse. She'd do it herself except she'd promised her services elsewhere to a group of hungry, thirsty workers. It wasn't the quiet, private homecoming she'd been hoping to have with just Jay, but as soon as everyone had gone and her father was safe in his own bed, she would go to him over at the shack.

They had a future to discuss and lost time to make up for, and she couldn't wait for the evening to hurry up and arrive.

'Let me help you with that.' Jay bounded down to help Meadow's father with the thick planks of wood he was hauling in front of the entrance to the old mine.

He'd had his quick, cold shower, and stopped by to make sure Meadow was all right on her own with the men who'd come for their promised refreshments. Thankfully, once they'd been fed, they were keen to get back to their own places. He wondered how many of them were farmers or, like Meadow's dad, obsessed gold hunters who couldn't get their next fix quick enough. However they made their income, he was glad to see them go and leave Meadow in peace. She'd protested when he'd insisted on staying but he didn't care if she knew them or not, he didn't want to leave her on her own with them.

He'd had to fulfil his promise to her father, though, so he'd left instruction for her to take a long, leisurely nap and he'd catch up with her later. Tonight, he wanted them to have a nice romantic time together, just the two of them and some home comforts. After last night he was going to appreciate everything he had here, and that started and ended with Meadow.

'Thanks. I don't want anyone else getting their hands

on whatever's in there. I mean, I wish I'd seen it for my-self but I don't want to risk another cave-in when it's al-ready going to be difficult to get back to the right spot.'

'Oh, I did take these. Sorry, I forgot all about them in the excitement. The screen's cracked, but it's a miracle it's still working, to be honest.' Jay pulled out the phone he'd spotted in the rubble on the way out and scrolled through the pictures until he found the couple he'd taken of the gold in the cave. 'They're a bit dark but it'll give you some idea of what you've got in there.'

Mr Williams set down the armful of wood to look at the photographs, his eyes growing wide. 'That looks promising, son. It'll take some digging and we'll have to filter it out…but I think we're onto a winner there. I can't thank you enough for finding it, and for looking after my daughter.'

Jay cringed, not comfortable with the praise, given the circumstances. 'It was my fault she got trapped in there. I'm not sure you've anything to thank me for.'

'My Meadow doesn't do anything she doesn't want to. If I'm honest, this is the happiest I've seen her in a while. She acts tough but she's got a soft heart, you know.'

He handed Jay his phone back, which was now dis-playing a candid pic he'd taken of her before the mishap, capturing that image of her digging in the dirt, her hair in a ponytail and the sun highlighting the freckles on her nose. She looked adorable.

'I know.' Jay had seen it for himself. Meadow gave everything to those around her, sometimes neglecting her own needs in doing so. Jay knew both he and her fa-ther were guilty of taking too much and giving too little in return. Which was probably why she'd been so wary of getting involved with him. She'd given him a place to stay, been his chauffeur and a shoulder for him when he'd needed one. All he'd done was nearly get her killed and take advantage of her when she was most vulnerable. It put what had happened last night in a different light and he knew she likely wouldn't have slept with him if they hadn't been in such a precarious position, not knowing if they'd live to see another day. If her father knew, he'd probably have sealed him inside the mine for good.

'She doesn't always act in her own best interests.' He fixed Jay with his unnerving icy blue stare, which said he had more than a suspicion that he was going to hurt his only daughter. Yes, he'd be lucky to get out of this one alive too.

'I mean, she should have ditched me years ago like her mother, but that girl wants a family so bad she couldn't cut me off. I know I'm lucky, and nearly losing her has made me think about what my life would be without her. She's the only person who comes to see me, who cares about me, and it's my turn to be the father she needs. That starts with making sure no one waltzes in and breaks her heart again. She deserves more than to be a passing fancy.'

'Yes, she does.'

Deep down, Jay had known that too, he'd just been too selfish to acknowledge it. He wanted her, he felt good when he was with her, but he couldn't be the man she needed. Meadow wanted someone who could give her that family she'd been denied, but how could he be part of that when he had plans elsewhere? The list he'd started with Sharyn had been their way of helping him move on from the past but he still wanted to complete it, maybe even add to it in the future. He certainly didn't think he was anywhere near ready to settle down, to put down roots and resign himself to a life looking at the same four walls again.

Lecture over, cogs whirring in Jay's brain as to what he was getting himself into, the duo fell into silence as they finished the job at hand. Jay knew he had a lot of things to think over, to be clear about what a relationship with Meadow would entail and if he was ready for it. The worst thing for them to do now was rush into something based on a night of good sex at a vulnerable time, and come to regret it later, to resent one another for being trapped in a relationship they knew could never work out. Meadow was still a home body who wanted a family and security. He was a nomad with adventures ahead of him.

It was becoming clear to him he should only make promises about a life together when they were sure that was what they both wanted. Otherwise, they should call it quits now.

Meadow had been watching the clock, wishing away the time all day, waiting for the hours to tick by until it was time to see Jay again. She'd had her shower and made sure she'd had something to eat to sustain her energy levels in anticipation of tonight.

In other circumstances, she would have found Jay's insistence on staying with her to feed the troops irritating, perhaps even condescending to think she couldn't look after herself, but she'd made that mistake before. It was his way of saying he cared about her and he wanted her to be safe. That sort of affection was something she'd been searching for her whole life. Even the hint of jealousy she'd thought she detected as he'd hovered around her gave her heart a lift that he cared enough about her to make his claim. Of course, if he overstepped the mark she wouldn't be long in putting him back in his place, just like that first night, but it was nice to be part of a couple again. Hopefully, tonight would cement that idea and they might even go official so everyone would know and his patients could stop flirting with him. Okay, so he wasn't the only one to get a little possessive when it came to members of the other sex getting too close for comfort.

'Are you sure you're going to be all right if I go out for a while?' She popped her head around her dad's bedroom door to make sure he was settled before she left. He'd been exhausted after the manual labour he and Jay had carried out earlier on so she'd insisted he get an early night and rest up. She'd left some snacks and drinks on his bedstand and put the TV on to keep him company.

Despite living on his own all this time, in her mind he was still a vulnerable man, as his accident had proven. His apology for the past, combined with his emotionally charged hug once he knew she was safe, had only made her want to take care of him more. It was clear he still needed someone to look out for him and for once in her life she was glad she hadn't severed all ties with him. He was the only family she had around her and she knew they loved each other in their own way. It was enough to know that now.

'I'll be fine. Have a good night,' he said, waving her away.

'Okay. 'Night, Dad.' She closed the door and checked her reflection in the hallway mirror. It was technically her first date with Jay, since the other times they'd spent together had happened organically and hadn't been preplanned. So she wanted to look her best. She'd taken the time to dry her hair and put some product in it so she didn't look as though she'd just rolled out of bed for once. If anything, she was hoping to roll back into one.

The thought of sharing one with Jay tonight put a smile on her lips as she dotted them with pink gloss. With a little make-up and a white sundress to show off her tan, she was hoping to make an impression when he opened his door to her.

Meadow hadn't counted on the backward flips her own stomach would do upon the sight of him.

'Hey,' he said casually and opened the door for her to come in.

She followed him inside the shack, which now smelled of his cologne and with the evidence of him living in it, his shoes by the door and his jacket hanging on the wall, she knew she'd never think of the place again without Jay in it.

'Thanks for helping Dad out earlier. I know he thinks he can do everything himself, but he's getting older and I worry about him.'

Her nerves were causing her to ramble a bit as she took a seat on the old sagging couch. Jay had sat in the single armchair, immediately creating some distance between them, and it had thrown her. In her imagination, she'd pictured them being reunited tonight like two long-lost lovers who hadn't seen each other in years, kissing each other senseless and not making it to the bedroom before ripping one another's clothes off. This was quite a different scenario.

'I know you do. You worry about everyone.' Jay set his

beer down on the table and she realised he hadn't asked her if she would even like a drink.

'Jay, is everything all right? You seem a little…off this evening.' There was something in his body language, in his abrupt manner that was setting her on edge. It wasn't the behaviour of the same man who couldn't keep his hands off her last night and who'd talked about a future together. Something had shifted between them and she wasn't sure what that was, how she could fix it, or if he even wanted her to.

Jay cleared his throat and shuffled further on his seat so he was almost sitting on the edge, elbows resting on his knees, head in his hands as though he was about to say something he knew she really didn't want to hear.

Her stomach stopped flipping and simply plummeted instead, as though she'd been enjoying a fun roller coaster ride and the wheels had suddenly come off. She had the urge to put her hands over her ears and block out whatever he was going to say next because she knew what was coming and couldn't stop it. He was going to break her heart.

'We didn't use any protection last night. You'll have to take the morning-after pill.'

'Yes, I suppose so. Thanks for the reminder.' She didn't know what else to say when none of this was how she'd expected the evening to go. Not only was he being distant and weird, but there was a coldness to him tonight she'd never seen before.

'I mean, I know we got carried away in the moment, and neither of us really thought we'd have to deal with the consequences, but you know we can still fix our mistake.'

'A mistake? That's what you think it was?' Meadow's

brain was firing with memories and feelings from last night and not once had he given her the impression that he hadn't wanted any of it. Now she was wondering if she'd been too caught up in the moment to see he wasn't one hundred percent into her. All of those feel-good endorphins which had been coursing through her body as she'd got ready tonight died instantly from the blunt force of his words.

He scrubbed his hands over his face before he spoke. 'What I'm saying is we didn't act on whatever feelings we may have for each other before last night and maybe there's a reason for that. We've both held back because, deep down, we know we're not right for one another, but last night was an exceptional circumstance. The danger we were in made us reckless, not least forgetting about contraception, and I can't afford to take that kind of risk.'

'I can take the morning-after pill. It's not like I was trying to trick you into having a baby, if that's what you're insinuating. I'm not so desperate to keep you in my life I'd do something like that.' She didn't know where any of this had come from. Yes, they'd been careless, but they could take steps to fix that, and to avoid a similar occurrence in the future. Except she got the feeling there was no longer a future involved.

'I know that, Meadow, but the possibility of a pregnancy got me thinking long-term. You want a family, a man you can settle down with, someone who will give you the stability you didn't have when you were younger. I'm not that man. I can't promise you I'll never have the urge to move on somewhere else or want to do something reckless, and that's not the sort of person you need in your life.'

This sudden turnaround was giving her whiplash when only a few hours ago they were looking forward to being together and having some fun. Now he was basically telling her he wasn't the marrying kind.

'Has my dad said something to you?'

'What? No. I've just had some time to think about what we're getting ourselves into.'

'You make it sound like I'm part of a dodgy business deal. I was just looking forward to us having some fun together, not expecting a lifetime commitment, or a judgement on my morals.' She got up out of her seat, forcing herself onto slightly unsteady legs to try and walk away with some dignity when he was gearing up to tell her they were over before they'd even begun.

'I'm sorry, Meadow. None of this is your fault. We're merely guilty of acting without thinking. Something which is completely out of character for one of us and proves what a bad influence I am.' Jay was doing his best to make light of the situation, to take the blame for things suddenly going awry, but Meadow couldn't find the funny side to it. Not when she'd already thrown her heart into the ring, not expecting to have it kicked around in the dirt.

'So, that's it then? Wham, bam, thank you, ma'am, but if we're going to live after all I don't want to tie myself down?' Meadow could hear the shrillness in her voice and hated herself for getting so emotional, but she'd really thought they'd moved past their differences. Loved up and anticipating another night with Jay, she'd convinced herself this was the start of something special. All the time he was probably thinking of a way out. Perhaps it was only last night's jeopardy which had pushed him over the edge into wanting her. Without that adrenaline-pumping threat of almost dying, she wasn't such an attractive prospect.

'I'll thank your dad for letting me stay and pay him rent for the month, but I think it's better for both of us if I move on. There are other places I want to visit, and things I want to do.'

'I thought you were done with the list?' She was clinging now to the last vestiges of her dignity, close to begging him to stay, if not for his benefit, for hers. Jay had come into her world and shown her everything she was missing. Without that excitement he'd brought into her day she didn't know if her old life would ever be the same again.

'I don't know. I don't know what I want right now.'

'But it's not me. That seems pretty clear.'

Jay didn't argue with her. He didn't even follow her to the door. Those simple inactions told her everything she needed to know as she stumbled back out into the night. The darkness hid her tears. If anyone had been watching her they wouldn't have been able to see her doubled over, the pain of losing Jay a physical wound which was going to take a long time to heal, if it ever did.

Jay was leaving her, felt no responsibility or desire to have her in his life in any capacity, and that was a difficult notion to come to terms with. She'd only ever been herself with him and that had proved insufficient for him to want to be with her. There was clearly something lacking in her personality which drove people away. The only person she still had in her life was her father, and that had been at her insistence, not his. It was becoming increasingly apparent the only person she could rely on was herself, and even that was in doubt, given her most recent decisions.

With past breakups she'd taken some time out for self-reflection, to try and figure out what had gone wrong in the relationship as she came to terms with it ending. Ultimately, as she'd usually been the one to call things off, she'd figured it was for the best, that things simply weren't working.

This was different. She'd known from the start Jay wasn't the safe option. That was why she'd kept her distance. Partly. Subconsciously, she thought perhaps she'd known she would be attracted to the danger he represented, that she would fall hard for him. She'd been trying to avoid this pain, the same feeling of rejection and being alone that she'd experienced through most of her childhood.

Except Jay had managed to break her heart as well as her spirit, and she didn't even have a catalogue of memories to keep her company. They'd only had one night. Not enough for her, but sufficient for Jay to know he didn't want any more. It was impossible not to take that personally.

The things she'd shared with him about her childhood and how it had affected her she'd only told him because he'd made her feel safe. She'd given him her trust, her body, her love, only to have it all thrown back in her face. It was a betrayal, yet she couldn't blame Jay for what she was feeling. He hadn't asked for any of it. She was the one who'd taken the risk, thinking she should be more like him and live in the moment. The mistake had been in believing it could last longer than that.

She had forgotten about using protection last night, but the idea of carrying Jay's baby would not have been the same disaster to her as it was to him. He was right, she wanted a family, the settled life she'd never had. But more than that she wanted to be with Jay.

Now, not only had she scared him off the idea of being together, he was leaving her dad's place, and it sounded as though she was losing her co-worker too.

She must have walked into the house in a daze since she didn't remember how she'd got there. It was only minutes ago she'd left, gliding out of here on a cloud of happiness as she went to meet her lover. Now that naïve version of her had been replaced with a devastated Meadow who was cursing her previous self for not being more wary.

When she went to close the blinds in the front room she saw car headlights outside the window. Before she got nervous about who would be out here at this time of the night, Jay emerged from the shack with his bag over his shoulder. Clearly, he'd made his decision to leave as soon as possible and in desperation had clearly phoned Marko for a taxi out of here. Perhaps he'd even done it before her visit, it seemed to happen so quickly, meaning nothing she could have said would have changed his mind about leaving.

As the car pulled away, plunging the room into darkness once again, she noted he hadn't even cared about her enough to say goodbye. It was then she allowed the tears to fall, knowing she was watching the love of her life drive away.

She could admit that now. She was in love with Jay, and probably had been from the moment he'd waded in to defend her honour in the pub that night. The knowledge that those feelings weren't reciprocated didn't make it any easier to see him leave. It only emphasised how much she'd lost when he was taking those unrealistic expectations of a happy family with him.

* * *

Jay got into Marko's car and looked back at the house until it was nothing more than a dot in the distance. He'd seen Meadow at the window watching him go and felt as though a crushing weight had been dropped onto his heart. If this had been a movie she'd have come running out barefoot after him, he would've stopped the taxi and met her halfway, swinging her around in the air and kissing her through his apologies for being an idiot. But this was real life and that wouldn't have fixed anything, only set them up for more devastation when he failed her again in the future.

He couldn't blame her father for this departure when he'd only told him what he already knew to be true. Meadow needed someone safe, who could be a good husband to her and a father to her children. Jay couldn't promise any of that when he still had things he wanted to do, places he wanted to see. It didn't mean he loved her any less, that this pain in his heart wasn't killing him. He'd grieved for Sharyn for a long time, and though it was only a relationship with Meadow he was mourning, those feelings were just as intense. It was still a loss, leaving his love with nowhere to go. That was why he had to leave now. If he stayed here, saw Meadow at work and on her father's property, he'd realise what he was missing and want to stay. He had to do this for her. No matter the pain it caused him.

His reward would be her future, and knowing she would find happiness with a man who could give her children and the family she needed around her. The only thing he knew about parenting was frightening and dark, and to his mind pretending that was what he wanted would only end up with him hurting Meadow. He'd be as guilty of trapping her in a nightmare as his father, and that was the last thing he wanted.

Though she might never know it, it was his love for her that was setting her free.

CHAPTER NINE

'DON'T YOU THINK we should just fly on up to the fair? I mean, we can still go if we get a shout, and we'll be on site should anyone be in need of medical assistance, but we could go and enjoy the carnival atmosphere while we're waiting,' Meadow asked their new flight doctor with the thought they might as well enjoy themselves along with the rest of the town while they were waiting for the next callout.

She hadn't had much fun in the two weeks since Jay had gone. Her father had been busy trying to get equipment in place to start mining the gold seam they'd found. He was in his element and totally rejuvenated by his new venture but she had stayed on in his house to make sure he didn't overdo things. It also made her feel closer to Jay, especially looking out on the shack which reminded her of him so much. That last night in particular, when he'd driven away.

She'd done her fair share of crying over him and for the first time in her life she found herself restless, her life here suddenly not fulfilling enough. As though Jay had taken a very big part of her away with him and she didn't know how to fill that void left behind.

'I don't think so. We have paperwork to do and we need to be at the base for any emergencies coming in.' Henry,

Jay's temporary replacement until they found someone permanently, was a stickler for the rules. Even more so than Meadow. She'd done her best to get along with him, but after Jay she found him very dry and boring.

He unbuckled his seat belt and exited the plane as soon as the engine had completely stopped, keen to get into the hub and file a report.

'Is it just me, or is he a bit of a jobsworth?' she asked Greg in the cockpit, annoyed that she couldn't spend the afternoon at the fair, away from the house and thoughts of Jay.

Greg laughed. 'That's rich coming from you, Miss By-the-Book.'

'What? Am I really that bad?' She liked to do her job well, but she hadn't realised it had earned her a nickname for her fastidiousness. If that was the case, it was a wonder someone like Jay had ever taken a romantic interest in her, and less surprising that she hadn't been enough to keep him here. To someone who'd travelled the world and experienced so many adrenaline-fuelled adventures, she too must have seemed dry and boring in comparison. Perhaps he'd simply seen her as a respite from the excitement, the human equivalent to a duvet day. The thought didn't improve her current mood.

'Not so much now, since Jay was on the scene. I think he had a positive influence on you.'

'You think?' She hadn't been able to find any positives since his departure, only negative feelings and space where he'd once been.

'You're not as uptight as you used to be, or defensive. I think he brought out your fun side. I hear he's in Sydney now.'

'Oh?' She'd been curious about what Jay had been up to and where he'd gone, but he hadn't made any contact with her since he'd left, and she hadn't wanted to look desperate by texting. Even if there was a message for him still waiting in the draft folder of her phone. She missed him, and she had hoped he would miss her too.

'Yeah, I think Kate was talking to him recently. He needed some paperwork or something for his new job. Anyway, talk to her, she knows all about it.' Greg unbuckled his seatbelt, set his headset down and climbed out of the cockpit, clearly ignorant of her thirst for more information.

'Thanks. I'll do that.'

Greg stepped out on the tarmac and helped her out of the back of the plane.

'I thought you made a good couple.' He shrugged.

'Me too, but I guess I'm just not his type.' It was all she could do to even give a half smile when all she still wanted to do was curl up in a ball and cry for everything she'd lost. They might only have known each other for a few days but it had seemed like a lifetime when they'd come to know each other so well, or at least she thought they had.

That instant explosive chemistry they'd had on the first night in the pub had always been fizzing away in the background but they'd shared so much more than physical attraction. The connection they'd had working together, the bond they'd shared over their difficult childhoods, and the simple pleasure of being in one another's company were things she doubted she'd ever have with anyone else. She couldn't believe she'd got it so wrong by putting her faith in him not to fail her when she'd spent most of her adulthood trying to protect herself. It proved just how quickly, and deeply, she'd fallen for him to give him that trust so easily.

'I don't believe that. I saw you two together, and the way he looked at you. Believe me, you were his type for the whole time he was in town.'

'Ah, but he's not in town any more, is he? I'm sure there's a much bigger dating pool in Sydney for him to dip his toe into and find his real type instead of his only option.' Meadow was well aware there were very few single women in town, just as there was a shortage of single men. It was the reason she blamed for hooking up with Marko that one time, and maybe Jay realised after their one night together that he'd settled too. She was fine as a passing fancy but anything more serious had never been on the cards.

'I don't believe that for a second. I saw you two that night at the pool playing doctors and nurses when you thought no one was looking.' Greg whistled a breath out through his teeth and Meadow blushed at the memory of being caught ogling Jay in nothing but his pants.

'Nothing happened. Not that night, anyway,' she muttered, half hoping he wouldn't hear her admission.

Greg chuckled. 'I'm a man, Meadow. Just because you didn't act on it doesn't mean he didn't want to. I can tell when a man is interested and when he's just grabbing the nearest chick for a good time. Jay likes a challenge, we both know that, and they do say opposites attract. Otherwise, why would our Miss By-the-Book have fallen for the pom with the danger streak?'

'What do you mean? I don't understand...' If what Greg was telling her was true, it didn't explain how easy it was for Jay to simply drive away that night after he'd ground her heart into the dust.

He took her by the shoulders. 'Meadow, you've a lot to learn about men. We run when we're scared.'

'But Jay wasn't scared of anything.' Except the dark, but he'd been able to get over that when she was there to distract him. She wondered who was there to hold him now.

'A man like that, always on the move, is running from something. I'm guessing this time it was his feelings for you. We're a skittish bunch, you know. One whiff of commitment and poof, we're gone.'

'But he was in a relationship before me. I don't think he had commitment issues per se.'

'Then you've got to ask yourself why else he would walk away from a woman he clearly had feelings for if it wasn't for his own sake.' Greg dropped that bit of wisdom and walked away, leaving Meadow to contemplate Jay's motivation from a different perspective. If it wasn't his feelings in question, as she'd believed, then it had to be something to do with hers. The sort of man Jay was, he wouldn't have wanted to cause her any problems and though her father insisted he hadn't said anything to influence his decision to leave, she wondered if that was true. After all, she'd told him she couldn't be with someone who wouldn't stay in one place, someone like her dad.

These past two weeks had told her that wasn't true. She'd been afraid to trust her heart with a rebellious soul like Jay, but it wasn't losing him that had made her so restless. It was not going after him and taking another risk that had made life so boring here now. The least she owed herself was to take one more chance and see where it led.

* * *

Jay stepped to the edge of the structure and made the mistake of looking down. Bungee jumping off the Sydney Harbour Bridge would have had any normal person's heart racing, but even with the wind whistling around him and only a safety harness preventing him from hurtling towards his death it wasn't the experience he had hoped it would be. It wasn't blocking out thoughts of Meadow, just as the swimming with sharks, moving to the city and starting over hadn't managed to erase her from his mind either. This was the last thing on the list and once he'd done this he didn't know what came next.

'Are you ready?' the instructor shouted against the wind as he adjusted his straps in preparation for the jump.

'Give me a moment.' Jay was only having second thoughts because he knew launching himself off here wasn't going to change anything, other than his perspective of the landscape.

He'd started his life over, something he'd done time and again on his travels with Sharyn, and something he'd had to do when she'd died. Yet since leaving Meadow he hadn't been able to settle. Ironic when he'd told her that was what he didn't want. Now it felt as though the only real excitement he'd experienced was when he'd been with her and everything else was boring and pointless in comparison. With Sharyn, he'd needed that buzz of jumping out of a plane or surfing giant waves to bond them together and get the adrenaline flowing. He hadn't needed to force anything with Meadow, except an excuse to leave.

With a deep breath and a glance back down, Jay tried to psyche himself up to take the leap. Like the whole list, he was only going along with this because he didn't know what else to do with his life or where to go, doomed to drift for ever. All because this big, brave man had been too afraid to tell Meadow how he really felt.

'Don't do it!'

At first, he thought he'd imagined the sound of her voice. Then he saw Meadow walking towards him on the platform, wearing a helmet and safety pads and picking each step very carefully. When she reached him she grabbed hold of him and hugged him tight, but he wasn't sure if it was because she'd missed him or that she just needed something to cling onto for safety.

'At least not without me.'

As Jay was attempting to figure out what was happening, the safety instructor began to strap her into a harness.

'Hey, you're not actually going to do this, are you? You don't just jump and hope for the best, you know.' He didn't know why she was here or what she was attempting to achieve, but he wasn't going to let her put herself at risk because he was the idiot who'd thought this was a good idea.

'I've had the safety talk and instructions. Kate told me you were planning this and I thought I would come and surprise you.'

'Why?' As glad as he was to see her, he couldn't understand what was going on, other than Kate having a big mouth. He hoped there wasn't a crowd from the base down below waving banners for him and turning this into a community event instead of a distraction from his lonely life. This had been his choice, even if he'd left Dream Gulley for Meadow's benefit.

She looked up at him with those big blue eyes he'd still

pictured in his dreams at night. 'I missed you. Perhaps I'm being stupid, but I thought we had something special.'

'We did, but—'

'Thank goodness I got that right, at least.'

'I just didn't want to let you down, Meadow. You need someone who'll be there for you, who wants to settle down and have a family. Someone safe.'

'Well, it turns out that's not what I need. Apparently, it's an Englishman with a death wish that's missing from my life. Who knew?' She was smiling up at him and, for the first time since he'd climbed up here, Jay's heart began to race.

'So where do we go from here? I mean, other than off this bridge.' He was afraid to believe that he could still have Meadow in his life when her sudden appearance didn't mean the things that made them incompatible would immediately evaporate. To go back again now would simply delay the inevitable again. That was why he'd ripped the Band-Aid off in the first place.

'This is the last thing on the list, right? I thought you might want some company to mark the occasion, so I took some time off. I know, I know, it's so unlike me, which is why I did, and flew here to be on this bridge with you. I want us to spend some time together and I'm willing to change, to do crazy stuff like this if that's what you need from me.'

'I wouldn't ask you to change, Meadow. I'm not even sure this is the kind of life I want any more. You changed me.' Jay laughed, knowing he'd rather be playing board games together or trapped in a cave, or making love, or doing anything as long as it was with her.

'I think we changed each other, huh? Things are kind

of boring without you around. So, what do you say we spend some time just hanging out and see how we feel?'

'Hey, guys, are you two jumping any time today?' The young instructor was standing with his arms folded, clearly still an adrenaline junkie who hadn't been tamed by love yet.

'I'm ready if you are,' Jay said, putting his arms around Meadow's waist now it appeared they were doing a tandem jump. This was the end of one chapter of his life and, hopefully, the beginning of a new, happier one.

'Yeah, let's get this over with so we can go do something fun,' she said with a grin. 'Now you've finished your list, we might even make one of our own.'

Jay couldn't resist stealing a kiss when she looked so adorable kitted out for her mission in trying to win him back. Not that it would take much persuading for him when he was missing her more than he'd ever thought possible. If Meadow had the courage to leave her safe place and stand here on the precipice with him, then he needed to take the plunge too. She was right, some time together without any pressure would soon let them know if they wanted to carry on past their adventures. Jay had a feeling that life with Meadow, whether they were working together, gold hunting or making dinner out of leftovers, would never be boring.

As they clung to each other and took that huge step into the unknown, Jay knew they were doing so with their eyes and hearts open. The biggest risk he'd ever taken.

EPILOGUE

'I REALLY THOUGHT you would have been better at DIY.'

Meadow was watching Jay attempt to put up shelves to house their growing collection of board games and photo frames of their madcap adventures. They'd even framed his completed list and added one of their own.

'Why? Because I'm a man?' He sucked on the thumb which he'd just hit with a hammer instead of the screw in the wall.

'No, because it involves dangerous things like hammers and drills and potentially maiming yourself.' She took his hand and kissed it.

'It's probably just as well we've hired people to do the essential repairs or this place would be in worse condition than when we started.'

After she'd followed him to Sydney and they'd decided they did want to be together, Jay had made the decision to return to Dream Gulley with her and start back at his old job. She'd spent so much time at the shack and on her father's land, he'd eventually told them they were welcome to live there permanently as a thank you for locating his long-sought-after gold. It had become their project to renovate the house into a home and with the place so busy with contractors and work going on at the mine, it no longer resembled the vast empty space she'd resented in her youth.

They'd found a happy middle ground, working and living together like any other normal couple, but every now and then they took a spontaneous trip to do something fun and exciting. She was happy and Jay seemed pretty content too. They had an agreement that if either of them wasn't enjoying their life together they would discuss it rather than let things fester. So far, so good.

'You can't be good at everything. You have many other more useful skills.' She danced her fingers up his chest, the sight of him attempting to make his mark on a home for them apparently her new kink.

'I don't like to boast, but I have been known to wrangle deadly snakes and discover gold in abandoned mines.' Jay set down his tools and put his arms around her waist, pulling her close.

'Hmm, I was thinking about the more fun, less deadly things you're good at.'

'There is still one thing I haven't tried. I don't know if I'll be any good at it, but you know I'm up for a challenge.'

'Oh? What's that?' Meadow's heart began to sink as she anticipated the bad news that he wanted to move on after all. Even if he wanted her to go with him, it wouldn't be the same as the life they'd made for themselves here and she would be reluctant to let go of it.

'Being a husband.'

Before she could process what he was saying or doing, Jay let go of her and went down on bended knee.

'Meadow Williams, I love you with every fibre of my being. Will you please do me the honour of marrying me?' He was holding out a black velvet ring box with a marquise cut diamond ring nestled inside.

Even if it had been a rusty old ring-pull he'd found outside with a metal detector she would have given the same answer. 'Yes. I love you too, Jay.'

Jay was reflecting the big grin she had on her face as he slid the ring onto her finger. 'I had it made specially, with permission from your father. The band is made from the seam of gold we found in the mine. A real piece of home to show you how much I love you. Maybe some day we'll even fill this place with a family of our own.'

Those simple words finally made her feel complete. Jay would never enter into a decision about getting married and having children if he didn't feel he could offer a stable home for everyone. It showed his conviction in his love for her to make such a commitment and Meadow loved him for pushing through his own issues for the sake of their relationship. He was letting her know she was loved and had a home where she was safe. It was everything.

* * * * *

RESISTING
THE BROODING
HEART SURGEON

TINA BECKETT

MILLS & BOON

To my dad, who loved serving his country.

PROLOGUE

SHANNA MEADOWS HEARD the sound first, before she fully comprehended what it was. Her mom was crying. Loudly. She slowly made her way toward the living room, realizing she was late for school. She hadn't meant to oversleep, didn't even remember her mom trying to wake her up.

The legs of the giraffe pajama bottoms she'd gotten last Christmas were still a little too long, and they dragged across the carpet with every step she took as she moved closer and closer to the sound. Maybe she should go back to her room and get dressed. Even if she was late, her mom could still take her to school.

Her dad had told her she needed to help around the house while he was gone, and she'd tried. She'd really tried. But now her mom was sobbing, and she could hear another voice in the room talking to her. A man's voice.

It wasn't her dad's. She was suddenly scared.

She came into the room and saw two men in uniforms, like the ones her dad wore on special occasions. "Ma'am, we want you to know that your husband was a hero. His sacrifice saved the lives of his troop."

Sacrifice? What did that mean?

Her mom's eyes suddenly swung her way, spotting her in the doorway. She dabbed at her eyes, which were really red and had a weird expression in them. "G-go back to bed, baby."

"But I'm late for school. Is something wrong with Dad?"

The two men stood like statues, not saying anything, but one of them glanced at the other.

Her mother closed her eyes for a second before looking at her again, drawing a deep breath as if she, too, was really scared about something. "You're not going to school today, Shan."

Not going to school? She always went to school unless she was really sick or there was too much snow on the ground. "But why?"

"Go back to bed, and I'll come talk to you in a few minutes."

As she looked into the unsmiling faces of the two men, who hadn't even said hello to her, Shanna realized something was very wrong. Something more wrong than not getting up in time to catch the school bus. And it had something to do with her dad. With the word *sacrifice* the men had used.

Suddenly, she *wanted* to go back to bed. To go back to sleep and wake up all over again. Wake up to the normal sounds of her mother getting breakfast ready and hollering that she needed to hurry.

Wake up to her mother *not* crying.

A normal day.

But today wasn't normal. And from the way her mom looked, and the way Shanna was feeling, days weren't going to feel normal again for a very long time.

If ever.

CHAPTER ONE

SHANNA PASSED THE wall commemorating military service at Everly Memorial Hospital and averted her eyes. It was a great acknowledgment of staff members' service, both current and past, but it tended to jar her every time she saw it. She normally tried to avoid this particular corridor, as it pulled at the cloak of positivity she tended to wear for her patients. For her mom, back when they were both grieving Shanna's dad's death. The word *sacrifice* still had the ability to rock her world, since she'd learned that her dad had found and attempted to defuse a pipe bomb found inside a box of food supplies and had been killed in the process. But he had saved lives that day. She and her mom had gone through some very hard times right after her dad's death, and her mom had never married again. Shanna didn't think that would ever change.

She couldn't blame her. After all, she was pretty wary of relationships, too, after watching her mom descend into a depression so deep that she'd had to be hospitalized after her husband's death. Shanna had gone to live with her grandmother while her mother received treatment, but the terror of somehow losing her mom, too, had never completely healed. She never wanted to live through a pain like that again.

She hurried down the hallway toward the elevator, away from the prints. She was a little late for work, which was almost unheard of for her, but traffic had been horrible today with an accident bringing the line of cars to a standstill.

Once on her floor, Maura, one of the nurses and a good friend, grinned at her. "I never thought I'd see the day Shanna Meadows was late."

"Ugh! Traffic was awful. How's it been today?"

"Actually pretty quiet. You have time to sneak away for a piece of cake for that new doctor we're getting, if you want. It's in the break room."

"Cake?"

Maura laughed. "I thought that might perk you up a bit. You looked a little sad when you got off that elevator."

She forced her face into a mock scowl. "Just irritated at some of the crazy drivers out there."

"Go get cake. It'll make you feel better. And bring me a piece, too, while you're at it, if you don't mind."

Maybe a dose of sugar really would help chase the weird sense of melancholy away. Or at least help her put on a happier face. "I don't mind a bit. I'll be back in just a minute or two."

With that, she pivoted and punched the button to call the elevator she'd just exited. The doors opened immediately. Wow, it really was quiet, if no one else had summoned the thing. She could only hope the day stayed that way.

* * *

"Dr. Vaughan, welcome to Everly Memorial Hospital."

The paper plates surrounding a large rectangular cake was evidently something they did for every new staff member, but it seemed weird somehow. He wasn't used to any kind of fanfare when he'd changed duty stations in the army. It was simply part of what was expected of you.

He smiled at Dan Brian, the hospital administrator, bypassing the cake and opting for a cup of coffee instead. People filed in and out, grabbing slices and murmuring their own words of welcome before heading back out to the floor. Actually, Zeke was anxious to get out there and join their ranks.

A stack of papers next to the coffeepot caught his attention, and he glanced at the Mark Your Calendars heading before perusing the rest of the flyer.

The hospital was evidently hosting a pumpkin-carving party for Halloween sponsored by a local charity as a fundraiser and to help boost community awareness of what Everly had to offer. His brows went up as he saw the words "All staff members are encouraged to attend." From his experience, "encouraged" was a euphemism for "expected." The party was planned for the day before Halloween, probably so that people with kids could still participate in their neighborhood activities on the thirty-first.

Great. The event was only two weeks away. He'd hoped to be able to stay low-key until he got a feel for the way the hospital ran. He was pretty sure it was nothing like his last post in Pensacola. Not that he missed it particularly. It held a mixture of memories both good and bad. But at least he'd been able to leave the area where his ex-fiancée still lived. The few times he'd run into her over the last couple of years, the encounters had been awkward. Kristen was now married with a baby. And her husband was definitely *not* associated with the military.

Yes, he'd been happy to move. Happy to be able to make the decision on his own, with no arguing, no debates, no negotiating. And his sense of relief at finally being able to shake off the shadows of his past was surprisingly strong. He was hoping to convince his parents to relocate from Jacksonville, since there were some wonderful specialists here in the Tampa area. It was part of the reason he'd chosen the city.

Compared with what his dad was going through, having to attend a pumpkin-carving party seemed a pretty minor inconvenience. As long as he didn't have to carve one himself.

He picked one of the flyers up and folded it, tucking it into the pocket of his lab coat.

Dan evidently saw the move and said, "We hope you'll join us for that. The kids have an absolute ball at it."

Zeke smiled. "How could I say no?"

"It's fun. I promise. Have you gotten settled in your office yet?"

He wasn't much for Halloween. It wasn't that he didn't like it. He'd just never been one for costumes or parties. "Not yet. I was just trying to remember where it was. If you'll just point me in the right direction…"

Dan started to say something, then the door opened, and a woman entered. Her hair was glossy black and hung straight, sliding like silk over her shoulders. Her eyes met his for a second before skipping past him to look at something on the table.

The cake, probably.

The administrator's brows went up. "Perfect. Shanna, would you mind coming over here for a minute?"

The woman's easy smile swung back their way. "Sure thing." Dark brown eyes met his again. "I take it we have you to thank for these tasty treats." She held out her hand. "Shanna Meadows. I'm a respiratory therapist and nurse here at Everly."

"Nice to meet you. I'm Zeke Vaughan. Cardiothoracic surgeon. And you all have a way of making a guy feel welcome."

She laughed. "If that's all it takes to win you over, then consider every day to be cake day."

No one could be that cheerful all the time. Or was she merely doing it for Dan's benefit?

As if hearing his thoughts, the other man smiled. "Shanna is actually in charge of making our Halloween party the successful community outreach endeavor that it's been over the five years she's been with us." He paused and glanced at her. "Have you had cake yet?"

"Nope. That's what I snuck in here for." She tossed a lock of hair over her shoulder.

"Can I talk you into getting it to go and have you

show Dr. Vaughan to his office and fill him in on the party? I'm meeting with members of the board in a few minutes."

"Of course." She bypassed the plates that already had some pre-sliced sections on them and cut her own piece. A chunky one. And then she cut a second slice.

For later?

That made him smile, for some reason. If she was peeved that she was going to have to entertain him for the next fifteen minutes or so, she didn't show it.

"Ready?" she asked. "Ever been to a costume party before?"

Costumes? Had the brochure mentioned that? "Um...not since elementary school."

She started to push the door open before stopping and turning toward him, somehow managing to hold both the door and her plates. "You're kidding, right?"

Okay, so maybe Zeke was the one who should be peeved. But he wasn't. There was something infectiously happy about Shanna Meadows. Something that made him want to take a minute or two longer to get to his office.

Now *that* peeved him. There was no way in hell he was going to let his thoughts circle around her. The sooner he shook her off, the better. But he was going to have to do it in a way that didn't offend her. Because it wasn't her. It was him.

One side of his mouth twisted up. Wasn't that a classic breakup line?

"I'm actually not the biggest fan of trick or treat. I'm just never home."

She finished pushing the door open, holding it for him to pass through. Then, still holding both plates in one hand, she somehow managed to spear a piece of her cake and pop it into her mouth as she approached the elevator. "And when you are home, I bet your porch lights are off."

"Huh?"

"You know. To make kids think you're not home."

When she said it like that, she really did make him feel like some old curmudgeon who ran little kids off his property just for kicks.

"Nope. I don't."

He just didn't answer the door. Not because he was mean. He just…forgot what day it was and normally didn't have candy in the house.

"Well, that's good to know."

They got to the elevator and waited as it ticked down floors, headed in their direction. He nodded at the cake. "Good?"

"The best. Everyone swears by this grocery chain's sheet cakes, and they are right." The elevator stopped and they got on.

Yes, he remembered that from his childhood when his dad was stationed at Naval Air Station Jacksonville in northern Florida. When Zeke chose to join the army rather than the navy, his dad wasn't mad or upset. Instead, they often had verbal skirmishes that ended in laughter. He still missed those jokes and fun times.

His dad was in the advanced stages of Alzheimer's disease. He and his mom were still in Jacksonville. It was where his father had loved serving his country. It was one of the reasons he'd chosen to retire from active duty a year ago and become a reservist. So he could spend time with his dad whenever he wanted.

He only realized Shanna had finished her cake and said something to him when the doors to the elevator reopened onto the fourth floor. He waited until she stepped off before following her. "Sorry, I missed that."

"Any idea what kind of pumpkin you'll carve?" She dumped her empty plate and fork into a nearby receptacle. "I try to keep track, so we don't have too many Baby Sharks—as in the children's song—in the competition."

"Carve?"

She looked at him like he had two heads. "Do you like to do a traditional jack-o'-lantern? Something elaborate? Spooky?"

"I thought we were just there for moral support while the kids carved them."

She stopped in front of a door. "Well, we are. But the staff also like to have a lineup of lit pumpkins. Before we help them carve their own. And the kids love going down that lineup and voting for their favorites."

"Surely in a hospital this big, not everyone participates."

"No, not everyone. And as for the size, you're right. Which is why a lot of departments team up to do one, or friends might band together and come up with a design."

And since Zeke didn't know anyone here, it was going to be a little hard to just toss his name into a hat and let someone else do all the work. Not that that was his style anyway. "Good to know."

He would say he would figure something out, but since the party was only two weeks away, it was doubtful that he would be able to devise a plan that would make him look like a team player. And actually Zeke did work pretty damn well in a team. After all, the military had ingrained that in him.

"I could help, if you wanted." As soon as the words came out, something in her face shifted and he wondered if she wanted to retract them. But despite his earlier thoughts about needing to avoid her, he was willing to jump at anything that was offered. Even if it came from a woman who set his nerves on edge.

"Aren't you already on a team?"

"I normally don't carve anything since I'm in charge of the party." She nodded at the door in front of them. "This is your office."

He took out a key ring on which he'd slipped the key Dan had given him. He slid the key into the lock and opened the door. "Isn't that a little hypocritical?"

"Excuse me?" Her head tilted and she fixed him with a narrow-eyed glance.

He'd meant it as a joke, but it had evidently gone off target. "Sorry, I was teasing. I was talking about not carving a pumpkin. And since you don't carve one, do you have any suggestions of a team I could join?"

She moved inside his office and sat down in one of the chairs, even before he had the light on. He hurriedly switched it on and watched her nose wrinkle as she looked around the small space.

"What?"

"I thought they would have given you the suite that your predecessor had."

"They offered. I told them I didn't need anything elaborate." He went behind his desk and sat in the chair. "I don't plan on spending the majority of my time here."

She looked at him for a minute as if he'd surprised her somehow. "I'll tell you what. If you buy a pumpkin, I'll help you carve it. I realize it's short notice on top of everything else you have to get used to."

"Don't feel like you have to." Although, he hoped she would. He certainly didn't want patients judging his surgical skills by his lack of talent in carving a pumpkin. Doing surgery on a human being was worlds apart from cutting into a pumpkin and hoping it came out as something recognizable.

"I don't *have* to do anything. I want to. I need to go see my next patient, so if you have any spare time today, we can get together and discuss some options."

Options for carving a pumpkin. This hospital took this a little too seriously, in his opinion. Or maybe it wasn't the hospital that did. Maybe it was the woman in charge of it who did.

Behind that cheerful exterior he thought he'd caught

glimpses of a quiet intensity, although he could be mistaken about that. But something about it intrigued him. Was there more to Shanna Meadows than what she showed to the world?

It didn't matter if there was. He wasn't here to try to solve puzzles other than the ones his patients presented.

"I actually don't have any patients scheduled as Dan thought I should just try to get settled in today and then start tackling my job tomorrow. I already have a bypass surgery scheduled."

"I know. Mr. Landrum. He was admitted this morning. I'm going to assess his breathing and do a treatment on him to try to keep his oxygen levels up until he can get the bypass tomorrow. He's actually who I was getting ready to go see. I just need to drop this piece of cake off at the nurses' desk."

Ah, so it hadn't been for her.

"Who ordered the treatment?" He wasn't sure what the protocol was in the civilian world, since he'd been working in military hospitals his entire career.

"Dr. Petrochki, since his last day was yesterday afternoon."

"There are a few other cardiologists who have hospital privileges, are there not?"

"Yes, but they don't reside at the hospital." She smiled, the act making her eyes light up. "And before you ask, no, they don't have to carve pumpkins. That privilege is reserved for hospital staff. Like you."

"Lucky me," he muttered.

She actually laughed at that one. The throaty sound

went right through him, as did the way her head tipped back, revealing a long length of neck.

He swallowed, trying to banish the sudden jolt of awareness that went through him. Hell, he hadn't had that happen in quite a while.

"It's a pretty popular event," she said. "Some of the surrounding doctors have been trying to get carving privileges along with their hospital privileges. Anyway, we can talk later, Mr. Landrum is waiting."

"Mind if I tag along, so I can meet him?"

"I think that might be a good idea, actually, if you're okay with starting your job today."

"The sooner the better." He stood and picked up the lanyard that had been laid on his desk and put it around his neck. "Since I still don't know where anything is located, can you lead the way?"

"Of course." With that she got up and slid from the room with a grace that had him scrambling to set himself to rights once again.

He'd been down the path of hospital romance once before. He didn't want to venture down that road again. Thankfully, Kristen had received an offer from a nearby civilian hospital soon after they broke up and had moved on. To a new life. A new partner. And he wouldn't have had it any other way. The trick now was to not make the same mistakes he'd made with her. Which meant that any weird vibrations that he got from Shanna Meadows had to be firmly placed in the nearest trash receptacle before they had a chance to take hold and root themselves in his head. And that's exactly what he was going to do.

They dropped off the cake to Maura, who eyed Zeke with speculation when she introduced him to her. Something about that irked her and she wasn't sure why. As did having the surgeon dog her steps. She knew that it was only natural for him to want to meet the patient he'd be operating on tomorrow, but something about him made her edgy. Something that had nothing to do with the party. She wasn't sure if it was the short, crisp hair that was slicked back from his head or his ridiculously straight posture, but he reminded her of someone. Someone she liked. She just couldn't put her finger on who that might be. His general apathy toward Halloween and the pumpkin-carving contest— something that she looked forward to every year— should have rubbed her the wrong way. Instead, she'd found it amusing, a challenge, even.

There was no way she wanted anyone at the hospital to think she was showing Everly's newest doctor any kind of favoritism by helping him. Maura had already raised a brow at her when she saw the new doctor. What would she do if she found out she'd offered to help Zeke?

It really wasn't fair to expect him to jump into his job and have time left over for something like the Halloween party. There were fourteen pumpkins already slated to be in the contest and Zeke's would make fifteen, the largest number yet. Dan was certainly happy with the way the party was making a splash in the community at large.

Mr. Landrum's room was in the cardiac care unit, which was on the same floor as Zeke's office and would make it easier for the hospital's resident doctor to do rounds. So before she could dissect her conversation with Zeke too terribly much, they'd arrived at the patient's room.

She turned back to glance at the surgeon, who'd grown silent behind her. "Ready?"

"Whenever you are."

With that, she took a deep breath and pushed through the door.

Their patient was lying propped up in bed, a cannula under his nose delivering a much-needed boost in oxygen.

"Good morning, Mr. Landrum. I brought you a visitor." She tipped her head sideways to nod at Zeke. "This is Dr. Vaughan. He'll be doing your surgery tomorrow."

Denny Landrum, at just fifty years old, had a strong wiry frame, but right now he was pale and ill-looking, and no wonder. He'd been working his butt off in his landscaping business, until chest pains had derailed him and driven him to find the reason for it. It was a good thing he had. Because he was almost 100 percent occluded in two major vessels. Once he got the surgery, he should feel like a new man. At least that was the hope.

Zeke stepped forward and pulled out a stethoscope

from his jacket pocket. "Nice to meet you. Mind if I have a listen?"

"Go ahead."

Shanna watched as Zeke went through the examination. She'd seen this done literally hundreds of times before with different doctors, but there was something about how intent Zeke was as he listened to the man's chest, the furrows between his brows deepening in concentration. His expression made her shiver. To combat the sensation, she crossed her arms over her chest and went through a mental checklist of things she needed to do during the man's breathing treatment once Zeke was finished.

She kind of hoped he left while she worked, but had a feeling that hope was going to be crushed. Because he seemed like a very hands-on type of physician.

Except when it came to things not involving patients. Like pumpkin-carving parties.

Well, he was going to learn that Everly Memorial took every part of its commitment to patients seriously. And that included mental and emotional care as well, which was where the thought behind the October event had come about: keeping morale of both patients and staff up with a fun activity.

Even though Zeke didn't seem like he needed anything to help him do that. Although looks could be deceiving. She hardly knew the man well enough to know what went on in his head, or what he was truly committed to, outside of his patients. She swallowed. And not all commitments came with happy, morale-lifting endings. Hadn't her dad's commitment to his military career led to his death?

This wasn't the same thing at all. Zeke's commitment to his patients wouldn't do that. Because he was a civilian and not likely to be dragged into a situation that was supposed to be keeping the peace but had ended up painting a target on the back of every man in his unit.

Zeke pulled his stethoscope from his ears and smiled. "Are you ready to feel better?"

"Yes. Whatever it takes. I have a wife and grandchild that are counting on me." He nodded at the table next to his bed, where a framed picture sat.

The surgeon smiled and went around to pick up the picture, studying it. "Who's who?"

"That's my wife on the left, my daughter and my three-year-old granddaughter. They're living with us right now. She had to...get away...leave a bad relationship."

Shanna's heart jolted. She hadn't known that. And the inference was that the relationship had been something worse than merely not being able to get along. Her fingers tightened around the treatment packet she held in her hand. Shanna knew the type. She'd seen them come through the hospital, periodically. Bruises and breaks that were explained away as accidents.

She couldn't imagine being a counselor tasked with unraveling the pain of betrayal and helping their patients find the courage to leave the situation. Or help a devastated wife deal with the loss of her husband to a senseless act. But she was thankful for them. Thankful that just such a specialist had helped her mom start looking outward again.

Time to put her mind back on her patient, since Zeke was returning the framed print to the table.

"Well, we're going to try to make sure you're there for them." He glanced at Shanna. "I think we have a breathing treatment that should help to clear out any congestion in your lungs."

"Shanna has been great. As has Dr. Petrochki. I was kind of hoping he could do my surgery—no offense. But he's evidently retiring."

Zeke smiled at him, seemingly unruffled by the fact that the man had basically said he'd rather have his former cardiologist perform his bypass. "He is. And I'd better hope I can live up to Dr. Petrochki's standards, then, hadn't I? I'll do my best not to disappoint you."

As if realizing how what he'd said sounded, Mr. Landrum was quick to say, "That didn't come out right, and I'm sorry."

"It's completely understandable. Do you have any questions I can help answer?"

He seemed to take a minute to think. "How long do I have to stay in the hospital after the surgery? It's busy season with lawn care right now. But then again, we're in Florida where it's always busy season."

"I'm thinking we'll need to keep you about a week. But as far as your business goes, do you have someone who can run it for a bit? You'll need to take it easy for the next six weeks to allow the grafted vessels to heal."

"I have a neighbor who's a landscape architect. He's

going to take on the clients who need to keep to a set schedule. The rest we're trying to stretch out the times between cuts until I'm back up to speed. I wish the old ticker had given me some advance warning, so I could have planned better."

Zeke touched his arm. "It did give you advance warning. You were very lucky."

Mr. Landrum's face cleared. "I hadn't really thought about it like that. But I guess you're right. Thank you."

The cardiologist glanced at Shanna, who felt kind of shell-shocked. His bedside manner was better than she expected it to be. Dr. Petrochki was a lot gruffer and tended to brush patients' concerns away. But he was very good at what he did.

"Are you ready?" he asked.

"Oh…yes." Feeling his eyes on her, she finished getting everything together and moved toward their patient and started his treatment.

CHAPTER TWO

SHANNA MEADOWS HAD been very good at her job. Earlier today as he watched her adeptly give the treatment, talking to Mr. Landrum as if he were a close friend and not just a patient, he could guess that she was probably as popular with her charges as Dr. Petrochki evidently was.

But partway through the therapy, it had started feeling like he was spying on her, so he'd given her a nod and had gone back to his own office to look at Mr. Landrum's chart, mentally agreeing with the workup and planning that his predecessor had done. He'd been very thorough, down to marking the location of the vessels he would have used for grafts, even though he'd already known he wouldn't be the one doing the surgery. He'd saved their patient a lot of time, since Zeke didn't have to repeat all of the diagnostic tests.

He glanced at his watch. He was supposed to meet Shanna for lunch in the courtyard to discuss the party. He probably should have insisted that they meet during working hours so she wasn't having to use her personal time to discuss hospital business, but she'd said she really didn't have a break in her schedule today, and since his would be filling up starting tomorrow, the sooner they met, the better for both of them.

He headed down to the ground floor, where the courtyard was, and went through the cafeteria line, picking out a sandwich and bowl of soup before exiting to the outside. Tampa's heat and humidity hit him almost immediately, but the shade of the palm trees in the outdoor dining area made it bearable.

Shanna waved to him from across the way. He headed over to her and sat down on the concrete bench across from her. She'd chosen a fruit bowl and salad. "No cake this time?"

"No cake. I already had my daily dose of sweets, so I'm going to be good for a couple of days." She said it with a smile that picked at something inside his chest. Something he recognized and had learned to be wary of.

What was it with her? Or maybe he should be asking what was it with *him*? He hadn't had especially strong reactions to women since his split with Kristen. And for it to start happening here...with someone he'd be working pretty closely with? Probably not a good habit to get into. Especially since he had no idea how she felt about the military. A subject that had caused so much strife with his ex.

His dad and grandfather had both been good men and had served in the navy, so Zeke's pride in military service had been instilled from a young age. Going into the army as a doctor had seemed the perfect marriage of his love of medicine and family pride. His dad's diagnosis had come just as he and Kristen had started dating, and maybe she'd been right in saying that he loved the army more than he loved her. But he couldn't just up and leave. He'd had a contract to fulfill, which Kristen just couldn't seem to grasp. And even if he could, it wasn't something he wanted to spring on his father, who was fighting his own battle. So rather than arguing, Zeke found it easier to just shut down every time the subject came up.

What he hadn't expected, however, was to come home one day to an empty house. While the loss of his dad was happening in slow, agonizing increments, Kristen had done the opposite and left him in one decisive move that had cut him to the core. Only afterward did he realize he'd probably rushed the relationship along to give his dad what he said he wanted most: to see Zeke happily married, and maybe even with a grandchild or two. He'd gotten neither. And looking back, Kristen's leaving had probably been a blessing in disguise.

His attention was yanked back to the present at the sound of Shanna flipping open a blue binder and thumbing through a couple of tabs before stopping on a page that boasted a kind of list. "Okay, so here's the chart of what teams are planning on carving for their pumpkin. We have everything from *Star Wars* to a comic book character planned. Take a look and see maybe what to avoid."

What to avoid would include not looking at her any more than absolutely necessary. So he stared at the sheet of paper instead. Hell, how on earth was he going to figure out what to carve when it seemed everything under the sun had already been chosen. How did one even carve a sunset into a pumpkin anyway?

"Do you have some kind of master list with ideas? Although I have to tell you, I'm not sure I can do much more than the traditional toothy jack-o'-lantern smile."

"Sure you can. There are all kinds of videos online of how to carve images on pumpkins. Almost anything you can imagine."

He thought for a minute. "Maybe since I'm a cardiac surgeon, I can carve some kind of heart."

Shanna's brows went up. "I take it you're not talking about this kind of heart." She formed a heart shape out of her joined hands.

Something about the symbol and the smile behind it made his gut twinge.

"Is that an option? I wouldn't need a video for that, since I think even I can saw a heart shape into a pumpkin."

"If you can do an actual heart, I think that would be super cool. And educational. And it would certainly fit a hospital setting along with a cardiologist." She pulled her phone out and looked at something. "How about along these lines?"

Surprisingly, there was a simple anatomic heart carved into a pumpkin. And it looked like it might actually be doable. Not like something that might require an engineering degree and special tools. "Can you send me that picture?"

"Sure? What's your number?"

He gave it to her and waited for a second as she punched something into her own phone. Then his pinged.

Only afterward did he wonder if it was a good idea for them to have each other's numbers.

Why not? It wasn't like they were going to be texting each other late into the night. Or that she would ever form a heart with her hands and mean anything by it other than work. This was not personal. He tried to remember exactly how things had started up with Kristen, but it was kind of a blur. They'd met at medical school, but he couldn't remember when things had changed from them being acquaintances to something deeper. Or maybe he'd blocked out a lot of the experience or maybe his dad's failing memory had superseded all other recollections from that time.

He knew one thing, though: continuing that relationship after it became obvious Kristen wanted a civilian doctor whose earning capabilities were far greater than that of a military doctor hadn't been his brightest moment. But it was a cautionary tale. He certainly didn't want to change hospitals again because of a relationship. Not that he'd actually done that last time. He'd simply gotten out of active duty when his contract was up and had chosen to leave his military hospital, which was ironic, seeing as that's what Kristen had wanted in the first place. Getting out of the area had simply been a nice side benefit, although he'd liked living in the Panhandle of Florida.

He glanced at the photo of the carved pumpkin. "I think maybe this is the one I'll do."

"Okay, I'll mark it down." She jotted something in her notebook.

He took a bite out of his tuna salad, finding it surprisingly tasty. Or maybe he was still used to military food, which tended to be bare-bones, since it normally focused on feeding large numbers of service people at once.

Studying her for a minute, he wondered how she'd become interested in respiratory therapy, although it was probably for the same reason any of them entered their specialty. Something piqued their interest and made them want to take a closer look. That had certainly been how it had been with him and cardiothoracic medicine. His biology classes had gone over the respiratory system and he'd been fascinated by how oxygenated blood was pushed through the body. The rest had been history.

His grades had been good enough to get him into medical school, and by choosing the military route, the army had basically paid for his education with the agreement that he would put in the time with the armed forces. It had been the perfect combination. He wouldn't change anything if he could. Other than his failed romance. He'd dated since then but had made sure they were both on the same page. He wasn't interested in anything serious. And at thirty-nine, he wasn't sure he ever would be. And his dad's memory was much worse now. At some point he would need round-the-clock care, which was another reason he hoped his mom would agree to move to Tampa.

"So tell me something good and something not so good about working at Everly."

He wasn't sure why he had asked the question, but it seemed like a fairly impersonal topic. He'd expected choosing a subject to carve into his pumpkin to take longer than it had. But it seemed rude to pick up his tray and move to another table, even if it was just to give her some time to herself.

She snapped her binder shut. "That's a hard question. Not the 'good' part, because there are really a lot of those. The hospital is good to its staff. At least that has been my experience. There's not much turnover and there are quite a few doctors who want in. As for the bad…maybe just the normal hospital soap opera stuff. It's obviously not in league with some of the television shows that depict everyone sleeping with everyone else, but there is an element of that that goes on in almost every setting."

Yes, he had experienced that firsthand. And knowing it went on here as well was a good warning to watch his step. He didn't want to be tangled up in any of that. Especially not this early after his arrival. Not that he wanted it at all. Kristen had proved to be a good inoculation against relationships.

"You're right. That seems to happen almost everywhere."

"So you've experienced it?"

This was one question he didn't really want to answer. "Let's just say it went on at the hospital I was at as well."

"Where were you?"

"At a hospital in Pensacola."

Her brows went up. "That's quite a change. Why Tampa?"

He wasn't sure why, but he didn't want to just vomit up everything about himself to her. The stuff about his dad's diagnosis and his previous relationship were things he rarely talked about, even to people he knew well. And to someone he barely knew? Not something he saw himself doing. Especially with some of the things he'd seen on the field. Unlike the good outweighing the bad, like Shanna had talked about, some of what he'd witnessed had been horrific. He wasn't anxious to bring up those memories, especially since it had taken time with a professional to work through some of those experiences.

Before he could think of a plausible explanation for his move, his cell phone went off. Followed almost immediately by Shanna's.

They glanced at each other before looking down at their screens. "I'm needed down in the ER. You?"

"Same."

He took one last bite out of his sandwich before taking his tray and discarding the rest of his lunch. Shanna did the same.

"Did your message give any details?"

"Nope. Yours?"

He shook his head. "No. Just that I was needed in the ER to help with a patient."

They made the short walk over to the emergency department and were flagged down by one of the nurses. "Shanna, we've got an acute respiratory distress in room one, as soon as Dr. Vaughan gets—"

"I'm Dr. Vaughan."

"Great. We're waiting on our pulmonologist to arrive at the hospital. He's been at home with a sick child and a pregnant wife. But he's en route as we speak. They're from Guatemala. Our translator isn't here yet, but Shanna speaks some Spanish, which is why we called her."

Once in the room, they found a child who was about two years old laboring to breathe, every respiration bringing a deep hacking cough that brought up thick mucus.

Zeke went into action, pulling out his stethoscope and hauling the boy's shirt over his head. He was painfully thin. Thinner than he should have been, and when Zeke glanced at the other child and the parents, they were all within normal ranges. "How long has he had this cough?"

Shanna switched to Spanish, her hands moving as she translated the question. The woman, who he assumed was the mom, responded.

"She says a few weeks. But Marco's had problems with colds for most of his life."

"How long have they been in the country?"

Shanna translated, the answer coming back as three

weeks. They were visiting family and hoped to move to the States in the near future.

He could hear congestion deep in the boy's lungs, and when he did bring up sputum, it was thick, with a texture he didn't expect. It raised a few warning flags, but he didn't want to jump to conclusions. Not yet. When asked if the child ate well, the parents looked at each other before talking to Shanna.

"They said he eats, but often doesn't feel well afterward. When he was a baby, the doctors told them it was colic and that he would outgrow it. But he's not growing like their other child did."

Zeke could see that. "Let's do a breathing treatment with albuterol and add some hypertonic saline to thin the mucus, and can you have someone call down to pediatrics? I want to get a sweat test, just to rule something out."

"Sweat test?" Shanna moved closer, speaking in low tones. "Are you thinking cystic fibrosis?"

Of course she would know what he was testing for. She was a respiratory therapist. There was every chance she had seen a case of this before at a hospital this size.

"It's a possibility. Just from the sound of his lungs and the fact that he has a history of lung infections combined with what I'm thinking could be malabsorption syndrome."

Cystic fibrosis was primarily thought of as a lung disease, but it attacked more organs than just the pulmonary system. The inherited condition also affected the digestive tract with thick sticky mucus that had the ability to clog the intestines or even create blockages.

Shanna called the nurses' station before preparing the treatment that he'd asked for. When she came over with the nebulizer, she held the molded plastic over Marco's nose and mouth, soothing him in soft tones when he seemed scared. Zeke made notes in the chart. "How long are they here in the States?"

She asked the parents and then came back with "Four more weeks."

Barely time enough to come up with a diagnosis, much less a treatment plan. One that would need to be followed scrupulously. "I want to make some phone calls when we leave here to their country and find a specialist I can refer them to. Can you help with translating and find out which part of the country they're from?"

"Of course."

Zeke had dealt with a couple of cases of cystic fibrosis before during his rotation, since if breathing was compromised, the heart could grow enlarged and need help pumping efficiently.

A nurse came in. "Dr. Rogers's wife just went into labor. He's had to turn around and go back home. Are you good? Do you need me to call one of the pulmonologists who has hospital privileges?"

"Let me see how the sweat test goes, so we know a little more about what we're dealing with."

The nurse nodded. "Someone should be here with the test in a few minutes." She then withdrew.

Fortunately the albuterol was having the desired effect and opening the airways, and Marco's breathing was discernibly less rattly, the coughing already sounding a little more productive than it had a few minutes ago.

Watching Shanna move around the bed with confident purpose, having the perfect amount of compassion and steadiness, he could see what a valuable asset she was to the hospital. The fact that she'd taken on the Halloween party—had been the one to introduce the festivities to the hospital, in fact—when it only added onto what were probably long, hard days, made something tug in his midsection.

Something he tried to squash.

But then, Kristen had been good at her job, too. But that hadn't meant they were compatible. They hadn't been. Not that he was assuming a fleeting sense of attraction would derail him toward a place he'd gone before. And hell, he'd just gotten to the hospital. What was he even doing thinking along these lines?

He purposely avoided looking up from his tablet, where he was typing his notes, until he heard Marco say something to his parents.

"What did he say?"

Shanna was looking at the boy with wide eyes. "He says he wants to play. And is asking if we have a train."

Zeke glanced at what Marco was pointing at on the wall. Sure enough, it was a picture of a toy train. In fact, he just realized that the entire room was decorated in colors that a child would like. He hadn't even noticed that. Maybe the hospital had different exam rooms geared toward different age groups. That would be quite an undertaking, but from what he was learning about how the hospital was run, it shouldn't be surprising.

"I don't know if we have a train or not. We used to have toys in the pediatric waiting rooms, but when COVID hit, they stored most of those away. I don't think they've brought them back yet, but let me go get one of the coloring packets that we keep for children."

"Thanks."

Yes, she was definitely an asset. As soon as the thought skipped through his head, he gritted his teeth. As were all of the staff who worked at the hospital.

While she was gone, another nurse came in with the sweat test. She was also good at her job. She didn't speak Spanish but was able to get across what she needed through pantomime. By the time Shanna came back with a colorful little plastic bag, the nurse had the solution that would promote sweating swabbed on the boy's arm and was waiting to collect some of the fluid.

"Everything going okay?"

"Fine." He realized his word was shorter than it should have been when Shanna looked at him with a frown. Probably wondering what he was so peeved at.

It wasn't her. It was him.

Hell, it was the same phrase he'd used earlier when thinking about her, and he didn't like it. At all.

But, more than likely he would be working with her on a regular basis even after Halloween was long gone, and unless he wanted to pack up shop every time someone caught his eye, he was going to have to learn how to deal with it. One way or another.

"Okay, I think that about does it," the nurse said. "I'll get this right over to the lab. We should have results within the hour, unless they're backed up with something else."

"Perfect, thanks."

Once she left, Shanna turned to him. "Do you want to keep them in the exam room? There's actually a small waiting room just to the back of the department, if you think they would be more comfortable there."

"Is that what normally happens in cases like these?"

"Yes, in case we get a sudden influx of patients who need rooms."

He nodded. "Let's do that, then." He glanced at what she was holding in her hand. "Maybe that will keep him occupied while they wait."

"I'll take them," she said.

"Thank you. I'll go see if we can pull a pulmonologist in from somewhere, since I have a feeling the results are going to show CF. I'll check on a genetic counselor as well, since if he does have the condition, they'll want to make informed decisions about having any more children from here on out."

Before Marco and his family fell completely off his radar, he wanted to make sure they knew about the Halloween party, so he reminded himself to mention it to them.

Seriously? Since when was he thinking this party was a good thing?

Since he'd met a little boy who needed something good on his horizon, since life was about to get much more complicated and was likely to stay that way forever.

It had nothing to do with Shanna, who was supposed to help him carve his own pumpkin. At least that was what he was choosing to believe.

CHAPTER THREE

"I NEED SUCTION!"

The second Mr. Landrum's heart restarted, his surgical field was covered in blood. Zeke went into crisis mode, trying to figure out where the blood was coming from. The surgical nurse's suction cleared a path for him to see long enough to tell that the first grafted vein was fine. But the second... Hell, the return of circulating blood had blown a hole straight through it. He hadn't nicked it, had checked it over before suturing it in place. There had to have been a hidden weak spot in it.

"Clamp! And let's get him back on bypass."

A clamp was slapped in his hand almost immediately and he closed off the vessel, promptly stopping the flow of blood. If it had been a small leak, he could have sutured it shut, but even though the vein had passed their precheck to make sure it could hold fluid, there was always the possibility that an imperfection had gone unnoticed.

They were going to have to redo the graft with one of the others they'd harvested. Hell!

He barely noticed someone swabbing sweat off his

forehead as the whir of the bypass machine took over. They'd harvested enough length from Mr. Landrum's saphenous vein that they could redo the bypass. He just hated to have the patient on the heart-lung machine any longer than necessary.

Working as quickly as he could, he undid the faulty graft and prepared to replace it. And God... He hoped there were no more surprises.

Shanna checked at the nurses' desk for what seemed like the umpteenth time. She'd been expecting a call to do a breathing treatment on Zeke's bypass patient, Matthew Landrum. But so far, he hadn't come out of surgery yet. And it had been six hours, longer than most of the bypasses she'd been involved with had taken.

Had something happened?

Lord, she hoped not. Not just because Mr. Landrum was a genuinely nice guy. But also because it was Zeke's first surgery at the hospital, and for some reason she wanted it to be a successful one.

Why? She should hope that all of the hospital's surgeries were successful.

And she did. This one just seemed...different.

Because of the surgeon?

No, of course not. His periodic glances her way may have sent her heart racing in her chest, but it was more than that. She had a feeling the surgeon would take it very hard if Mr. Landrum didn't pull through.

He'd already had to break the hard news to young Marcos's family yesterday afternoon that the child did indeed have cystic fibrosis. And even though treatment options over the years had increased life expectancies, it was still a life-altering diagnosis. And Marcos would need specialized care his entire life.

His face, as he'd explained the situation and as she'd translated, had been tense, his eyes on Marcos, who'd been busy coloring a train.

And then he'd told the family about the pumpkin-carving party, which had actually shocked her, asking if she had a flyer the family could take with them.

Her eyes had met his and there had gone her heart, pounding like crazy in her chest. It was a ridiculous reaction, and she'd taken the opportunity to murmur that she would go get one of the pamphlets. Once outside the door, she'd leaned against it for several seconds to catch her breath before heading for the information desk, where a stack of notices for the Halloween party were kept.

Shaking off the memories and wanting to do something besides just thinking of what had happened yesterday, she decided to actually walk through the doors where the surgical suites were housed, since she was between patients at the moment. She didn't know what that was going to accomplish, since she didn't have X-ray vision. In reality, she just needed something to do besides hang out at the nurses' desk.

One of the doors to Surgical Suite One opened and a nurse came out looking somber.

Oh, no! Something *had* happened.

Then Zeke came out, tugging his surgical mask

down as he did. He didn't look much happier than the nurse had.

"Zeke…" Her voice faded away, unsure of what she could really say or do that would make him feel any better.

His glance swung toward her, and a frown appeared between his brows.

She definitely should have hung out by the nurses' desk if his expression was anything to go by. But she was here now, and she needed to somehow explain her appearance outside the door of his operating room. "Mr. Landrum?"

"He pulled through, but he gave us a couple of scares."

"He did? Pull through, I mean? The nurse that just came out of there…"

He nodded. "It was one of her first surgeries, and it didn't go like clockwork. One of the veins we harvested for the bypass had a weak spot in it and it blew out just as we were closing him up. We had to go back in and stop the bleeding and redo the graft with another portion of the vein we'd harvested. The surgery took twice as long as we'd hoped it would, and honestly, I thought we were going to lose him when it first went sideways." He tugged off his cap and rolled it up with the mask he'd removed seconds earlier.

"But you didn't. Lose him, I mean."

"No. We didn't. Thank God." He glanced at her again. "I need to go talk to the family, but do you want to go get a coffee after I do? If you don't have another patient, that is."

His frown deepened as if he hadn't been sure why he'd made the offer. Maybe he just didn't want to be alone, which Shanna could totally understand. And she didn't have the heart to say no. Especially if he needed to talk things through.

"I don't. I was scheduled to work with Mr. Landrum after his surgery…" She thought fast. "Which is why I was hanging around. And yes, I would love a coffee."

"He'll need some time in recovery before that treatment. How about if I meet you by the doors to the ER in about fifteen minutes?" He hesitated again for a second. "We can talk more about the pumpkin carving."

Of course that was why he wanted to go to coffee with her. It wasn't just to decompress after a difficult surgery. Something in her deflated, and she suddenly didn't want to go with him. But she'd already said she would. To back out now would be awkward and might make him think his request for coffee had held a lot more meaning than it actually had.

No. She had to act as nonchalant as he seemed to be. "Okay, there's a coffee shop called Top Grounds around the corner. Why don't I just meet you there. You'll be close to the hospital if Mr. Landrum or the hospital suddenly needs you."

"Perfect. See you there in a few minutes."

She nodded, then turned to go, wondering what she was thinking to even consider going to coffee with him.

When she got there, the shop was busier than she'd

expected it to be. She should have asked what he wanted, and she could at least order it for him. But she hadn't. But she could get hers and save a table, if there were any.

Fortunately, by the time she ordered her iced vanilla latte, a table had opened up and she snagged it, sitting down and taking a sip of her cold brew. She normally liked her coffee hot, but Tampa temperatures were steamy today, and she'd wanted something that wouldn't make her feel like she was going to melt.

She was on her second sip when she spotted Zeke entering the shop. He'd discarded his scrubs and, with his erect bearing and dark-washed jeans and a white button-down shirt, if she didn't know he was a surgeon, she would take him for an executive at some financial agency somewhere. There was no sign that he'd been engaged in a battle for someone's life not a half hour earlier. A couple of women who were at another table watched him, one of them whispering something to the other, who elbowed her, before they both giggled.

Is that how Shanna looked at him? Lord, she hoped not, although her eyes had followed his every move as well. To combat that, she turned to study the decor on the walls. All of it was coffee paraphernalia, from French presses to faded recipes that included coffee. It really was an interesting shop. One of the places she tended to frequent since it was on her way to work from her house...the one she'd spent a lot of her childhood in after her dad had died. Her mom had signed over the title a few years ago, when she decided she wanted to downsize to one of the nicer condos in the area. Being a Realtor had its perks when it came to ferreting out good deals on homes.

Her thoughts were interrupted when Zeke pulled out the chair across from her. She glanced at the table of other women and noticed one of their mouths turned down. They probably thought they were an item or something. If only they knew. But even that thought didn't completely quench the little shiver of satisfaction that he was sitting at her table and not theirs. Even though he would never be hers. Nor did she want him to be.

Was she trying to convince her libido of that? Or just giving it a heads-up that nothing was going to develop between them? Ever.

He nodded at her drink. "Cold coffee?"

She smiled at his tone and countered, "Hot day."

"Good point. It is pretty warm out there."

And yet not a hair on his head was ruffled, nor was there the slightest mark of perspiration on his crisp white shirt. If she'd had that on, she would have been dripping wet. As it was, she had a dark-patterned scrub top on for a reason. It was loose and cool and very forgiving of spilled food, drinks or sweaty days.

"Everything still okay at the hospital?" she asked.

"If you're talking about Mr. Landrum, then yes. He'd just been wheeled into recovery when I left."

"So the graft blew? Is that very common?"

He dragged a hand through his hair. "I've never had it happen. The harvested vessel was tested and showed no signs of defects, but I'm glad it chose now to fail rather than a month or year from now. But—" a muscle worked in his jaw "—I really thought I might lose him."

She couldn't stop her hand from covering his for a second before pulling it away. "But you didn't."

"Not this time." She almost didn't hear the low mutter. Maybe he hadn't meant her to.

Had he lost another patient to something similar? She almost let the comment go by without saying anything, but there seemed to be a wealth of pain in those words. "Sometimes things just happen. Things we can't foresee or control."

Like the prick of tears behind her eyes as the thought of her dad suddenly went through her mind.

"You're right. But that doesn't mean I want it to happen on my watch."

"I get it." It sounded like something her dad would have said, and was probably what led him to try to defuse that bomb. To shake off the thought, she added, "How is Mr. Landrum's family doing?"

"They're just glad he made it through, which I'd never had any doubt of, until the moment blood started pouring out of that vein. The vein that I'd just finished suturing in."

Maybe Zeke really had needed to talk things through. To decompress from what had almost happened. She was suddenly glad she hadn't backed out of coming.

"There was no way you could have known. And when the unthinkable happened, you were able to figure out how to fix it. That counts for a lot."

He looked at her for a long moment. "Thank you for that."

She couldn't seem to look away from him, until she saw movement at another table. The women who had ogled him were getting up to leave. Lord, maybe she really was just like them. She cleared her throat. "Do you want any changes to his treatment? As in do you still want me to do breathing treatments with him starting today? Or do you want me to wait?"

"This afternoon is fine. His aftercare will remain the same, although I'm going to do some imaging with contrast before releasing him to make sure there are no other unexpected surprises, since the replacement graft was taken from the same saphenous vein."

"You think it could fail, too?"

"Hell, I hope not. But I don't want to take any chances."

"I don't blame you. Will you keep him longer?"

He shook his head, taking a sip of his own steaming brew. "I think we'll keep him a week, like I would with most other bypass patients, and then let him finish his recovery at home. Unfortunately insurance companies don't cover cardiac rehab the way they once did, so I'll send home some detailed instructions upon discharge and hopefully get a home nurse out there who is well-versed in cardiac care."

"I could probably stop by his house on my way home to check in on him from time to time, if you think it will help."

He pursed his mouth. "I doubt his insurance would cover that."

"What if I went as a friend?"

His frown deepened. "But you're not. His friend, I mean."

She probably shouldn't have said anything. She had a feeling the hospital wouldn't really approve of her making house calls. And maybe a personal visit wouldn't even be covered under her current malpractice umbrella. She needed to check.

"I wouldn't give treatment, unless the orders were there, obviously. I was just thinking of seeing how his color and affect seemed." She wasn't sure how to retract her offer without it being weird. But she wanted to make sure that if there were problems during the healing process, they were caught early enough to be treated. After all, if her mom's descent into depression had been caught earlier, maybe she wouldn't have needed inpatient care. But there was no way to know that now. All Shanna could do was provide the best care she could for her own patients.

"Sorry if that came across wrong. I was thinking of making sure you were compensated for your time."

"I don't do it with all of my patients, but part of my licensing covers home health treatments when needed. If I ever get tired of working in a hospital setting, I wanted another avenue available to continue practicing what I love. So far, I still get a lot of satisfaction from working with the team at Everly Memorial, though."

With no house payment, she could certainly afford

to take a cut in pay if she needed to explore other options. But right now, there was no need.

"Then, as long as the hospital doesn't object, that would be great."

A warm satisfaction went through her, although it wasn't like he was patting her on the back for anything. Just expressing that he had no objections to her checking in on their patient.

Their patient.

Well… He really was, right? She was taking part in his care, no matter how small that part might be.

"Sounds good." She tried to shift gears, since he'd been the one to mention their reason for having coffee together and she needed to steer their conversation to less personal grounds. For her own sake. "So about your pumpkin. What do you need to know?"

He stood and tucked his hand in one of his front pockets, pulling out a piece of folded paper before sitting back down. "I looked up various diagrams on hearts and came up with this. Does this look carveable?"

She unfolded the sheet and looked at it. There was a simple pictorial image of a heart, with the major vessels coming off it. "This should be doable. We won't carve completely through the pumpkin for all of it, just through some of it, so that the light will shine through. That will give it some depth."

"Can't I just carve straight through it?" He studied it for a minute. "Wait. I think I see what you're saying. There has to be some connective tissue or it will all just fall into the pumpkin."

"Connective tissue." She laughed. "Once a surgeon, always a surgeon. But yes. That's what I'm saying."

"And are you going to offer a class? Pumpkin Carving 101?"

"Funny you should ask that. Next week, in fact, I am offering a quick-and-dirty how-to class in the staff lounge for anyone who wants a little instruction on special techniques."

One of his brows went up. "Not that I'm asking for any special consideration or anything, but I thought you were going to help me with mine."

"I am. But what I didn't offer was to carve it for you. That wouldn't be fair to everyone else."

"You're assuming you'd win."

She smiled, thinking of the blue ribbons she'd won with her dad. "I may have won a contest or two in my younger days. But I'll admit, I've never once attempted to carve a heart—at least the organ—from one."

Even after her father had been killed, carving pumpkins had been her way of keeping his memory alive. She'd done more and more elaborate carvings as the years went by. The only reason she didn't enter her own carving in the hospital's party was that as the organizer, it seemed like a conflict of interest. So she'd been content to let other people shine. Her goal was not only to promote the hospital, but to keep the spirit of Halloween alive, something that seemed to be dying out little by little.

"When is your course?"

"Next Saturday at one p.m. Since most scheduled surgeries tended to happen on weekdays, it seemed to be the day when at least a member or two of each team would be able to come. If they need it. Some folks have been through the course before and already know what I'm going to demonstrate."

She took another pull on her straw, surprised at how much talking she'd been doing and how little drinking. Especially considering that Zeke was almost done with his own cup. How had that happened? She was never usually this talkative. She was friendly, yes. But she didn't normally monopolize the conversation. Maybe it was just to avoid talking about anything deeper. Anything that might make her look at him the way those other women had. "Sorry. I think I've been talking way too much. Tell me more about Mr. Landrum's surgery. You said your harvested vessel came from the saphenous vein?"

"That's right. It's my preferred vein, just because the diameter tends to be closer to those of the heart. Although many surgeons use the radial artery as well. Have you seen bypass surgery?"

"Once during my training, but only because I asked to observe. I find it fascinating, although I wasn't exactly sure of what was happening from where I sat."

Zeke scooted his chair closer to hers, taking the diagram he'd brought with him and setting it on the table between them.

Her pulse immediately picked up its pace with his

proximity and the light tantalizing scent of something coming from his skin. Soap? Shampoo?

He didn't seem like the type to wear cologne, although how could she know that for sure? And she wasn't going to ask him. Instead, she listened as he explained an overview of the surgery, using his finger to point out the different vessels that could be bypassed.

She could listen to those deep gravelly tones forever and never tire of them. Which was a dangerous thought, especially since she had been trying to steer the conversation clear of deep subjects. More tables in the café were now vacant besides the one with the women.

How long had she been here with Zeke, anyway?

Probably long enough. And yet she wasn't about to stop him midexplanation, so she leaned forward on the table and listened as his words painted pictures that she could visualize in her head. It was as if she were there for Mr. Landrum's surgery.

And when he finally finished, she realized she'd been holding her breath, which now whooshed out in a way that was far too loud for her liking.

He immediately glanced at her. "Sorry. I know that was long-winded."

"No, not at all. I could picture it. How on earth do you deal with the stress of surgery? Of knowing that things might not end well?"

"I try to concentrate on what I need to do, and when, and leave the rest to whoever controls life or death. Because it normally isn't me. I simply do a job and hope it's what the patient needs to survive."

"And if it's not?"

"Then the patient dies. And that's where I get stuck in my thoughts, reliving each and every move I made during surgery. Was there anything I could have done to prevent it? Was there anything the patient could have done to improve their chances for survival? Sometimes it's just the luck of the draw. No matter how hard I try. No matter how hard the patient tries to prepare… death sometimes happens. Genetics? Timing? Surgeon? There are so many variables. It's not often that we know the entire reason. Sometimes the veins are too calcified to hold sutures well or there's not a good vein or artery to harvest because of vascular disease or damage. Or there are injuries that are too devastating to overcome."

His voice hardened on that last sentence. Probably thinking of senseless deaths caused by human violence.

"I get it. It's the same with the lungs. Sometimes there's too much damage. Or sometimes the pressure in them is too high and it eventually causes respiratory failure that no amount of treatment can prevent. Or there's cancer. Or COPD. Or any number of lung diseases."

"Like cystic fibrosis."

"Yes. Like cystic fibrosis. Thank God cases like Marcos's are not a dime a dozen. And with genetic testing, people can make informed choices about things like getting pregnant."

"So if you carried the gene, you wouldn't have children?"

"It's a recessive gene, but if my partner and I both

carried the gene, I think I would choose another route, if I wanted to have a baby. Like adoption. Or donor eggs. Actually, if I carried the gene and my partner didn't, I might still choose a different avenue to become a parent, so that I didn't pass the gene on to my offspring."

"I tend to agree with you, although I know it's each person's choice about how to handle their own genetic information." He glanced at his watch. "As fascinating as this discussion is, I'd better head back to the hospital to check on Mr. Landrum. Do you have time to do a breathing treatment, if he's awake enough to do one?"

"Yes, of course. That's why I came down to the surgery wing. I only have a couple of patients today, and fortunately nothing has come through the ER that involves breathing. So I'm available."

Almost immediately, she wished she could take back that last sentence. And from the way Zeke's eyes jerked toward her, he must have heard the unfortunate wording. But she wasn't about to stutter her way into an even bigger mess, so she pretended there was only one way her words could be construed.

"Great. Are you ready?"

Her drink was still only half-gone, but she could stick it in the staff lounge fridge and retrieve it later. "Yep. I'll bring mine with me."

They walked back to the hospital together, Shanna searching for some sort of small talk that might fill the time but coming up blank.

"Did you hook Marcos up with a lung specialist?"

"I did. One of the local pulmonologists has agreed to take him on pro bono, since the family has no medical insurance. He'll get treatments while he's here in the States." He smiled. "And his parents said he keeps pointing at the pumpkin on the flyer you gave them. I'm pretty sure they'll be here for the party."

"That's great. It'll be good to see him. And I'm so glad he'll get treatments. Were you able to find a specialist in Guatemala?"

"Not yet, but I put a call into the American consulate there, and they're checking into it."

She smiled and touched his hand again, the warmth of his skin sending a tingle through her. "Let me know if you need me to back you up or translate for you. I'd love to help that family."

There was a moment of silence after her statement.

Realizing she was still touching him, she shifted so that her arm fell back to her side, heat sliding into her face.

"I'm sure they'll appreciate that. And I might need a translator if I have to treat him again."

"I'd be happy to. Even though my family is from Cuba rather than Guatemala."

"Is the Spanish that different?"

She rocked her head from side to side. "It depends. There is a lot in common. But there are words in their version of Spanish that we don't find in our form of the language. But we can get by, for sure. And context carries a lot of cues, even when certain words are unfamiliar."

"So since your last name is Meadows, is your mom the one who's Cuban?" He stopped and frowned. "I guess Meadows could be a married name…"

"Nope. It's my maiden name. And yes, my maternal grandparents came over to this country as political refugees due to some of the civil rights violations that were going on at the time. Their last name was Gutierrez."

"So you learned Spanish from them?"

She nodded. "And my mom, who is still fluent, although she speaks English most of the time now."

They rounded the corner, and Shanna could see the hospital on the next block. It was huge, its modern white facade taking up almost an entire city block.

"Did your dad learn how to speak it as well?"

"Some." Her mouth twisted. "Unfortunately he passed away when I was ten, so I don't remember that part of him."

"I'm sorry, Shanna, I didn't mean to pry."

"You weren't. He's been gone a long time." Although the hurt and finality of his death were still things she was working through.

"Did your mom remarry?"

She shook her head. "No. He was the love of her life. I'm not sure she'll ever meet someone who can measure up to my dad."

Then they were at the hospital and entering the doors. Thankfully by that time, their conversation turned back to Mr. Landrum and his upcoming breathing treatment. And she could forget that the sensation of her fingers sliding across his hand had caused her own breathing to stop for a moment. Good thing those women from earlier had already left the coffee shop, or they might think she and Zeke really were an item.

Even though she knew for a fact that they were not. Nor would they ever be.

CHAPTER FOUR

ZEKE DIDN'T SEE Shanna for a couple of days after that first breathing treatment with Mr. Landrum. It was as if she were purposely choosing to do his therapy when Zeke wasn't around. Which was ridiculous. How would she even know when he was on the floor or doing rounds?

It was simply dumb luck that had them avoiding each other's paths. He should consider it a godsend, if anything.

Watching her animation as she talked about various things had had his eyes glued to her face, where each expression flitted across it in record time. He couldn't remember the last time he'd been that fascinated with what someone had to say, and he wasn't sure why she held him enthralled. Maybe because of the way she'd talked about heart surgeries. As if they really fascinated her, rather than it merely being politeness that had her asking about his job.

He'd never grown tired of operating on the heart. As many poems and songs that had been sung about that particular organ, it was no wonder that hearts had so many problems. They were battered and bruised by the emotions of life. And yet he'd actually found the heart was a pretty tough cookie. It could be ravaged by disease or even stress, and yes there was actually a broken heart syndrome that could be deadly, but it was a pretty resilient organ.

As if he'd summoned her, Shanna came rushing around the corner so fast that she almost careened into him. He gripped her arms to keep her from making contact with him. Probably because with his thoughts the way they were, that could prove disastrous. If her hand touching his while walking down the street could go through him like a current of electricity, imagine what body-to-body contact would do to him.

Hell. Something he did not want to think about.

"Sorry, Zeke. I'm late for Matthew Landrum's treatment after a case of acute asthma came through the ER. I just finished with it."

"Mind if I come with you? I haven't seen him since this morning and wanted to check in again before I left for the day."

"Sure. Were you able to get his imaging done?"

"It's scheduled for tomorrow. I'm hoping we can get him released by Friday."

The day before her pumpkin-carving seminar.

Now why had that thought slid through his head? One thing had nothing to do with the other.

"That's great. Isn't it sooner than you'd planned? Or did you mean a week as in a workweek?"

"No, I'd originally planned for a full seven days, but he's doing remarkably well after all he went through in surgery. He's strong and young enough to bounce back from this faster than someone in their, say, seventies or eighties. Not that I've done that many surgeries on people that old." The military didn't exactly have a thriving geriatric community in its ranks, although he had seen some older vets come through the last military hospital he'd been stationed at. It was very different from the fieldwork he'd done, where injuries from electric shock or, God forbid, things like explosive devices could cause catastrophic damage that needed lifesaving measures. Although even in the civilian world, he would surely be called on to treat some of the same things, like gunshot wounds or other types of trauma.

"Wow, being discharged that early is great news."

"Yes, it is." He noticed she didn't say anything else about going to the man's home to check on him. Had she asked the hospital about it and been vetoed? Or was she simply going to try to fly under the administration's radar and do it on her own?

"So you'll still get to come to the class on pumpkin carving?"

"I will. I have the weekend off, although I'm on call Sunday, should something urgent come into the ER."

She nodded. "Weekends can either be a dead zone or we could be up to our eyeballs in patients."

He was personally hoping for a quiet weekend. He still needed to find an apartment or place to stay, since he'd spent this last week in one of those long-term hotel rooms. It was noisy far into the night, although it could be worse. "I'm hoping to have time to talk to a Realtor about locating more permanent living quarters."

She frowned. "Where are you now?"

"In a hotel."

Her eyes widened. "Yikes. My mom is actually a Realtor, although she's not as active as she once was. I could have her put out some feelers, unless you'd rather find someone who isn't a relative of a colleague."

"Actually, that would be great, since I don't know anyone in the area, or know who to ask about reputable Realtors in the area."

"I promise, she'll never try to strong-arm you into something you don't want. If anything, she's probably seen as too honest about the properties she comes across, but she's seen people burned on homes that turn out to be money pits. She's also a very good judge of a property's value."

"That sounds exactly what I need. How do I contact her?"

"How about I see if she's available after our carving class, and I can take you to her condo and introduce you."

He hesitated for a fraction of a second. She must have noticed because she quickly changed her words to, "Or I could just give you her phone number and let you set that up yourself. You can just tell her you work with me."

"I wasn't turning down your offer. I just don't want you to feel obligated to take me over there in person. You're already helping me with this pumpkin thing and did a great job translating for me with Marcos's parents. I don't want to seem 'extra.'"

"Extra?"

He laughed. "It's my mom's way of saying someone is being needy or a nuisance. She'll say, 'You're being a little *extra* today.' Don't tell me you've never heard that expression."

"Nope. Never." She smiled. "But I kind of like it. And no, I don't think you're being 'extra.' You're new to the area, and a place like Tampa can seem over-whelming to people who haven't lived in tourist cities."

"I lived in the Panhandle before this, so I am a little acquainted with tourist meccas like Destin. A place that's nice to visit, but complicated to live in without getting annoyed at the constant crowds."

"I can imagine. So why on earth choose Tampa? It's pretty touristy, too."

He again hesitated over his reply, and he wasn't sure why. It just seemed that every time he mentioned being in the military people had one of two responses. Either they gushed over him, thanking him for his service, or their faces closed as if expecting him to dive into a narrative on all he'd seen and done. Kristen's face had done that a lot in the weeks before he moved out. For some reason, he didn't want to know which camp Shanna fell into. "I wanted to change locations, with-out completely leaving Florida. So Tampa seemed to fit the bill."

"Enough that you're ready to house hunt. Even with

the Halloween party hanging over your head? You didn't seem like a fan when we met."

"I've just never been one for parties or pretending to be something I'm not." Which had been one of the problems with his ex. Even if he could have opted out of his military contract at that time, he hadn't been ready to do that, not with what his father was facing. And the military was all he'd ever known. They'd paid for his education, for God's sake. Even now he wasn't quite ready to throw it all in. The reserves were his way of having the best of both worlds.

Shanna was going to find out eventually when he had to go to a training weekend or was deployed. The hospital knew. But he'd not told any of his colleagues yet, either. Maybe he wanted to be seen as the person he was—as a surgeon—rather than some cardboard cutout that people thought military personnel were.

"I can see that about you. Your lack of pretense, I mean. Honestly, it's kind of nice."

A warmth appeared from nowhere, spreading through his chest at the speed of light.

It means nothing, Zeke.

Even if it did, he wasn't in the market for a relationship. Because although he'd said he didn't like pretending, wasn't that kind of what he was doing? He wasn't exactly lying about who he was…far from it. But he had purposely withheld a significant piece of information about his background. But really, why would Shanna need—or even want—to know his life story?

They were colleagues. Just like she'd said a moment or two ago.

"Thanks. And, yes, to you introducing me to your mom. I would very much appreciate it. Now are you ready to go see Mr. Landrum?"

"Anytime you are."

With that, they walked down the hallway, chatting about the patient and work stuff rather than things that were of a more personal nature. And that's exactly how he wanted to keep it.

"Okay, so each of you has brought in a picture of what you'd like to carve into your pumpkin, right?"

There were about seven people in the room, including Zeke, who was again impeccably dressed. Not that he was going to stay that way for long. Not with pumpkin innards squishing through his hands or splattering onto that light blue shirt. She would have a hard time containing her amusement when that happened.

Except wasn't laughing at someone considered cruel?

Yes, it was. And she hoped she wasn't that.

"I've placed a set of tools beside each of your pumpkins and we're going to do a test one. We're not even going to do your planned carving, because I want you guys to do that on your own. But what I am going to teach you is how to use the carving instruments to get a different combination of depths and looks to your pumpkin. You'll have to plan out when and how to use those skills on your own drawings."

"Why did we bring them, then?" The woman who

asked the question wasn't being rude. Shanna could see that she was genuinely puzzled.

"I wanted to take a quick look to tell you whether I think you can easily execute the image on a pumpkin or whether I think you should try for something more simple."

She walked over to Zeke's drawing, which still had the creases from where he'd folded it. The paper had been warm when he'd pulled it free from his pocket and had…

No. No thinking about how it had made her feel. This was about everyone in the room, not just him. She held it up so everyone could see it. "This diagram of a heart might seem complex, but it's really not that involved. It'll make an excellent subject for a pumpkin."

She placed the paper back by the pumpkin she'd provided for a sample carving. Then she went to each of them, looking at their pictures and telling them why the image would work or why it might be difficult to achieve. "Don't let this discourage any of you. I want you to succeed. And part of that includes being honest about how hard something might be to carve. Any questions?"

"Do the carvings need to be related to medicine or anatomy?"

"No, not at all. We've had everything from Cinderella's castle to various animals like whales or dogs, or even people."

She went back to where her own pumpkin was sitting, along with a picture of a jack-o'-lantern. But not the everyday kind. This one had a toothy human grin that she would partially carve, along with eyebrows, and various creases that would happen when someone smiled. "Okay, I assume you all know how to cut open a pumpkin and clean it out. But we're not going to go in through the top like most people do. Instead, we're going to take off the bottom so that we can place our pumpkin over a faux candle. It'll make balancing the pumpkin a little easier than if it were rocking on its normal base. So let's go to work. There are disposable plastic aprons on your chairs if you're worried about your clothes getting dirty."

She wondered if Zeke would utilize the plastic cover.

Since she'd worn old clothes that had splotches of paint on them, she didn't bother with an apron. Instead, she flipped her pumpkin on its side and began cutting a circle out of the thing's bottom, making short work out of it. She then pulled the plug out, a lot of the innards coming with it. "Cutting this way also makes it easier to clean it out."

Glancing up, she saw they were all still sawing at their vegetables, and then heard an oath come from somewhere nearby. When she glanced to the side, she saw that Zeke—sans apron—had sliced all the way through his pumpkin, the knife exiting through the side. She couldn't hold back a laugh that she did her best to disguise as a cough. "We're not trying to create stab wounds in our pumpkins. We just want to take off their bottoms."

Too late, she realized how that sounded and her face

turned to an inferno. A couple of people giggled. She wasn't sure if it was because of what Zeke had done or because of what she'd said. And she really didn't care. At this point, she just wanted to get through this.

"Thanks for that clarification." Zeke's reply was dry, but at least he was smiling.

A minute later, he'd removed the base of his pumpkin and was using a spoon to scoop out the stuff inside. So far, he was still clean as a whistle. The urge to toss a handful of pumpkin guts his way came and went. That would not be professional. At all. And the last thing she wanted anyone to think was that she had some sort of crush on the hospital's newest staff member.

Because she didn't.

But what she had done was offered to introduce him to her mom. That might be considered unprofessional, too, right? Or would it just be seen as being helpful? Because that's all she'd meant by it.

Right?

And then there was her mom. She might jump to the wrong conclusion, too. Except she would be wrong. It wasn't like she was inviting Zeke to be her roommate or anything. Not that she would. Because she couldn't see herself remaining immune to the man for long, if she actually had to see him day in day out. In casual clothes or, worse, running shorts or accidentally seeing him in whatever he wore…or didn't wear to bed at night.

Her face exploded with fire. She turned away for a minute, pretending she was arranging her carving instruments in a specific order. When she glanced around the room, hoping no one had seen her reaction, she saw that most of them had finished cutting open and cleaning out their pumpkins. There were just two more who were still working. "Let's talk tools while we're finishing up."

"We have some punches, some engraving tools, a peeler, some scrapers and various other things that you can feel free to experiment with. You can check them out to use on your actual pumpkins that you enter into the contest, or you can buy your own set. It's completely up to you. Any questions so far?"

One of the techs said, "I could see a good sharp scalpel being useful for this."

"Absolutely. If you have access to some surgical tools, or even a drill with different-sized bits, you can create some amazing designs with just a few simple techniques."

Zeke glanced at her, and she quickly looked away and began talking again. "I'm going to walk you through carving the design I've chosen. Maybe share this with your team and see how you can adapt the different techniques for your design."

Shanna took them step by step through carving the mouth first, answering any questions and going around to help those who needed extra help. "There is no right or wrong way to do this. If you cut deeper into the pumpkin than I do, then your light will be brighter in those areas. If your cuts are more shallow, less light will get through. The idea is to have some areas that go all the way through the pumpkin and others that will help create various areas of light and shadows that will give interest to your depiction."

She could tell Zeke was a surgeon by the way he went about carving his. He paused to plan out each carved groove and execute it with a precision that made her swallow. What other things was he this precise about?

Sex?

The word came and went before she was prepared for it. Oh, Lord, maybe she was developing a crush on the man. Which would be beyond mortifying, since he'd shown zero interest in her. And Shanna didn't have the best track record with men. For some reason, her interest in someone waned almost before it appeared. Most of that was probably residual fear of loss from her dad's unexpected death. One day he'd been in her life, smiling and alive, and the next he'd simply been gone. There'd been no open casket. Nothing other than a metal box with a flag draped across it. The memory of how cold that metal had been when she'd touched it still had the power to sear her emotions.

She shook the thoughts away. But at least they were better than flickering mental images of Zeke slowly undressing in front of her.

Well, hell. She took a wrong angle when carving the space between the teeth and pierced all the way through the pumpkin, much like Zeke had done when cutting open his pumpkin. Her mouth twisted in irritation, but she forced a laugh. "And as you can see, mistakes happen to the best of us. But don't let it get you down. You can make your mistakes into 'happy little whatevers' like that television artist liked to say."

The class laughed. About a half hour later, her pumpkin was done and a tea light underneath made it come to life. Even her boo-boo wasn't all that noticeable.

She went around from person to person, helping them with trouble spots. When she finally got over to Zeke, she found him, head close to his pumpkin, lines of concentration as he finished up the last little touches on his creation. It was different from hers, but much better than she'd expected it to be from the way he'd talked.

"It looks like you're about done."

"It could be a little more precise." He eyed it with a critical glance that made her smile.

"This isn't brain surgery. Or heart surgery, for that matter. We're allowed creative license with no right or wrong way to do it. Watch. Let's put the light under yours."

She switched on the candle and slid it into the opening under the pumpkin, then set it down. The carving's toothy grin was the thing that stood out the most. She smiled. "It looks kind of like the Cheshire cat from *Alice in Wonderland*."

She drew everyone's attention to the difference between his carving and hers. "See? They're different. But they both draw your eye to particular spots. Just like all of yours will."

Five minutes later, all the pumpkins had their candles turned on and she switched off the light in the room. It made the place magical, just like it always did. She shivered as she looked at all of the carvings. "Good work, you guys. You should be proud of yourselves. Any last questions?"

"How far in advance can we carve our entries?"

"Great question. I wouldn't go more than a couple of days ahead with the way we're doing these carvings. As the pumpkins dry out, parts of them will begin to shrink, changing the look. Anyone else?"

They shook their heads.

"Okay, then consider yourselves officially inducted into the league of pumpkin carvers. Go out and practice or find new designs. Whatever you need to do to get ready for the party. And don't forget your costumes."

"Costumes?" This came from Zeke, and she glanced over at him. "I'm sure I mentioned that one of the other times we talked. It's part of the fun. So yes, if you can, the hospital would appreciate it."

She wasn't sure, but she thought she detected the slightest of eye rolls from the cardiothoracic surgeon. She chose to ignore it.

"If you need to check out your tools, please put your name on the sheet by the door. And the pumpkins and tea lights are yours to take with you."

Almost everyone came over to thank her with smiles, along with some good-natured laughter about how much harder pumpkin carving was than their jobs at the hospital.

Zeke hung back, letting everyone else leave before

he came over to her and handed her the tools. She swallowed. God. Had it been so awful that he was going to pull out of the contest?

"I don't understand," she said, glancing down at the case where every tool was back to the pristine, clean condition with which it had started.

"I'll get my own set," he said.

"Does this mean you actually liked carving it?"

"It means I prefer to buy my own set of tools." But this time he smiled, softening the words. "You'll probably never hear me say I actually like carving pumpkins or dressing as outlandish characters. But it's for a good cause, and I'm pretty sure Marcos's parents are bringing him to the party. I don't want to seem like a..."

"Scrooge? Halloween-style?"

That got a low chuckle out of him. "Maybe. Are we still on for meeting your mom?"

"Yep. She knows we're coming and will probably have already done quite a bit of research, knowing her, even though she has no idea what you're looking for yet."

"Honestly, the sooner I can get out of that hotel, the better. Eating takeout every night is getting old. And the walls are a little thinner than I might like."

He didn't say what those walls being a little thinner might be referring to, but all she could picture was a headboard banging late into the night. She gulped, horrified to have pictured herself spread out across a bed with Zeke...

With Zeke nothing. And he was probably talking

about a television that was turned up too loud. But when she glanced at him, she got the feeling she'd been right the first time.

"Well, hopefully she can find something you like sooner rather than later."

"Yes, let's hope." He glanced around. "I'll help you get this cleaned up and we can drop my pumpkin off at my office. Then we can go."

She was kind of surprised he hadn't just dumped his carving into the big trash can that she had set up in the room for cleanup. But it made her feel good. That maybe he hadn't completely hated doing it. Although it could be for exactly the reasons he'd mentioned—that he didn't want to disappoint Marcos and his family.

Well, if that was the only reason, she should be glad for it.

And so that's what she was going to try to be. Glad.

Shanna's mom was cordial and super organized. She already had a binder with his name on the front of it and potential properties for him to look through so she could get an idea of his taste.

He smiled over at Shanna. "I see where you get your love of notebooks with dividers."

Grace laughed. "I think we both get that from her father. He was super…organized."

Hadn't Shanna said her dad died when she was ten? He couldn't imagine losing his father at that age. Couldn't imagine losing him now, honestly. And it was happening. Little by little, and there was nothing Zeke could do to stop it. When he glanced over at Shanna, she was staring at her mom as if looking for something.

Grace sent her a quick smile and said, "I'll be back in a minute."

He sat on a large gray sectional sofa, binder opened to a listing of a small bungalow, while Shanna's mom left the room. With her dark hair and brown eyes, she looked much like her daughter, who was currently sitting on the far end of the sofa.

He turned his concentration back to the listings and flipped to the next page.

Hell, there were more houses available than he'd expected. Honestly, probably any of them would do, but he wanted Grace's take on areas within a reasonable distance from the hospital. He didn't really want to be a half hour away, stuck in bumper-to-bumper traffic during his commute, if he could help it. Maybe he'd gotten spoiled by how close he was now. But staying in a hotel forever wasn't the best choice, either.

Shanna had been pretty quiet. Maybe she was just tired. Or maybe she was regretting bringing him to meet his mother, despite her earlier words. Well, he wouldn't stay any longer than necessary.

That pumpkin-carving class had been something else. Watching Shanna flit from person to person, helping them figure out difficult areas, was a revelation. No wonder she seemed to be so good at her job. She was able to multitask in a way that surprised him. He tended to be laser focused during surgery and found that things that broke his concentration were annoying.

He tended to like quiet in his surgical suite. He knew of medics in the army who liked to have music blaring as they patched up wounds both big and small, but he preferred a quiet scene with minimal chitchat. Just the stuff that needed saying. He'd only had a couple of surgeries at the hospital so far, Matthew Landrum's and two that had come through the ER. He was still getting used to the way things were run at Everly, but so far he'd been pleased at the level of skill he'd found at the hospital.

"Find something?" Shanna's voice interrupted his thoughts and he turned to glance at her, realizing he'd stopped turning pages again.

He glanced down and saw that it was a two-bedroom, one-bath fixer-upper. No, that probably wasn't the best idea for someone who ran on coffee and adrenaline. "No. I just have no idea what I'm even looking for."

She scooted closer and glanced down at the listing. "That's quite a way from the hospital. You'd have to cross the Sunshine Skyway every day on your way to work."

"That's the big bridge?"

"Yep. Crossing it daily is something I would consider a nightmare. But then I'm not a huge fan of heights and avoid that bridge whenever possible."

He smiled. "I didn't think anything scared you."

She shrugged, her glance flickering to the doorway her mom had gone through. "You'd be surprised."

She didn't elaborate on the other things that frightened her and he didn't ask.

"So where do you suggest I look for places?"

She moved even closer. "May I?" She nodded to the book.

"Of course."

Her fingers touched his as she reached for the plastic page protectors her mom had slid each listing into. He moved his hand, trying to make it seem more casual than it was. Her touch had gone through him like an electric shock and the urge to feel it again made a ball of tension coil inside him, just like when they'd drank coffee together and she'd covered his hand with hers.

He'd been shocked by his response then. Evidently that hadn't changed between that day and this one.

She flipped the page to the beginning. "If I know my mom, she probably put these in some kind of specific order, the closest properties to the hospital toward the beginning of the binder. Ah, yes. See here? This particular apartment complex is just a block away from work. But if I remember right, these are small units, maybe not much bigger than the hotel room you're currently in."

"I don't need much. But I would like something in a quiet place. Being woken up in the middle of the night isn't my favorite way to spend an evening."

Her face turned a pink shade that he found more attractive than he should have. "I can imagine. Living in any kind of hotel room wouldn't be my idea of fun."

"It's not. Which is why I'd like to find something else pretty quick."

The rhythmic thumping against the wall in the room next to his had happened on a couple of nights and had made him grit his teeth, trying not to imagine what was taking place.

She smiled, the move crinkling the skin near her eyes in a way that was damn attractive. She'd never mentioned a significant other, but then why would she have? For some reason, though, he didn't think she was involved with anyone. She wasn't checking her phone constantly the way he'd seen some of the other staff members doing.

Her attention went back to the binder as she flipped another page. "Are you looking for an apartment, or a house?"

Really, he'd thought either one would be fine, but thinking about the upkeep involved in having a yard… Maybe an apartment or condo would be better. This place hadn't been all that far from the hospital. It had taken maybe fifteen minutes to get here. "Are there any units in this complex in that binder?"

"This complex?" A look of alarm crossed her expression before she wiped it away.

"What? Do you live here as well as your mom?" Maybe she didn't want him living nearby. But why? Was she afraid he was going to hit on her?

Hell, hadn't he just wondered if she was involved with anyone? He hoped he wasn't sending off some kind of stalker vibes. But then again, she wouldn't have suggested he talk to her mom if she was genuinely worried about it, right?

She shook her head. "No. Actually, I live in the house I grew up in after my father... Well, for a lot of my school years."

After her dad had died? Her demeanor right now didn't invite questions, though, and he couldn't blame her. He rarely mentioned his dad's diagnosis. But when he'd gone into the reserves, he'd wanted a duty station that was close enough to his parents that he could make it over there in a few hours by car. He'd done his research and there were some great facilities that specialized in memory care. Now all he had to do was get his mom to agree to move.

It was strange to see the man who'd been such a strong, powerful force in his life whittled down to a shell of his former self. His mom had been a bastion of strength, though, much like Shanna's mom seemed to be. Much like Shanna herself seemed to be.

Grace came back into the room, carrying a wooden tray with an elaborate array of meat, cheeses and small slices of crusty bread spread over it.

"You didn't have to do that. I'm already asking a big enough favor."

"It's nothing. And it's fun to dip my toes back into the housing market."

Dipping her toes? From the number of pages in the binder in front of him, it seemed more than just that. She probably did like sorting through properties. "Have you been a Realtor long?"

"About twenty-five years. I had started taking courses, and then when Jack was killed, it made finishing a necessity."

"Jack?"

"My late husband. Shanna's dad."

CHAPTER FIVE

GOD, WHY HAD her mom had to mention her dad's death? She made herself as small as possible when Zeke's gaze swung to her.

"You mentioned your dad died when you were a kid. I'm sorry. I should have realized."

"It happened a long time ago."

Grace spoke up. "Jack is the reason Shanna likes Halloween so much. They used to carve pumpkins together. They won quite a few ribbons."

Why had she ever thought bringing Zeke here was a good idea? Her mom was an open book, rarely feeling the need to hide anything from those she met. No matter how uncomfortable it might make her daughter.

"That explains a lot," Zeke said.

Did it? He had no idea what it was like to lose a parent for a reason that was so stupid that it boggled the mind. A pipe bomb, of all things. They'd cleared the area of IEDs, only to have a bomb hidden in supplies they had ordered. If not for her dad, a lot of men would have died. Instead, it had been just her dad.

Her chin went up and she decided to challenge

Zeke's words, although she wasn't entirely sure why. "Exactly what does it explain?"

"Why you took it on yourself to create a Halloween event at the hospital."

Her ire deflated almost as quickly as it had risen up. Because he was exactly right. Halloween was a way she could keep her dad's memory fresh and vibrant in her head. How often had she thought about how her dad would appreciate some new tool or carving technique? He would have been a much better teacher than she was at classes like the one she'd held earlier today.

But he wasn't here. And while her mom still loved going to parades that honored the armed forces, Shanna wasn't quite as quick to stand there and wave a flag. While she understood the need to help keep world peace, how many fathers had died—just like hers had—trying to attain what seemed like an impossible goal?

Shanna had decided long ago that she wouldn't date a military man, just because it would always be in the back of her mind that the unthinkable actually did happen. Probably more often than she realized.

But she wouldn't tell her mom any of that. She was proud of her husband. Proud of his unwavering commitment. Proud of the way he'd loved her and his daughter with the same unwavering devotion.

It was on the tip of her tongue to ask about his own parents, but it didn't feel right prying into his personal life. If she hadn't liked her mom laying it all out there, Zeke probably wouldn't appreciate a direct question, either.

Her mom must have sensed that things had become awkward, because she handed Zeke a plate and urged him to have some of the items on the charcuterie tray. It was one of her mom's favorite things to make. And she was good at it. Maybe because she had one at most open houses that she'd held. They had always been such a huge hit.

Zeke selected a few items, placing them on the small plate in front of him. When her mom gave her a pointed look, she took a plate and did the same, although she'd never really felt less like eating. For one thing, she was worried about her mom. The same way she always worried about her whenever she talked about her husband's death. Like Shanna, she was a master at hiding her emotions. It was another reason she avoided talking about her dad. She never wanted her mom to slide down into another pit of despair.

"So I was asking Shanna if there are any units available in this complex."

Ugh. Of course he hadn't forgotten the question. And honestly the condo community was big enough that even if he bought one of them, they wouldn't necessarily run into each other every time she came to visit her mom. So what was the problem with him living here?

Maybe it was just knowing that he *was* there, even if she never saw him in the flesh.

Her mom sat on the other side of Zeke and flipped

through several pages. "Actually, there are three units available. Two two-bedrooms and a three-bedroom."

"Two bedrooms would be plenty. I don't entertain much at all."

He didn't? For some reason, she'd gotten the idea he could have any woman he wanted. And maybe he could. Maybe he just chose not to do his "socializing" at home. Or maybe his surgeries were so stressful that he chose a quieter life when he was in his own space. She couldn't blame him. Her own social calendar wasn't exactly filled to the brim, except during Halloween. Once the hospital party was over, she'd go back to her own quiet corner of the world.

"Bayfront Condos has a pretty big footprint, but it's a nice quiet area." She smiled. "If you tend to throw wild parties, you might run into a bit of trouble with the homeowners' association."

She'd heard some of those homeowners' associations could be pretty nitpicky with what they allowed or didn't allow within the community. But HOAs definitely had their place. They were probably the reason there were no wild parties going on late into the night.

"No wild parties. In all honesty, I probably wouldn't be here all that much. When I have a few days off, I'd run up to see my folks in Jacksonville."

So his parents were both still alive. Did he realize how lucky he was?

Probably. And since he liked to go see them as often as possible, they must have a pretty good relationship.

She was happy for him. But it also removed some of

her reticence about him possibly living in her mom's condo association. After all, if what he said was true, he really wouldn't be there a lot.

"Would it be possible to see one of the units?"

"Sure. I have the code for the lockboxes. And the units are all empty at the moment, so we wouldn't have to worry about notifying the owners. So you said two-bedroom, right?"

"Yes."

Grace scooped up a slice of sausage, spreading what looked like mustard from a little pot on the piece of meat before popping it in her mouth. "Shanna, do you want to come?"

What was she going to say? No? That she would just hang around her mom's condo and wait for them to come back? That would seem churlish somehow. So she stood to her feet. "Sure. I wouldn't mind see-ing the units, either."

"We'll take my car. It's not that they're far, but Flor-ida's downpours sometimes come out of nowhere."

Zeke smiled, and she found herself staring for some reason. The curving of his lips carved a divot in his left cheek that was attractive in a way she couldn't explain. She'd seen plenty of dimples before, but this was more than that. It was more of a craggy line that her fingers itched to explore.

Not that she would ever get the chance. Nor did she want that chance. Right?

"Sun showers were what we called them," he said.

"We do as well. The sun can be shining, even as the rain is pounding on the sidewalks across the city."

"Any other properties that strike your fancy that you want to go see?"

"I haven't had a chance to look at all of them. Is there any way I can take that binder back to the hotel with me and look at it in more depth?"

"Of course. It's what I meant for you to do with it."

"Thank you for taking the time to put it together. I know it must have taken hours."

She smiled. "It's as much my passion as Halloween is my daughter's."

"I can certainly appreciate that."

Zeke's passion was probably his work, from what she'd seen. He saved lives and helped his patients have more quality years doing what they enjoyed. Like Mr. Landrum.

And even Marcos, even though the boy wasn't specifically Zeke's patient. But he could have done what other doctors had done. Sent the boy and his family home with antibiotics to fight an infection that wasn't at the heart of his problems. That cycle had probably happened more than once.

They piled in her mom's SUV and drove less than five minutes to another section of the condominium. Like the section her mom lived in, this area had pristine white buildings surrounded by lush green and floral landscaping. Shanna couldn't imagine living anywhere else. Tampa was beautiful with its white Gulf beaches and ocean breezes.

"It's in this unit on the ground floor. The other two-bedroom is on the third floor, depending on which you'd prefer."

"Are they exactly alike other than what floor they're on?"

"No, they're decorated completely different. One has a beach cottage vibe, while this one is ultra-modern. Obviously, you can have it redone according to your own taste. I'll take you to see the other one after this. It's on the far side of the property."

Walking up to the door of an end unit, Zeke nodded. "I like that it's on the end."

"Yes, those units don't come up for sale very often." She punched a code on the lockbox and it snapped open, letting her retrieve a key to the unit, which she used to open the door.

Swinging it wide, she motioned for Zeke and Shanna to go in ahead of her. Shanna was surprised by how different this place was from her mom's cozy-looking decor. Ultra-modern was right, from the chrome and leather furniture, down to the white marble flooring, which was devoid of a rug or anything that might soften the space. The dining room table was an expanse of glass with chunky chrome legs and accompanying white upholstered chairs.

She frowned. It was too cold. Too stark for her taste. But maybe that's what Zeke liked.

He wandered around the unit, not saying much, and her mom didn't push him for an opinion, instead letting him explore the unit at his leisure. It's what made her such a good Realtor.

"How many square feet is this unit?"

Her mom didn't consult her listing, just said, "Eleven hundred. The second unit we'll see has the same basic layout although it has a master suite with a bathroom, whereas this one doesn't."

"I see."

They followed him to the hallway, which had three doors along it. All closed.

He opened the first one and revealed a smallish bedroom that was in keeping with the theme. It boasted a silver, shiny tubular headboard, white bedspread and white plush carpeting. "Is this the master?"

"No, this is the guest room. The master bedroom is the last door on the left."

The bathroom was also all shiny furnishings and fixtures that bounced light onto every possible surface. She wrinkled her nose, only to have her mom frown at her.

Okay, she knew she wasn't supposed to have an opinion. After all, she wasn't going to be sharing this space with him. Or any other space for that matter. But somehow she'd be disappointed if this was the place he chose.

Guys were supposed to like modern minimalist, weren't they?

"Do the furnishings come with the unit?" he asked.

"They do. They're included in the price."

"I see."

He opened the door to the last room and Shanna almost laughed. While it was modern as well, it had some sort of faux animal hide tossed diagonally across the bed. It looked like…giraffe? But it seemed so impractical as to be almost ludicrous.

"Okay, I think I've seen all there is. Do you have time to run to the other unit?"

"I do."

Locking the place back up, Shanna was glad to be back out where there were at least splashes of color from the landscaping. All that white would drive her batty in no time flat. She'd have to get rid of most of the furniture in order to live there.

Whether Zeke loved it or hated it was impossible to tell. The man would make a great poker player, his face giving nothing away.

When they got to the next unit, they had to walk up two flights of stairs and the unit wasn't on the end like the other one had been. But since there were only three floors, there would be no one above his. The second her mom opened the door, Shanna fell in love. She was right when she said it was decorated like a beach cottage. But while she normally thought of those as filled with soft blue colors and muted flowers, this wasn't overly feminine. This place also had its share of glass surfaces, including the round dining room table, but it was softer. The dining room chairs were made of light whitewashed wood and there was a gas fireplace, which struck her as humorous in this part of Florida. But there were chilly days here for sure, and the idea of a glass of wine while watching the flames dance held an appeal that the other unit hadn't offered.

Large, bleached pieces of coral were artfully placed on flat surfaces, and there was a large round clock over the fireplace. She was glad there wasn't a television perched there, although it probably would have been convenient to have one in that spot.

She glanced at Zeke, whose face was just as impassive as it had been in the other unit. The appliances in the galley kitchen were high-end and, while they were stainless, it still didn't have a cold feel. Maybe because of the tiles of the backsplash, which looked like they'd had some sort of paint technique applied to give them a softer appearance. She reached out to touch it, expecting it to be delicate or easily scratched, but it wasn't. It felt almost like concrete.

"It's called German smear. It's a technique that's popular in homes today," her mom explained.

"Is it concrete?"

Her mom nodded. "It's a mortar that's kind of smeared on to create a textured surface. It's where the name of the technique comes from."

"I'm surprised by how nice it looks in here."

Zeke glanced at her. "So you like this, do you?"

She bit her lip, knowing she'd probably broken one of her mom's unspoken rules, but it was too late to take it back. "I really do." In her own best interest and so as not to earn herself a lecture later on, she kept the rest of her opinion to herself as Zeke walked from room to room.

The master bedroom boasted the same whitewashed beachy-looking furniture, the low chunky posters of the bed seeming to be in keeping with the rest of the unit. And no giraffe hide tossed across this bed. Instead there was a white bedspread, whose nubby textured pattern reminded her of sand somehow. And when she followed him through to the bathroom, she stopped in her tracks. This was a study in muted luxury. A soaking tub that stood on the far wall was what you saw when you first entered the space. A white distressed board was placed across the span of the tub, and on it was a dark brown candle that gave the impression of tree bark. Again, not too feminine. The shower had a sprayer on either side of the space, making it obvious it would hold two people easily.

She did her best not to picture Zeke in that space with her, but it was a struggle. One she was losing. She finally backed out of the room, waiting in the bedroom, instead. That didn't help. Because she could picture some nameless couple exiting the bathroom, soaking wet and falling onto the luxurious bedding.

Nameless couple?

Not so much, because the couple wasn't nameless at all. She was picturing her and Zeke. Again.

What the hell was wrong with her? She'd had a couple of relationships in the past, but they always fizzled out pretty quickly. And she'd never had fantasies like these. With her mother standing nearby, of all things.

Worse was that she might be picturing herself twined together with the cardiac surgeon, but there was no evidence that he was doing the same with her. No surreptitious glances. No hooded looks.

Just a man who was looking for an apartment rather than a partner.

And she wasn't in search of a partner, either. She was happy the way she was. She had a career she loved, friends that she went out and had fun with on a regular basis. She didn't need a man to make her life complete.

So what was that gnawing sensation in her belly when she remembered the way those women had looked him over in the coffee shop the other day?

Well, if it was any consolation, he hadn't even noticed them. At least not that she was aware of. Ha! If she'd been one of those women, she'd have gotten the same oblivious reaction from him, more than likely.

They came out of the bathroom and Zeke's gaze slid over her before shifting to the bed. Her insides turned hot. It had to be a coincidence. She'd simply been in his line of sight, that was all. But even so, the way it had made her feel sent off warning bells inside her. Because what if he did notice her at some point? What if he was willing to share his bed with her? Would she go along with it?

Evidently that was a no-brainer judging from her reaction.

Zeke turned to her mom. "Does this also include the furnishings? Everything we see?"

The way he said it intensified the heat inside her as if he were referring to her. He wasn't. And she had better scrub that thought from her head, before it burrowed deep and threatened to taunt her late into the night.

"It does. Right down to the linens and cutlery."

"Can I see that listing again?"

She handed him the binder and watched as he studied the specs and probably mulled over the price, whether it was in line with what he was willing to pay.

"I like this one, actually. I think I'd like to put an offer in on it."

Yes! The internal fist bump she gave herself was way out of line. Especially with her initial dismay that he might choose a condo in this particular complex. And her mom would have given her "what for" if she could read her thoughts. But despite all of that, something inside her was stoked that he would choose this place over that cold, emotionless unit they'd just come from. This place had emotion. And despite the cool whitewashed color palette, there was a heat that ran just below the surface.

Or maybe she was getting herself confused with the condo.

But the image of his glance going to her before sliding across that bed would be one that she was going to have a hard time banishing, no matter if he'd been picturing her sprawled out on that bed or not. Because she could do enough picturing for the both of them.

And right now, she was wishing she hadn't come with them. Wished she had simply introduced him to her mom and then driven herself home. She didn't want to know what his future place was going to look like.

And she certainly didn't want to picture him naked in that shower, being pummeled by hot streams of water, which would pour down his hair and sluice down his chest before finding other areas in which to play.

Oh, God, this had been such a huge mistake. Was it wrong to hope that the contract didn't go through? And that he would find some other place to live? A place she couldn't actually picture in her mind?

"Are you sure you don't want to look any further?" Her mom was the consummate professional. She didn't want him to look back and have buyer's remorse later on.

His glance went to her again before jerking away. "I think I've looked far enough. I know what I want."

He knew what he wanted? Okay, maybe she wasn't imagining it. Surely there'd been some hint of awareness in those impossibly blue eyes.

But even if there were, it didn't mean that either one of them had to act on it. In fact, that could prove to be a disaster since they worked together professionally. She'd seen some pretty ugly breakups after hospital romances. The last thing she wanted were the pitying glances she'd given others who'd been through exactly that.

It did make her feel better, though, that she might not be as crazy as she'd thought.

And she was still weirdly happy that he'd liked the beachy condo rather than the first one.

"Okay, let's go back to my place and we'll write it up."

This was probably where she should make her exit. "Well, I'll head home and let you two talk business."

"Nonsense," her mom said. "We should go out and celebrate. That is if Zeke is okay doing that."

"Actually, that sounds good." He looked at Shanna again. "Thanks for suggesting your mom. This process was a lot more painless than I expected it to be."

"You've never bought a house before?"

"Nope. Never. But there's a first time for everything, right?"

"Absolutely," her mom said. "And I can't imagine a better place than the one you picked out. It was honestly my favorite out of all the ones in that binder, although my taste doesn't always line up with someone else's, so I try not to do much in the way of trying to influence my clients."

"And I appreciate that. I really do."

They got back to Grace's place and wrote up a contract. He'd been glad to get out of the place, because he'd noticed Shanna's eyes light up when she'd seen that shower, and it had sent all kinds of crazy thoughts spinning through his head. And if he had read her right, she'd had the same kinds of ideas. And watching color infuse her face when his gaze had landed on the bed had given him a sense of satisfaction that was far too appealing. Far too dangerous.

And he'd actually been glad her mom was there, because it meant he couldn't act on any of those impulses. It had probably saved him a lot of grief in the long run. A brief romp in the bedroom was one thing, but there was something about Shanna that seemed to hint that she wasn't one to blithely have one-night stands. He wasn't sure how he knew that, but it was there in the way she didn't openly try to figure out if the attraction was mutual and then let him know she was there for the asking.

Which meant he needed to tread a lot more carefully around her. Needed to watch his step and make sure he didn't do something that might hurt her without meaning to. He hadn't wanted to hurt Kristen, and he didn't think he had. She'd been the one who'd wanted to exit the relationship once she realized he wasn't going to leave the military for her. Leaving the service was something that needed to happen on his own terms. When the timing felt right. And it hadn't back then. And it still didn't. It was why he'd opted to go into the reserves once his required time on active duty had ended. Maybe it was as a tribute to his dad. He wasn't quite sure. He just knew that right now staying in felt like the right thing to do.

But changing from active duty to reserves also meant that base housing was no longer available for him to use like it had been before. So buying his own housing was new to him. He could certainly see how it would have its own benefits in that he would be investing in something that could increase in value.

"So how soon before I hear something?"

"We'll probably hear back on whether the offer was accepted pretty quickly. In the meantime, we need to get you preapproved for a mortgage, but I can help you do that. It'll also give you a ballpark figure of price ranges, in case this particular unit doesn't work out."

The problem was, he really wanted it to. His credit rating was excellent and doing some quick figuring in his head, he should be able to afford the payments on the condo with no problems.

Grace signed off on the contract and Zeke also signed where she'd indicated. "I'll go ahead and send this over to the listing Realtor and go from there. Be right back. You and Shanna decide where you want to eat."

The second she left the room, he went over to one of the windows and looked out onto the property. The lawns were well manicured and tastefully landscaped. In the distance he could see some kind of pond with a misty spray erupting from the middle of it. Florida had a lot of these that, while beautiful, also helped deal with the runoff that came with inches and inches of rain per year. They also attracted gators. The funny thing was, most people who weren't from Florida feared the creatures. But for the most part they weren't aggressive unless they'd lost their fear of humans, even though they were a danger to small pets that ventured too close to the edge of those areas.

He glanced at her. "Do you get many gators in Tampa?"

"Our fair share. Although you probably got some, too, when you lived in the Panhandle, even though winters can be colder. The Okefenokee Swamp in Georgia has quite a few, even."

"They do. I've canoed the trail there many times."

She smiled at him. "Me, too, actually. It was always a popular destination spot when I was in college."

"So you preferred canoeing to the night life?"

"After a busy day at school, the last thing I wanted to do was go out and party. There were certainly those who did, but the group I hung out with was pretty boring."

"You? Boring? Not a chance."

Surprisingly she smiled at that. "I don't know whether to take that as a compliment or a cut."

"A compliment for sure. I was pretty boring myself." Except for the times when duty had called on him to treat wounded soldiers in less-than-ideal circumstances. But those were his memories. Memories that he'd struggled with. He didn't need to push them off on her.

"So if I agree with you, will you get mad?"

"You think I'm boring?" He sat up a little straighter.

She laughed. "How can anyone who doesn't embrace all that Halloween has to offer be anything but boring?"

"I liked carving that pumpkin. Does that earn me any brownie points?"

A flicker of surprise crossed her face. "You did? I thought you were just being polite."

One thing he wasn't going to say was that part of the reason he liked it was because she'd made it interesting. By her body language. By the way her tongue peeked out of the side of her mouth when she was concentrating on a particularly intricate part of carving her pumpkin. The way she was able to laugh at herself when she'd accidentally punched a hole through the pumpkin when doing the teeth.

"That surprises me. Doesn't my expression give away my every emotion?" His lips canted sideways when her face transformed from shocked confusion to one of irony.

"Very funny. I remember thinking that you'd make a great poker player with how little your face moves. You'd make a great spokesman for Botox."

"Botox. I think that's a slight exaggeration."

Her head tilted. "Maybe. You do have slight lines right here." She touched the corner of his eyes, the sensation of her fingertips sliding across that area sending a shudder through him.

Right then her mom walked back into the room and Shanna jerked her hand away so fast it probably gave her whiplash. Well, if his expression was stony, hers was the opposite. She looked mortified and embarrassed.

Grace looked from one to the other, but before she could draw the wrong conclusions, he said, "I had a spot of dirt on my face. She was brushing it away."

Shanna's shoulders actually sagged in relief. He really should warn her that her body language gave most of her thoughts and emotions away.

Like when she'd looked at that shower and made him see it through her eyes.

"Okay, are we ready to go eat?" Grace asked.

Yes. More than ready. The sooner he got out of this condo and pressed reset on this crazy day, the better. Then tomorrow, everything could go back to normal.

At least he hoped it could. Because if not, he was in big trouble. A kind of trouble that could creep up like a gator and bite him in the ass when he least expected it. The key was to make sure he didn't let it.

CHAPTER SIX

"SORRY, GUYS, CAN I catch up with you at the restaurant? The listing agent wants some more information. Zeke, are you willing to go up to the listing price if needed?"

Shanna stood there shell-shocked. She knew her mom well enough to know she was telling the truth. There was no matchmaking involved here, but still...

"I'm willing to go ten thousand over the listing price, if there are other people trying to get it."

"Great, that's all I needed to know. Let me know where you wind up and I'll meet you there as soon as I can."

She looked at Zeke. "Don't feel obligated to go if you don't want to."

"I'd like to find out if I'm in the running for the unit or not. Unless you don't want to go."

Great. Now if she said no, her mom was sure to look at her a little more closely and wonder what was going on. "I'm fine with it, just didn't want you to feel pushed into something you don't want to do."

Like she did right now? It wasn't that she didn't want to go. She did. And she wasn't sure why. Maybe she was better off not knowing, though. Surely it had nothing to do with getting a peek inside the man's head as far as his taste in decor went. Surely sitting with him in a restaurant without her mom was better than having her analyzing everything either of them said or did.

Although why would her mom do that? Unless Shanna gave her reason to. And if she knew her mom, she would probably become so immersed in the game of buying and selling that she might not make dinner at all.

Leaving just the two of them. Her and Zeke. And a roomful of other patrons. Her mouth twisted. It wasn't like they'd be at a private table in a secret room in the restaurant. Something that only happened in the movies.

"I don't feel pushed."

Shanna had to scramble to figure out what he was talking about. God. He was simply responding to her last statement.

She nodded as if she wasn't totally discombobulated. "Do you like Cuban food? There's a place on the bay that is authentic. The owner is my second cousin, actually."

Her mom nodded. "You'll love La Terrazza. I'll call if there's a problem on this end. In the meantime, go and enjoy yourselves."

At least with Tereza there, there could be no footsies under the table. Not that there would be. Why on earth had she offered to introduce him to her mother? It would have been better off to leave their relationship where it was. Which was exactly nowhere. He could have found his own Realtor and Shanna wouldn't now be introducing him to yet another member of her family.

Suddenly eating at her cousin's place seemed like a very bad idea.

"Why don't we take my vehicle, and you can ride back with your mom?"

Okay, maybe this wouldn't be such a disaster after all. She wouldn't be forced to play the awkward games of being dropped off at the condo.

"That sounds like a plan."

Grace paused with her thumb poised over a button on her phone. "Give Tereza a big hug from me." Then she held the phone up to her ear. A second later she was headed for the kitchen, the binder in her hand as she read something from the listing.

Her mom was super nice in person, but as a Realtor she was nothing if not efficient. And a little bit ruthless. It was rare for her to lose a sale once she had her mind set on it. And it sounded like she'd just shifted into that persona. Lord help whoever that listing Realtor was.

"I guess that's our cue to head out," Zeke said.

His car wasn't what she pictured a high-powered surgeon to drive. It was an SUV, but not the newest model. Did she really judge people like that?

Lord, she hoped not. Her own ride was a five-year-old model, but it was clean and purred like a kitten. It was also a lot lower to the ground than his.

She stepped onto the running board and into the vehicle, letting him slam the door behind her. Once he got in, he looked at her. "Top up…or down?"

Her eyes got wide. "What?"

"The top to the car." His mouth twisted. "I guess that could have been construed as something else entirely."

"Obviously I knew you didn't mean my top." Except that is what she'd thought for just a second, before she realized she was being ridiculous.

"So my question remains. Car top up or down?"

"Down, please. It's warm out today and it's not often I ride in a convertible." She reached into her purse and pulled out a clip for her hair. The last thing she needed was for it to be tangled in one huge knot when they reached La Terrazza.

"Down it is."

He started the car and pushed a button and the roof accordioned onto itself, folding down in stages until it disappeared into the frame of the car. Once they moved out of the parking lot, the warm air sifted past her skin and she raised her face to the sun and let the currents flow over her. It revived her, much as the sea breezes had the power to do when she sat in the soft powdery sands of the Gulf and listened to the seabirds as they went by.

"Have you ever seen the sunset over the Gulf?"

"Only from the Panhandle, but I assume it's even more magnificent sitting on a beach that faces west."

"You need to see it. So very gorgeous."

He glanced at his smartwatch. "I would say we could cross the bridge into Clearwater before dinner, but we still have an hour and a half until sunset, and if your mom is planning on meeting us at the restaurant..."

"I know." She sighed, trying not to make it sound as wistful as it felt. It had been quite a while since she'd actually made time to sit on the beach. It was another of the things she'd loved to do with her dad...walk along the shoreline and watch for dolphins that liked to play along the coast. It had been more than twenty years since his death. And while his memory would never die, there were times when she had trouble bringing his face into focus, times when she couldn't remember how his shirts smelled as she nestled against his chest and listened to his stories.

Zeke looked over at her. "Tell you what. If we can't do it tonight, you'll have to take me to your favorite spot sometime, so I know where to go to see it."

Just as they pulled into the parking lot of La Terrazza, her cell phone buzzed in her purse. When she pulled it out, she saw it was her mom. "Hi, Mom. Did you get your calls made?"

"I did, but I'm not going to make it to dinner. A friend called and she needs me to come over and look at some discoloration on her wall. But tell Zeke that the owner accepted his offer and will pay closing costs. We did have to go up to list price but didn't have to go over it. He'll need to come in and get his financial stuff together for the mortgage company."

"That's great news." She held her hand over the speaker. "Mom said the owner accepted the offer at list price and they'll pay for closing costs."

"Tell her thank you, for me."

"He says thanks."

Her mom gave a few more details and then said goodbye. She had to go look at discoloration on a friend's wall? That sounded fishy to her, but no way was she going to let Zeke know of her suspicions. "The bad news is she's not going to be able to make dinner. She's off to help a friend who has an issue with her house."

"Okay." He paused a second or two. "So what would you rather do? Go to dinner? Or head to Clearwater?"

"Clearwater, unless you're starving."

"With that meat and cheese tray your mom had, I have to admit, I'm not super hungry."

"Me, either." She shot him a look. "Are you sure you wouldn't rather just drop me off at my mom's and head home, since you don't have to fill out any more paperwork on your future house? Congratulations, by the way."

"Thanks. And you forget, I have no home right now. Just a hotel room that leaves a little to be desired as far as peace and quiet goes."

"It'll take about forty minutes to get to Clearwater Beach, but it's worth it, and we'll hit it just before sunset. If you're sure you want to go."

He nodded. "I'm sure."

Shanna explained that Clearwater Beach was actually a barrier island, connected to the mainland through a long causeway. Since he grew up on the east coast of

Florida rather than the west, it was like entering a different world. There were no large waves like they had in the Jacksonville/Saint Augustine area. Just white sand and calm clear waters.

And he was used to going to the beach to see the sun rise rather than to watch it set. It was one of the funny things about Florida. Its long and relatively narrow shape made it possible to watch the sun come up over the water on one side and then drive across the state to the other side where you could watch it set over a different body of water.

The trip over had been nice. A little too nice. He'd enjoyed her touristy chatter about the things that the west coast had to offer, and he'd also enjoyed watching her twist her hair back up into its comb when too many strands escaped. They played around her neck and face, the silky locks looking far too inviting.

Yes. He was glad she'd wanted the top down. It was probably the only time he'd ever see her so…*disheveled*, although that wasn't really the word he was looking for.

He wracked his brain for another one that would better fit what she looked like from where he sat.

Sexy. Yes, the woman looked sexy as hell with the top of her scrubs ruffling in the stiff breeze, the slightly V-neck offering peekaboo glances at the skin just below its border. Not that he could take his eyes off the road long enough to ogle. And not that he would. But his imagination was working overtime at filling in some very tantalizing blanks.

He got to the end of the causeway and when they

were beachside, he stopped, pulling off the road and looking at her. No more fluttering. No more peeks. But, damn, he was glad, because things were starting to get a little more uncomfortable with every mile they traveled. "Which way from here?"

"Let's turn right and go past Pier 60 and sit on the beach. The pier is neat, but it's bound to be crowded right now."

"So that's the pier?"

"That's it. A fishing and tourist mecca. And a great place to catch the sunset…if you're a fan of crowds. And I don't advise coming out here during spring break."

That made him laugh. "Noted."

He glanced to the left. Pier 60 was a long dock that hung out over the Gulf. And true to what Shanna said, there were people crowding the rail on its west side. It had what looked like shelters along its stretch and then in the middle of it there was an actual building. Scattered on the sand surrounding the area were vendors selling everything from truck food to umbrellas. "What is that structure on the pier?"

"It's a bait store and shop. Let's drive down a ways. It'll be easier to park and the crowds won't be so terrible."

They traveled until they found a public parking area and Zeke pushed a button to raise the top. She glanced at him and laughed. "Well, it's not super obvious we work at a hospital, is it?"

They both still had their lanyards around their necks,

and while he was in jeans and a shirt, Shanna was in dark blue scrubs with pictures of elephants all over them. He smiled. "I think your getup is a little more obvious than mine." He dropped his lanyard into a compartment in his vehicle. "Do you want to leave yours inside as well?"

"Yep." She pulled it over her head and slid it into her purse. "If you're going to lock the car, I won't bother bringing anything with me."

"I am."

They climbed out of the vehicle, and he locked the door.

Then they were walking toward the beach. Shanna kicked off her rubber clogs and stuffed her socks inside them, opting to carry them rather than keep them on her feet. She had glittery pink polish on her toenails that shimmered in the sun. Somehow it fit her to a T.

They stepped onto the beach, and he soon saw that it wasn't as hard-packed as some of the beaches on the other coast. He ended up taking off his own shoes to make walking in the sand a little easier.

"I was wondering if you were going to tough it out."

"I figured I'd have to take them off sooner or later. But remind me to take my cues from those around me."

Not one person still had their shoes on. It made him smile. It had been a while since he'd actually stood barefooted on a beach. Maybe not since Kristen, although she wasn't much of a beachgoer. They'd visited a nearby beach in Panama City probably twice during their relationship.

His mouth twisted. Looking back, they'd had more arguments than good times. Especially in the last year of their relationship. But, still, to come home to an empty apartment had been a jolt he'd never quite gotten over. Maybe because he knew that someday he would visit his mom and have to face an empty bed where his dad would have slept.

Something cramped inside him and he forced it to release its grip. That day was not now. His dad was still with them, even if he was slipping away little by little.

He'd been to see them before moving to Tampa, but the urge to make the four-hour drive was strong. Maybe with this next trip, he could broach the subject of moving them to the area. There was even that ground-floor condo he'd looked at today, and he was sure there were others like it in different parts of the city.

But for now he would focus on what was here in front of him. The beach. The sun. And the sand. His dad would have liked the pier and the fishing. If they moved in time, maybe he could still bring him out here and help him do some of the things he'd liked the most.

She walked a little farther down the beach and then found an area away from people and dropped onto the sand, giving no thought to the lack of a towel. "Mmm... it's still so warm."

He blinked before she answered his mental question. "The beach. It's still warm from the sun."

She patted the sand next to her. "Try it and see."

He settled onto the beach and closed his eyes. She was right. The beach held on to the heat from the sun, even though that orb was hanging a little lower in the sky than it had been fifteen minutes ago. He was glad they'd come here rather than the restaurant. Glad that Grace hadn't been able to come, although he felt a twinge of guilt over that feeling.

There were people gathering their things who'd obviously been out here almost all day. Some of them sported tans, while others looked so red they had to be painful. It was clearing out.

It was...nice. Nice to sit here after coming out on a whim. Nice to see the way she sat cross-legged on the beach as if it were the most natural thing in the world to do.

And maybe for her it was. But for him?

Not so natural. But he could see how it could become so. And he'd better enjoy it, because he couldn't see himself coming out here on his own very often. And asking Shanna to join him periodically was... impossible.

He would not...*could* not do that. Because sitting here with her felt natural and good.

Without a word, she unclipped her hair and lay back on the sand and when she did...

Oh, hell. When she did, his body shifted into another gear. One that moved in slow motion and yet seemed to coil in readiness. He tried to stare out over the water as the sun edged lower in the sky, but try as he might, he couldn't stop his peripheral vision from moving back to her and imprinting what it saw on his brain. So he closed his eyes and refused to look. At her. At the sun.

"Zeke, you're going to miss it."

When he peeked, he saw that she was propped up on her elbows rather than stretched out. He wasn't sure that was any better, but if he went back to hiding behind closed lids, she was going to want to know why, and there was no way he was going to tell her the real reason.

"Just enjoying the breeze."

Like hell he was. But she was right. The sun was now a fiery ball in the sky, and it had started painting colors along the horizon, the red tones piling on top of each other until it became a kaleidoscope.

It was so different from the sunrise. Maybe not the colors, but the emotional sensation of a day nearing completion.

He liked it. Maybe too much. "It's beautiful."

"I haven't been out here in forever. I'm glad we came."

"Me, too."

They spent several minutes just watching the sky transform before it started shutting down the show, a heaviness beginning to darken the beach and the water.

Her soft voice came from next to him. "Sometimes you can see dolphins playing near shore. There's nothing like it on earth."

Oh, he could think of a couple of things. But they weren't things he could admit to himself, much less to her. "I'm sure it's beautiful."

She turned her head to look at him. "It is. It's amazing."

Something about the shadows that played around her cheeks, her eyes—her lips—gave her an air of mystery that made him swallow. "Yes, it is. It's amazing."

They stared at each other for a very long time before he did something he shouldn't. Something that was going to get him in so much trouble.

But it was as if the sunset was reeling him in, whispering that everything would be okay, even when he was pretty sure it wouldn't be. When he reached out and traced his finger over one of her cheeks, she didn't move, eyes still on his.

As if his decision were made, his hand moved to her nape, his palm curving over the soft surface he found there. And then lowering his head, his mouth found hers.

CHAPTER SEVEN

THE TOUCH OF his lips sent her soul soaring into the heavens. She had consciously asked for this, but she knew that something inside her had been hoping this moment would come ever since they'd gotten into his car. She couldn't stop her body from turning toward him, or her arm from reaching up and curling around the back of his neck.

He was as warm as the sand. No. Warmer. And the heat from his body was melding with her own until she couldn't tell where he ended and she began. But what she did know was that there was nowhere she'd rather be than right here. Right now.

And if they stayed like this much longer, she wasn't going to be able to move. Wasn't going to be able to stop...

She didn't want to stop.

But if she didn't...

She might come to care too much. And if he left...

Forcing herself to stop clinging to him, she put an inch between them, then two.

He stared at her for a second before letting her go

so fast that she would have fallen back onto the sand if he hadn't steadied her.

"Hell, Shanna, I'm sorry. I have no idea where that came from."

She did. It was the magic of the sun and the water. That's all it was. That *had* to be all it was. Because she didn't want to risk it being any more than that. Her life was good as it was. She was happy with it.

Right?

Yes. She was.

She forced herself to respond to his apology. "It's okay. I'm just as guilty. Let's chalk it up to the sunset. It tends to cast a spell on you."

"Right. The sunset."

But as he dragged his hand through his hair again like he'd done earlier, she sensed he was struggling with something.

Well, so was she and it had nothing to do with the setting. But she'd better get herself back under control, or she could be setting herself up for a world of heartache. She didn't do relationships. Didn't want to. Some people might get their happy endings, but she and her mom sure hadn't. And the thought of having to go through a pain that great again was too much.

Not that Zeke had even mentioned anything about getting involved or making this into anything other than a silly mistake.

Only it didn't feel silly. So she needed to get up and move before she let herself get swept away again.

"Well, it's getting dark. Are you ready to head back to the car?"

"Whenever you are." He stood to his feet and reached a hand down to her.

She hesitated before placing her hand in his and letting him help her up. But thankfully he didn't hold on to her once she was on her feet. In fact he released his grip the second she was up. But where there should have been relief, there was just a sense of emptiness that seemed to drain the beauty from the sunset she'd just witnessed.

Was she doing the right thing by closing herself off from relationships? The other times she'd gone out on dates she could have definitively said yes. But this time?

And tonight hadn't even been a date.

It was more than that.

The words whispered through her like the warm ocean breeze. A breeze she needed to get out of if she had any hope of walking away from this without embarrassing herself.

They walked to the car in silence and when they got inside, Zeke made no mention of putting the top down, and she was glad. All she wanted to do was get home and forget that kiss had ever happened. Whether that was possible or not was yet to be seen.

All she knew, though, was that she needed to try. Or she might be setting herself up for a world of pain.

Shanna straightened the crown on her head, yet again. Was he going to show?

Fiddling with the display of pumpkins, she wondered if Zeke was going to back out altogether. She hadn't spoken more than ten words to him since he'd dropped her off at her mom's house with yet another apology. Somehow that second "I'm sorry" had been worse than the first. It had a ring of finality to it that had made her face heat.

Every day since then, she'd been tempted to text him and ask if he needed help carving his heart, but didn't trust herself to be around him any more than necessary. And since he hadn't contacted her outside of work, she was afraid any move on her end would have an air of desperation to it.

She'd seen him over the last week, but anytime they'd run into each other, he'd been noticeably standoffish, which made her doubly glad that she'd given him a cheerful wave before walking from his car back to her mom's condo. At least he wouldn't think she'd been hoping for more than a kiss.

Actually, it would be unbearable for him to think that. As it was, her mom had wanted a rundown on all that had happened after they left her place. Shanna had made her explanation as short and succinct as possible, leaving out any and all details that might make her mom think it had been anything other than two colleagues spending a casual hour or two together.

And it was pretty obvious that Zeke regretted what had happened on the beach. Two apologies and a week of avoidance had gotten his message across in no uncertain terms.

He didn't want a relationship, he didn't want friendship. He probably didn't even want to have to work with her anymore. She should be glad.

And she was. Glad the decision had been taken out of her hands.

Her mom said they were still in contact about the condo and were getting the mortgage stuff in order. Things were going swimmingly, according to her mother. Her mouth twisted. She was really glad they'd left her out of it. She hoped the best for him. But right now, the less she had to interact with him, the better. If she were honest with herself, it was a little odd to be on this side of the equation. It was normally her putting the brakes on things with men. And she would have in this instance as well, if Zeke hadn't had his own foot so firmly on them that she could practically smell the rubber burning as the wheels screeched to a halt.

It made her feel foolish and downright stupid.

So, yeah, she wouldn't be surprised if he was a no-show tonight. She tried to figure out how to space the pumpkins a little farther apart rather than leave a blank spot where his would have been.

"I think you're going to have a great turnout tonight as always, Shanna. Congratulations. This may be our biggest night yet." Dan, the hospital administrator stood looking at the lineup of pumpkins.

She smiled at him. "So you're dressed as…let me guess." She put her finger on her lower lip. "A hospital administrator?"

"Very funny. I'm still on duty. I do want people to

take me seriously when I'm greeting the patrons and patients alike."

"I know. I'm kidding."

"You, on the other hand...look amazing."

He gripped her hand and held it up as he surveyed her Glinda the Good Witch costume. With its layers and layers of frothy pink tulle and huge puffed sleeves, it was a little harder to walk in than she'd expected it to be. As was the tall pink crown that felt like it might topple off her head at the slightest movement, even though she'd bobby-pinned the heck out of it. Her hand crept up yet again to make sure it wasn't hanging sideways.

Nope. Still there. Which was a little more than she could say for her pride, which still stung.

"Thank you." She made what she thought might be a Glinda-esque curtsy just as the doors opened and in walked a pirate. A tall upright figure that... She blinked, stopping midbow as she realized that was no pirate. It was Zeke, looking incredibly stunning, and nothing like Johnny Depp. With his broad shoulders, he filled out the loose white shirt that he'd cinched with a wide black leather belt, his black jeans not quite what she would envision as pirate gear, but the boots they were tucked into certainly were. God. He looked yummy.

And he was carrying a pumpkin.

All her lies of being glad he might not come flew out the window. She was glad. Incredibly, irrationally glad. And that made her pull up short.

Realizing she was still holding Dan's hand, she let

go and gave him an apologetic smile. "Sorry. I was worried Zeke was going to ditch the event, but it looks like he's brought his entry after all."

"That's a good thing. Especially since I met a young family waiting in line outside who asked for Dr. Vaughan. They were speaking Spanish, but I understood a little of it."

"That's wonderful. Zeke... Dr. Vaughan will be really happy they made it." She wasn't too embarrassed to be caught calling the cardiologist Zeke, since staff members tended to use each other's first names. Dan, obviously, had to be more formal when talking to the public about hospital staff.

Zeke came over to them, taking in both her and Dan. "I ran into traffic, sorry I'm late."

She smiled. He actually didn't seem as distant as he had for the last several days. "I was just about to give up on you."

"Were you?"

She ignored the question, glancing at the black leather bands on both of his wrists and the gold hoop in his ear. Wait... She looked closer. "Did you actually...?" She touched the earring.

"Pierce my ear? No. It screws on the back. I feel a little like my grandmother."

That made her laugh. "Believe me, you don't look like any grandmother I've ever seen."

"Neither do you."

Dan had walked off to greet more of the staff, leaving her to handle Zeke on her own. "Thank you. I think."

"That's quite the outfit. Are you from that kids movie with the ice and the song that everyone was singing for a while?"

"Frozen?" Her brows went up. "No. Try an earlier generation."

He shook his head, looking blank.

Seriously? He didn't know who she was supposed to be?

"It has a tornado? And Kansas, and ruby slippers…"

"Of course. *Wizard of Oz.*"

"Yes. And you're a pirate, obviously." Realizing he was still holding his pumpkin, she motioned him toward the empty spot. "Here, put that down."

When he set the pumpkin in place, her eyes widened. He'd done the diagram of a heart just like he said he was going to do but this… This was great. "Wow. You carved this on your own?"

"I did. It took me almost the whole day yesterday."

"I am seriously impressed. I may have to hand in my carving tools and let you take over my class."

"No thank you. I'm still not comfortable in this getup, but I did like carving the pumpkin. How did Dan get out of dressing up?"

"He says because he's greeting the public and needs to be recognizable. It's the same story every year."

"Funny how that works for him but not for anyone else."

She smiled. "Well, you can't blame him. He has to be ready to answer questions and schmooze with potential patrons. It's kind of hard to do that while dressed as Peter Pan."

Zeke's eyes cut back over to the administrator. "That's an image I won't be able to easily erase."

Neither was the one of Zeke leaning over her on the beach as he got ready to kiss her. He'd been soft and approachable and far too sexy.

But it hadn't lasted. Then again, it was probably better this way. In fact, she knew it was.

"Well, you'd better hang on to that mental image, because that's about as close to a costume as Dan is ever likely to get." She glanced at her watch. "We have about five more minutes before people start filing in."

"What am I supposed to do?"

"Just kind of mill around and be in character, if you can."

"In character. I don't think that's going to work for me. But I can walk around and talk to people. But saying 'Argh, matey!' is out of the question."

"It's okay. Just be you. I don't think I could imitate Glinda's voice very well, either. But I can nod and curtsy enough to get the point across, I hope."

"I'm sure other people are brighter than I am and will get it right off." He glanced at the line of pumpkins. "So I don't need to stay with mine?"

"Nope. They just have numbers on them since we don't really want anyone to know who carved what. Otherwise it could become a popularity contest."

"One I wouldn't possibly have a chance at winning." He grinned.

He was very wrong. Which was why they'd changed the way the contest was run after that first year. Because Zeke could certainly win a popularity contest based solely on who he was. "Don't sell yourself short, Zeke. Cardiothoracic surgeons are always the life of the party, right?"

He leaned closer. "Argh...matey."

That made her laugh, just as the doors opened and people started filtering in, heading straight for the candy line or the pumpkin-carving contest. "That's our cue."

"Okay, see you on the other side."

"Oh, I almost forgot. Marcos will be coming in. Dan saw the family in line outside. He'll be looking for you."

"Okay, thanks. I'll keep an eye out for him." He gave a quick salute and headed off.

Something passed through her head at the speed of light, before she lost whatever it was. About Zeke?

She wasn't sure. But she was glad things weren't as chilly between them as they had been for the last week. Maybe things were looking up. But whatever it was, right now, she just needed to concentrate on her duties and stay in character for the next couple of hours.

Zeke was almost talked out and his bandanna kept sliding down his head, forcing him to push it back up again. He felt ridiculous. Although Shanna had seemed happy enough to see him.

That surprised him after how he'd acted for the last

week. It was as if he'd been afraid she would suddenly morph into Kristen and start urging him to give up being a reservist. Actually, he wasn't sure if she even knew he was in the military. He hadn't told her. But he knew how hospital gossip chains were.

That kiss had been an impulsive move. And for someone who rarely did something without thinking it through, it had turned him sideways. But here Shanna was acting as if it had never happened. Maybe he'd made a bigger deal out of it than he'd needed to.

And wow, she looked like she was dressed for a formal ball with that puffy dress on. But it fit her perfectly, as if it had been custom-made with her in mind. He'd had a hard time trying to figure out anything to wear. He'd finally settled on a shirt he'd found at a thrift store and some cheap boots and a bandanna. But there was no way he was wearing striped pants that looked like they belonged in a B pirate movie. He'd also forgone the eye patch. But no one seemed to be looking at him like he was something to be pitied. As far as costumes went, there was a mix of traditional and silly, and he really enjoyed seeing the kids dressed up as different characters.

Then a family came in that he recognized. Marcos and his parents. While his parents were dressed as anything other than themselves, Marcos was wrapped round and round in strips of white cloth. He waved at the boy and his parents, wishing Shanna was there to translate. Instead, he fingered one of the cloth wrappings and gave the boy a smile and a thumbs-up sign.

While still thin, the child had a rosier hue to his skin today, hopefully evidence that whatever treatment the pulmonologist had him on was working. At least for now.

It was hard to tell what the future held for the child, but hopefully the parents would get some counseling on how to handle each stage of the disease as it came. The important thing was to be scrupulously consistent with his medications and breathing treatments. It would help hold the disease at bay for as long as possible. If he ended up in the right place at the right time, there was always the possibility of a double lung transplant when his own lungs became too compromised to deliver enough oxygen to his body.

Suddenly Shanna was there, greeting the parents and smiling at Marcos and gripping his little hand in her own.

"Se ve saludable."

Marcos's mom and dad responded to whatever she'd said with nods.

"Se siente mucho mejor."

She glanced at Zeke. "They said he feels much better."

"I'm happy to hear that."

Shanna translated the words for the family, who nodded with smiles.

She talked to them for a few minutes more, before sending them on their way. "I explained to them how to vote for their favorite pumpkin. They wanted to know which one you made, and I had to tell them it was a secret. Although if they think for a few minutes, they'll figure it out."

"Thanks for rescuing me. I'm taking this as a sign that I might need to learn a second language."

"If you're going to stay here for any length of time, it probably wouldn't hurt. There are a lot of places that teach Spanish."

"I'll keep that in mind." He looked over. "Well, I'll be damned."

Coming down the walkway with a walker, his wife supporting one of his arms, was Mr. Landrum, who'd just been discharged on Friday. To say she hadn't expected to see him was an understatement. Zeke shared her surprise. "Should he be out yet?"

"Probably not, but from what I've learned about him from his family, he's a pretty stubborn guy. Which may be why he survived that surgery, even after all hell broke loose."

"I'm glad he did. Is his insurance going to cover any cardiac rehab?"

"Unfortunately, no. But I'm working on a plan to help with that."

"A plan? What kind of plan?"

Before he was able to say anything else, though, Mr. Landrum reached them, holding his hand out for Zeke to shake.

Zeke looked at him. "Do you think being here tonight is wise?"

"Maybe not. But climbing on that tractor this afternoon was probably not the brightest idea, either."

He felt his face twist in outrage.

Mr. Landrum broke in before he could respond. "I'm joking. Even I'm not stupid enough to try to go back mowing grass. At least not right now. In a few weeks, it'll be another matter."

"Six weeks. You need six weeks for those bypasses to heal. Six weeks to regain your strength. To do anything before that time is just inviting disaster."

"I hear you. Six weeks. Got it." He glanced to the side. "Now excuse me while I go and vote on pumpkins. I think I may have guessed which one my friendly neighborhood cardiac surgeon may have carved."

"Oh, you do, do you? Well, good luck. I might surprise you."

"You already surprised me. When you did my surgery and gave me my life back. I don't know what I can ever do to thank you."

"You can start by giving yourself time to heal. By not taking on too much too soon."

The man's wife looked at him. "Are you listening, Matthew?"

"I'm sure you're going to remind me again and again."

"Yes, I am, until the message makes it past that thick skull of yours."

"Message heard and received." He gave her a smile that was filled with a mixture of love and exasperation, the way true love should be. "Now can we get off the nagging train?"

"Yes. But when you get too tired, you need to let me know."

He gave her a tired nod. "I think you'll know before I even say a word."

They slowly made their way over to the first pumpkin on the block, waiting behind a line of other people who were also trying to cast their votes.

Shanna said, "Think he'll listen?"

Glancing over at the couple and the way Mr. Landrum's wife had her hand over his on the walker, he nodded. "I think he will. I don't think he has a choice. And honestly, he's a lucky man to have her."

"I was just thinking that very thing."

Their glances caught for a moment or two before breaking apart. He realized what he'd said was true. Matthew Landrum was a very lucky man to have someone who loved him enough to tell him the truth. Who loved him enough to lay down the law in an effort to keep him safe. It didn't mean he'd always do as she told him to do, but what it did mean was that he wasn't going to want to leave her before it was his time to go.

It was a love like his parents had. But how was that love going to look six months from now? A year from now, when the only one who remembered was his mom?

He didn't want to think about what that kind of loss would look like.

Shanna gave them one more look before backing away. "Well, I need to go over to the pumpkins and try to get a preliminary count once the crowds thin out a bit."

"Okay, I'll see you later. Anything specific you want me to be doing?"

"No, just mingle with the crowds. This is supposed to raise community awareness of the hospital's needs. Every year, we seem to get a large grant from someone who goes through the line, but who wishes to remain anonymous. And I think that's partly due to the way the doctors and other staff show they care by being here. Not everyone can or does come to the party."

One brow went up. "It was a pretty strongly worded flyer."

"Yes, it was, but that doesn't mean that people always care enough to participate. Or some have second jobs or pressing family needs and just don't have the time. But for those of us who do, it's an important event in the life of Everly Memorial."

"I'll try to remember that next year."

"See you later. Make sure you stick around to hear final results of the contest."

"Honestly, I don't care if I win or lose. It's been a good experience. Much better than I thought it would be."

The smile Shanna sent him warmed him through and through. And then he walked away and made his way into the crowd, to do one of the things that he liked the least: make small talk with people he didn't know.

Shanna couldn't help it. Her eyes sought him out time and time again, trying to be careful that he didn't catch her looking at him. But, of course, he had a couple of times, earning her either a raised brow or a slow smile that seemed to burn right through her. And each time, she expected to find herself in a fluffy, melted heap on the floor. The change in his attitude from this past week was enough to make her head spin. But who knew how long it would last. She could fall for the man far too easily. And that thought was enough to scare her into averting her eyes. At least for a few minutes.

Somehow she rallied and went about her job, keeping track of the votes tallied up by the various pumpkins. They'd all done a great job. There was Zeke's heart, and Dr. Murphy's depiction of a newborn baby. There were also funny ones like an appendix attached to a string of intestines or even a dog holding a ball.

Everyone had gotten at least one vote, and since the staff weren't allowed to participate in that part of the event, it showed how hard they'd all worked to make this year's Halloween party something that would be remembered for months afterward.

There were only five more minutes of voting left and the crowds had drifted away from the pumpkins and were busy playing the carnival-style games or bouncing in the inflatable house that they'd erected in the courtyard. And the weather had been perfect. Just like that night on the beach. No rain in sight and balmy temperatures that had morphed into a slightly cooler evening that provided some relief to those who were manning the booths outside.

As soon as the winner of the contest was announced,

she'd send everyone out of the room so she could turn off the lights and get some pictures of the jack-o'-lanterns in all of their glory, lit by just the glow of their battery-operated tea lights.

And then they'd line those who were in costumes up and get some shots to send to the local news sources. She'd already spotted one of the television news crews wandering around taking videos and pictures of the events.

There was always a tiny spark of pride and thoughts of how much her dad would have enjoyed this night. How he would have put his heart and soul into it, even if he had no skin in the game. Oh, the memories they could have continued to make together if not for that terrible night. If he hadn't had to play the hero. If, instead, he'd been safely at home with his wife and daughter.

But he wasn't, and none of her selfish thoughts were enough to change that. And while his loss still had the power to bring her to tears, she went on doing what she could to try to make him proud of her, wherever he was.

The timer on her watch went off and she went over to the pumpkin display, catching the last few votes as they were cast before putting up a rope in front of the ballot boxes to show that the time had passed to select a winner. Then she and Dan opened each box and pulled out the remainder of the ballots, adding them to the totals they'd tallied earlier and marking them on the sheet she'd made up for that purpose.

"Okay, looks like we have a winner," Dan said. "Are you ready for me to announce it?"

She smiled. "I am."

The hospital administrator climbed onto a small podium, where a band had been playing earlier, pulling the microphone from one of the stands. "Okay, here's the moment you've been waiting for. To see which one of our talented staff carved what you declared as the best pumpkin."

People gathered around as he talked a little bit about the history of the party and named her as the mastermind behind it, something that always made her feel a little uncomfortable, since it really was a team effort. But she smiled and did her best Glinda curtsy, holding her long magic wand out to the side as she did so.

"So if we call your team's name, please come up and collect your prize."

It always struck her as funny, because the prizes were vouchers to the hospital cafeteria, which wasn't really the most popular hangout at the hospital. But Dan had always said it was better to keep the prizes in-house to support the things that they were trying to do and promote.

"In third place, we have Newborn Baby by Dr. Murphy and the Everly Women's Center."

A bunch of hurrahs went up and a cluster of five people, headed by the ob-gyn herself, Beverly Murphy. They handed out a gift certificate to each team member. Shanna carried the plate containing the pumpkin over to the group so pictures could be taken.

"Congratulations," Dan said. "And now, in second place, we have an unusual entry. Zeus and his Lightning Bolt, carved by the radiology department." That garnered several laughs as people got the connection between the imaging department and a bolt of lightning. She was actually surprised that entry hadn't won the grand prize. It was well executed, and this team had won several years in a row.

Pictures were taken and their prizes were handed out. And then Dan once again brought the microphone to his mouth. "Our grand-prize winner came as a little surprise to me, since Radiology normally has this one in the bag, but I just want to say that it really does fit who we at Everly are as a hospital. I hope we're seen as a place where you are cared for when you're ill. Where you're supported as you heal. And where you're comforted when you grieve. More than anything, Everly has a heart for this community and for you. Our winning pumpkin is The Heart by the newest member of our team, Dr. Zeke Vaughan. Dr. Vaughan, come up here, please."

Shanna looked around to try to see where he was, but there was no movement in the crowd.

Dan glanced at her, and all she could do was shrug. Surely he hadn't gone home. He knew how important this event was to the hospital. Of course, he probably hadn't expected to win. But still. She couldn't see him leaving without stopping to tell her.

Then a voice came from a nurse who was standing by one of the doorways. "Dr. Vaughan has had an emergency and is with a patient."

Shanna's eyes went wide and she searched the crowd for two faces that should be there. She saw Marcos with his parents, but when she looked for Matthew Landrum, she didn't see either him or his wife. Maybe he'd gotten tired and had gone home. But as her eyes scoured the room, she saw a lone walker standing over by a door.

Oh, no! Was that the one he'd used?

She wanted to rush from the room and find that her fears were unfounded. Instead, she had to stand there and do her best to smile as Dan smoothed over Zeke's absence.

"Like I told you, folks, Everly Memorial has a big heart. Our cardiac surgeon is proving that point tonight, by putting his patients first. But we'll get his prize to him. Thank you all for coming out to support the hospital and its mission. And our party is still going strong, so enjoy yourselves and be safe going home. We love you all."

There was clapping as Dan hopped from the podium and came to where she was. "Any idea what happened?"

Shanna blinked moisture from her eyes. "No, not for sure. But one of Zeke's patients—a double-bypass case who came out tonight—is nowhere to be seen, and I think that walker is the one he was using when he came in." She nodded at the wall where the mobility device was still sitting unclaimed.

Dan nodded. "Let me know if you hear anything. I still have to go around and talk to people, but come and find me."

"I will. I need to get pictures—"

"I'll take care of that, Shanna, just go find Zeke."

She found him. Zeke sat in the empty cardiac waiting room, a surgical cap gripped in his hand. He was in scrubs. The boots he'd worn with his costume and that fake earring were the only evidence of the part he'd played less than an hour earlier.

There was a defeated look to the droop in his shoulders and the way he leaned forward as if in physical pain.

Her heart cramped, and she stood frozen for a minute before forcing herself to move.

She touched his shoulder before sitting down beside him. "Hey. Are you okay?"

A muscle worked in his cheek, and she thought for a minute he wasn't going to answer her. A sheet of ice seemed to encase her with a cold she'd never known before. She'd had patients pass away before, but there was something about the way Zeke was just sitting there that told her the outcome wasn't a good one. He shook his head.

"Mr. Landrum?"

"Yes."

"Oh, Zeke, I'm so, so sorry."

"He threw a clot while I was standing there talking

to him and his wife. I tried. I opened him up, tried to find it. Dammit. I couldn't. Couldn't find it."

She wanted to weep. What could she say? Certainly nothing that would make him feel any better. Dan Brian was right about one thing. This heart surgeon truly did have a heart.

She put her arm around his neck and laid her head on his shoulder, trying just to be there for him.

His head went back to lean against the chair cushion. She thought her own heart was going to break. That patient had seemed so happy, so alive less than an hour earlier, bantering back and forth with his wife.

"Hell." His voice was rough. Graveled. A sign he was in danger of losing his composure completely. "Any chance we can get out of here?"

If people didn't think doctors mourned over patients, here was a prime example that that wasn't true. There were some people who just made an impact on you, and their loss...

"Absolutely." She would shoot Dan a quick text and let him know what had happened. He would understand. He'd be the first person to tell Zeke to take some time to himself. And the administrator was the consummate professional. He could cover for her and would probably do a better job than she could do herself.

While he got up to throw his soiled scrubs in a receptacle, she sent off a text, letting Dan know what was going on.

Her phone pinged.

Got it. Tell him to take some time. I've got this.

With shaky fingers she typed back.

Thnx.

When Zeke came back, she looped her arm through his. "I know a back way out."

He didn't say anything but let her lead him through a hallway where janitorial supplies were kept near a back entrance, where workers could come and go. She'd needed to leave through this same exit more than once, for this same reason.

Twilight was just falling as they made their way around the deserted side of the building. They'd have to go back to the parking area where they might run into people, but hopefully not anyone who would know either of them.

She found her car and dug for her keys, unlocking it. Zeke hesitated for a second before getting in.

"Do you want me to take you home?" She climbed in her own seat.

He gave a pained snort. "Home. No. The last place I want to go is back to that hotel."

Shanna understood that feeling completely. "Let's go back to my house. I can make you some coffee or tea. Whatever you want." She started the car.

Before she could pull out of the space, warm fingers touched her chin, turning her to look at him. "Why are you doing this? Especially after the way I've acted this last week."

Her chin wiggled for an instant before she got it back under control. "Because I've been there. I've lost people I care about."

His palm cupped her other cheek, easing her a bit closer until he pressed a kiss on her lips. It was soft and fleeting, but said everything that needed to be said.

Then she put the car in gear and pulled out of the lot, heading…home.

CHAPTER EIGHT

ZEKE LEANED HIS head against the seat rest, trying to get the images out of his head. The ones of soldiers he'd worked on and lost. The cries of pain and fear as they were brought to him in hopes that something could be done. Sometimes it could. Sometimes it couldn't. He'd been to counseling to come to grips with what he'd seen out in the field.

But here he was at a state-of-the-art hospital and he couldn't save a patient he'd worked on eight days ago? A patient he'd almost lost on the table during bypass surgery, but who'd somehow come back from the brink. And look where that had gotten him: lost to a damn clot. Something so ridiculously stupid. It was a gamble anytime surgery was performed, but with each roll of that wheel he hoped for a winning number.

And, damn, he'd wanted Matthew Landrum to win. Had willed his heart to start beating again as he cracked open his chest and performed cardiac massage.

All for nothing.

Shanna hadn't said anything since that kiss a few minutes ago, and he could kiss her all over again just as a thank-you. The last thing he needed was platitudes or words that were meant to comfort him, but which would do the opposite. He needed time to rage in his head against the kind of deity who would give back life only to take it again days later.

What seemed like an hour later, but was probably a lot less than that, she pulled into the driveway of a modest home, pressing a button to open a garage door before driving the vehicle inside.

Without a word, she exited, and he followed suit. What he really wanted to do was lie down and sleep for a while. There was a bone-weariness in him that he hadn't felt in a long time.

She led him through a kitchen to the living room, where she nodded at him to sit, then disappeared into the kitchen. He toed off his boots and propped his feet on the long leather ottoman that sat in front of the couch.

Matthew Landrum's wife was going home to an empty house. Tomorrow she'd be planning a funeral for a man whom she thought would be beside her for years to come. Only he wouldn't be.

How long before he went through that same loss with his dad? He closed his eyes.

Shanna came back in with two cups of coffee. He took one and drank a gulp, the brew burning his throat on the way down and hitting his stomach with a force that he welcomed.

She curled up on the couch next to him, her bare feet peeking out from beneath that ridiculously huge dress. Part of the skirt spilled over onto his thighs, and he stared at it. He pinched a piece of the fabric and rubbed it between his fingers. It was a mixture of scratchy weightlessness that defied explanation.

But maybe some things didn't need explanations.

Like that kiss on the beach?

He took another pull of his coffee and glanced over at her. She'd removed that tall crown thing that had been perched on her head, and her hair was falling out of the clips that she'd used to hold it in place.

And God. She was gorgeous. There was something magical about her that was as inexplicable as her dress. As that kiss on the beach. Something that drew him to her time and time again.

His fingers traced her cheek as she watched him, her own coffee cup in her hand. "Thank you." He nodded at the mug he was holding.

"You're welcome."

But still he didn't pull his hand away, exploring the planes and curves of her jawline to where it met her earlobe, which was heavy with a dangly gold earring. He gently tugged at it, hearing a slight intake of breath as the side of his hand brushed against her throat.

Did she feel it, too? This strange pull of emotions that seemed to be winding silken threads around him?

"Zeke…" The breathy whisper came just as his fingertip touched her bottom lip. He set his cup on a tray that was lying across the ottoman and slid his fingers into the hair at her nape and tugged her closer.

This time, she was the first to make contact, her mouth sliding onto his with a gentleness that sent his other hand up to cup her face and hold her in place. It was the softest, sweetest touch he'd ever experienced, and his eyes closed to take it in.

Shanna pulled away for a second, like she had at the beach, but when he frowned and opened his eyes, he saw she was just setting her coffee cup on the side table next to the couch.

Then she was back. And this time the kiss was stronger. Warmer. Infused with a sense of urgency that matched the one growing inside him.

And this time, there were no people around. No reason to stop.

He hauled her onto his lap, her poofy skirt enveloping them both. It was heaven and hell all rolled into one sweet package. One he didn't seem to be able to resist.

When their lips met again, her mouth opened with a heady question mark that he was more than happy to answer. His tongue slid against hers, and she made a sound deep in her throat as she shifted on his thighs so that she straddled him.

Oh, hell. The pressure of her against him was almost his undoing. But somehow he held it together as he gripped her hips. The top of her dress clung to her ribs and waist, and he had no idea if he could get it off her.

Or if he even should.

His palms slid up to find her breasts, kneading them. And the answer to her dress was suddenly answered. Yes. He should.

He drew away from her lips, his mouth trailing to her ear. "Is there an easy way to get this dress off of you?"

"No. But nothing good, is ever easy, right?" She gave a soft laugh and nipped at his lips. "There's a zipper in back. Pull it down."

Reaching behind her, he found the little tab and tugged. It slid along the tines much more easily than he'd expected and he got it as far as her waist. Which was all he needed for right now.

He peeled the fabric down her shoulders, past breasts that had no need of a bra.

The sight was his undoing. Pressing his hands against the bare skin of her back, he drew her to his lips and found his first nipple...then closed his eyes as the sensation of tight, puckered skin met his tongue. Oh, yes. She was definitely all heaven. At least right at this moment.

Drawing her deeper in his mouth, he reveled in the way her back arched and she moaned, her hands holding him to her as if afraid he might leave.

Hell, he wasn't planning on going anywhere.

Except here. His hands tunneled beneath all of that fluffy fabric until he somehow managed to find the bare skin of her thighs, gliding up them until he reached the edge of panties that were warm and silky. Some kind of lace.

His thumb eased under the elastic at one leg and encountered a moist heat that made his body tighten with need. A need so sharp that he ached to finish it now. But he couldn't, not yet. He touched the juncture of her thighs, and she shuddered against him, as if she felt the exact same thing.

As he moved to yank his wallet from the back of his jeans, he let go of her breast so he could find what he was looking for. At least he hoped it was there.

There. He pulled the packet free, even as Shanna stood to her feet.

He looked up at her, wondering if she was calling a halt to things, but instead, she reached under her skirts and pulled her panties down, kicking them to one side, her breasts jiggling in a way that made his mouth water.

Then instead of taking her dress off the rest of the way, she lifted her skirt around her hips. "Put it on." She smiled and looked at the packet.

Ripping it open, he eased his zipper down and released himself, then slowly rolled the condom down his length.

Shanna's teeth came down on her lower lip. Then with skirts still gathered in her fists, she climbed back on top of him.

"You're going to keep that on?"

"You object to role-playing?"

Hell, when she said it like that, no he did not.

The skirts fell around their hips, and she reached under them and found him, taking him in hand and stroking in a way that made everything in him rise up in a rush.

His hands went to her breasts, still bared to him, and he murmured, "I need to be inside of you, Shanna. Soon."

"How about right now?" The hand that was stroking kept going, but her body shifted, edging up and forward until he felt that same heat he'd touched earlier. Slowly she eased onto him, sliding down in a single smooth motion, and he jerked with pleasure when she reached the bottom. Her hands came out from beneath her skirts and untied the ties at the neck of his white shirt, her fingers curling around his bare shoulders.

"Hell, Shanna."

She rose and fell, her eyes on his face as she squeezed around him. But it wasn't enough. He needed more. His hands went to her waist and moved her with purpose. Deeper, harder, his own hips lurching up with each downward movement. He pressed her breasts to his face as he breathed in her scent.

Then he could stand it no more. He carried her down to the couch, so that she was on her back, and he was in between her thighs, the costume making things even hotter, although he had no idea how that was possible.

Her feet pressed against the arm of the sofa as he thrust into her over and over, mouth meeting hers and kissing her with a ferocious need that he couldn't remember ever feeling before. One arm went under her hips, tilting them up to change the angle. She immediately went still and moaned, then began pumping her hips wildly against him. He couldn't tell where she started and he ended, until she gave a long, keening cry and strained against him. Then he felt it. That crazy pulsing of her body that traveled up his shaft and pushed him over the edge in a single thrust. He drove into her again and again until there was nothing left.

Then slowly, with a stealth that caught him unawares, the urgent need morphed into a slow, sated calm that took over his body. Took over his mind.

Hell. What had just happened?

He had no idea, but suddenly he was exhausted. Somehow he managed to shift their positions until she was lying on top of him, his arm wrapped around her and holding her against him.

All he could feel was his breath, moving in and out of his body, releasing the tension of a day that had gone so horribly wrong. He let his eyes close. Not to sleep. He just wanted to lie here for a minute and absorb all that she was and all that had happened on this couch.

Just another minute or two and then he'd get up.

Shanna was up and showered by the time he woke up. She'd lain there for almost a half hour watching him sleep, before realizing she was dangerously close to falling for this man.

But why not? She'd seen the best and worst of him.

At least she thought she had.

And she trusted him. Her dad's death and her mom's resultant depression had given her more than enough reasons not to venture into serious relationships, but this was different. Zeke wasn't likely to encounter a land mine in Tampa or be ordered to work under dangerous conditions.

But she needed to give herself a little more time to be sure. Right now her emotions were all jumbled up over what had happened last night. Both to Mr. Landrum and what had occurred in her house.

She knew that when faced with trauma, sometimes the body craved a proof of life that could only be achieved one way. Zeke couldn't be blamed for doing what his instincts told him. And she'd been just as eager.

Neither one of them had stopped to think about what happened afterward. Or how they would handle it. It would be so much easier if they'd gone to his place, so she could slip away before he woke up. But that would be cowardly.

Especially if she was wanting to test the waters and see how dangerous they felt.

They were both adults. They could face what had happened. Right?

At least she was now fully dressed in normal clothes, since she needed to be at work in an hour. She was going to have to wake him up soon, though, because she was his ride.

Ugh!

Tiptoeing back to the living room, she startled when she realized his eyes were open and he was looking straight at her.

She licked her lips. "Hi."

"Hi, yourself." At least he had the throw she'd tossed over him in the middle of the night, because as she'd found out last night, a naked Zeke was damned near irresistible.

She waited for him to say something further, but when he remained silent, she couldn't stop the question. "Are you okay? After everything that happened at the hospital, I mean."

His eyes closed for a second or two before they opened again. "Not quite. But I can't change anything. At least not about that. What I am sorry for is what happened here. I honestly did not come here with any intentions other than to find someplace to decompress. I'm not sure how that all changed."

It was what he needed.

And if she was honest with herself, it was what she'd needed as well, after fantasizing about him at that condo. Not to mention that tantalizing kiss on the beach afterward, which had given her even more material for her dreams.

But the reality of what had transpired last night had blown her dreams out of the water. Sex with him had been so much better than anything she could have imagined.

"I was just as guilty as you, so no apology needed. But I do have to be at work in an hour. I can fix you some breakfast, if you'd like."

"No need. I'll just grab something at the hotel."

"About that… Do you want me to drop you off there at the hotel? Or at the hospital to get your car?"

He blew out a breath. "Another thing I'd forgotten. I didn't drive here." He seemed to think for a minute. "I don't have anything pressing this morning. If you could just take me to the hospital, I'll go home and change and then come back."

"Okay."

She frowned. They were tiptoeing around each other in a way that felt awkward after her thoughts about romance and whether or not it was possible with him. He was kind of making her feel like it wasn't. Or at least that it wasn't what he wanted. After all, did you really apologize if you were hoping things would continue in the same vein?

She knew nothing about his life before he'd come to the hospital other than the fact that he'd lived in the Panhandle before moving to Tampa. Had he ever been married?

Divorced?

Well, she was pretty certain that he wasn't currently married, but his relationship status really was something she should have asked before she hopped into bed with him.

But people had short flings all the time, right? This wasn't any different from that. In fact, it was easier, because then there was nothing waiting to surprise her around the bend. Not that there would be. The other guys she'd been involved with had been marvelously simple. But the attraction had fizzled out almost before it began.

"Do you want to shower?" she asked.

"Yes, if there's time."

"There is." At the moment, she was more worried about dropping him off by his car, where people coming into work could see them and jump to all kinds of conclusions. And more and more she was thinking they would be the wrong conclusions.

Before she could move away, though, he reached up and wrapped an arm around her, hauling her down to sit beside him. She looked at him in surprise, unable to think past the fact that he was naked under that blanket.

"I know this was all kind of crazy, but when we both have a spare moment, I'd like to sit down and talk about what happened."

"Talk?"

"Yes. About where we go from here. What it all means."

Okay, so it didn't sound like he just wanted to ske-daddle out of here and never mention this again.

And where they went from here? Did that mean what it sounded like?

Her thoughts swirled around and around going no-where, so she finally just said, "I think that's a good idea. Let me know when you have some free time."

"Can we go to dinner somewhere tonight?" He gave her a slow smile. "Especially since our last dinner plans never happened."

They hadn't. Because they'd wound up at the beach instead.

So yes. Dinner sounded promising. Much more so than "I have a space from four to four fifteen free—why don't we talk then."

"I would like that."

With that, he dropped a kiss on her temple and then stood up, the blanket falling away to reveal skin as bare as it had been last night. She gulped as he gathered his clothes from the floor. That was her signal to get the hell away from him before she ended up being late for work and had a whole lot more explaining to do.

Why the hell was he so nervous?

Maybe because this was the first time since Kristen had walked out on him that he was actually entertaining the thought of getting involved with someone again.

And was he entertaining that idea?

He thought so. But this time they'd opted to meet at the restaurant, and Zeke was not going to count on sex after their meal. In fact, it would probably be better if they didn't wind up in bed.

He didn't see any sign of her car in front of La Terrazza, the place they'd planned on eating at a week ago.

Just then his phone pinged.

Am inside. Fourth booth on the right.

Okay, she must have parked behind the restaurant.

I'm here. See you inside.

As soon as he entered the restaurant, his eyes found her. And she looked just as good as she ever did. She'd changed from her scrubs into a pair of dark jeans and a navy gauzy tunic that she'd cinched at her waist with a metal link belt. Her hair was swept back into a high, sleek ponytail that looked both classy and casual. She gave him a quick wave as if unsure whether he'd spotted her.

He had. And he found himself smiling as he strode toward her table.

"I'm not late, am I?"

"No, I'm just a little early."

He slid into the booth and nodded at her glass. "What are you drinking?"

"I'm kind of a stickler about not drinking and driving so it's sweet tea. But you can have whatever you want."

"Tea sounds good."

As if summoned, a waitress appeared to take his drink order and handed him a menu. "Another sweet tea, coming up. Do you need a few minutes?"

"Please."

She left and Zeke opened the menu only to find that the names of the dishes were in Spanish, even though the descriptions were in English.

He glanced at her. "Any suggestions?"

"The red beans and rice are kind of a Cuban staple. So is the *ropa vieja.*"

He had no idea what she'd just said, but the way it rolled off her tongue was sexy as hell. "The rope what?"

She laughed. Also sexy. And a torpedo to his senses in more ways than one, when he'd hoped to keep his wits about him. *"Ropa vieja."* She said the words slowly this time. "It actually translates as 'old clothes' in English, but believe me, it tastes nothing like that. It's unapologetically Cuban. And delicious."

"Okay, then that's what I'll have."

Their waitress returned to the table, and Zeke sat back as Shanna ordered their food in Spanish, carrying on a short conversation with the waitress, who chuckled at something she said. When she left to turn in their order, Zeke was tempted to ask if they'd been laughing at him, before deciding he was being a little paranoid. So instead, he said, "I like hearing you speak Spanish. Did your dad understand the language?"

She gave a half shrug that made her ponytail swish. "He understood more than he spoke, but my memories of him are from my childhood, so it could be skewed a bit. But I'm sure he knew at least some words, since my mom spoke Spanish quite a bit at home."

"You're lucky. I always thought it would be nice to be bilingual."

"It's definitely an advantage in Florida." She smiled again and canted her head to the side. "You don't speak anything besides English?"

"Unfortunately, no. I know words here and there in a few other languages but don't have any extensive knowledge of them."

"I get it. It was hard for my mom to start speaking exclusively in English after she met my father."

"But they made it work."

"Yes, they did."

He hesitated, but didn't want to go through a stilted meal while an elephant lounged on the sidelines waiting to be noticed. "How did they, coming from two different worlds?"

She sighed and seemed to think for a few minutes.

"They did come from different worlds and had some barriers to overcome, but they loved each other enough to make those things kind of slide away. Stay out of reach, unless they had a disagreement. Then they never let those times get in the way of the good. Their good times. My parents loved each other despite everything that might have stood in their way. Until he died."

"And your mom didn't regret being with a man who ultimately couldn't stay with her?"

She took a breath before blowing it out. "My mom really struggled after my dad died. So much so that it's made me wary of relationships. Are your parents still together?"

He twisted his lips trying to decide how much to answer, before realizing he needed to tell the truth. It might make a difference in how she saw him. Especially since he was thinking about going out with her periodically. He hadn't been diagnosed yet when Kristen left and he was pretty sure that would have been another strike against him.

He chose his words carefully. "They are still together. But my dad was diagnosed with Alzheimer's a couple of years ago. It's progressed enough that he's not always sure of who people are and it's starting to get noticeable in his speech. He has trouble choosing his words sometimes."

"Oh, Zeke, I'm so sorry. Where do they live?"

"In Jacksonville at the moment, but I'm hoping to convince them to move to Tampa in the near future.

In fact, I was thinking about that other condo that was for sale on the ground floor."

"Right, that would be perfect, if he has mobility issues."

He put his straw in his drink and took a quick sip. "Yes, that's exactly what I thought."

"It must be hard for your mom."

"It is. Just like your dad dying must have been hard for you and your mom."

"It was pretty devastating. My mom went through a period of depression after he passed away."

He nodded. "My dad hasn't passed yet, but there are times when it seems like the person he was when I was a kid is no longer there. And that's the hard part, I think, for her. She loves him deeply, but I'm not sure that's something he necessarily understands, nor can he reciprocate."

He hoped that made sense.

"I can see how it would be really hard."

The waitress came back with their food in record time, setting the dishes in front of them with a warning that they were hot.

He waited until she was gone before smiling. "But that's not why I wanted to come to dinner with you."

"No? I was so sure that you wanted to pry all of my family's secrets out of me."

He leaned forward. "I'm not concerned with your family's secrets. I'm only interested in you."

And there. He'd said it. Hopefully there wasn't a stalkerish feel to his words.

"Are you?" Her finger reached out to trail down the hand he'd placed on the table. It was enough to send a shudder through him.

"Yes." He hurried to add, "But I'm not trying to rush you into anything. I'm just hoping you might want to go out periodically and see where things lead. No pressure. No hurry. I've been in a bad relationship once before and so I'm a little more cautious on that front."

"I hear you. And I'm in favor of everything you just said about going out but keeping it casual. At least for now."

Hmm... He didn't remember anything about it being necessarily casual. But she was probably being the smart one in wanting to go even slower than he might have been thinking. "So...parameters?"

She laughed. "Now you sound like a heart surgeon."

"Do I?" Something about the way she said that amused him. "Does that surprise you?"

"Not at all. In fact, it kind of turns me on."

Okay, now he was in danger of not getting through this meal at all. And as much as he'd love to just say to hell with it and drag her back to his hotel for another dose of what they'd had the last time they were together, he really did want to be smart about this.

As if she sensed something in his manner, she added, "But I really do want you to try the *ropa vieja*. After all, if you don't like Cuban food, we may as well just call it quits."

And just like that, she'd steered them back into safer waters. Where they could hopefully get to know each other a little better, and he could find out whether these feelings that had begun to percolate inside him were worth pursuing, or whether they should stop while they were ahead—before they ruined their chance to at least maintain a professional relationship.

His first bite of meat surprised him. It was bold and full of spice and flavor that reminded him of Shanna. It was deliciously different. And he liked it. A lot.

Liked her. A lot.

"So?" She was looking at him with an expectancy that made his chest tighten.

"I love it."

She seemed to relax into her seat. "I am so glad. Not everyone likes rice and beans."

"Well, I haven't tried those yet. But I do like both of those things, and if they're even half as good as the meat is, then I'm going to be a fan for life."

By the time he finished the meal, he could definitely say he was a fan. Of both the meat and of Shanna. She was sweet and funny and seemed so very real. But there was an underlying sensuality that made him sit up and take notice time and time again. And if he hadn't declared sex off-limits for at least tonight, they would have wound up back in each other's arms. But instead, he settled for getting to know her better. And hopefully in the process was laying a more solid foundation than the one he'd had with Kristen.

A foundation that wouldn't be washed away with the first wave that might come their way.

CHAPTER NINE

SHANNA WAS STILL feeling weirdly satisfied as she headed into the hospital eager to see her first patient of the day. Their dinner last night had been a huge success. And for the first time in her life, she felt like she might have found something real with a man. Something she might actually want to hang on to for a while.

Or maybe even…forever.

Was it even possible? Was this how her mom had fallen in love with her dad? Because Shanna couldn't definitely say she was pretty near admitting to herself that she might just care deeply about Zeke.

She turned the corner to head to the elevator, realizing she'd wound up in the hallway that recognized those who had served in the armed forces. But for once it didn't send a chill through her. Maybe because of what was blossoming between her and Zeke. She let herself look at them for once.

There weren't a whole lot of pictures. Maybe fifteen or so out of hundreds of employees. But her gaze stopped on a man who was screwing something into the wall at the far end. A hook. Maybe they had a new hire that used to be in the military.

She started to steer around him when she caught sight of something lying on the ground. A picture of a man in uniform. She was almost past the workman when something stopped her, and she looked again.

There was something about the posture and the slight crease on the left cheek of his serious, unsmiling face. A sense of foreboding rose up within her and she couldn't make her glance go any higher, as she tried to suck down a quick breath or two. Then she realized how weird it must seem for her to just keep standing there. So she forced herself to look at the image again, focusing on the man's eyes. She swallowed and a clawing sense of fear and panic suddenly overwhelmed her.

God! It was Zeke. A little younger than he was now, but still very recognizable.

Despite that dinner last night, she still knew so very little about him. She tried to itemize what she knew. He'd had a bad relationship, which made him wary. *Check*. His dad had Alzheimer's, a terrible diagnosis that had pulled at her as he'd described him to her. *Check*. He'd come from the Panhandle. *Check*. A place where there were military bases. *Check and double check*.

How stupid could she be? It all made sense.

She licked her lips, trying to think. It wasn't like he'd lied to her, or avoided telling her. The subject had just never come up.

But when he'd been discussing loans with her mom, shouldn't he have mentioned that he qualified for VA financing? Maybe he had done that over the phone or something. Or maybe he wasn't even in the military anymore. Could it be that simple?

She cleared her throat. "These pictures are all of men who are no longer active duty, right?"

He shrugged. "I'm just paid to hang the pictures. I don't know anything about them."

"Okay, thanks."

That had to be it. There was no way they could work for the hospital and still be active duty, right? This was just a way of recognizing past service.

But she wouldn't know for sure…unless she asked him.

Over another dinner?

And what was she going to say if he was still somehow connected with the armed forces? But again, she didn't see how he could be anything but discharged. And it had to be an honorable discharge, or they wouldn't hang him up, right?

But it still felt like he'd hidden something important from her. Probably not on purpose. Maybe he just thought she wouldn't care. But then again, she hadn't told him about her dad, either. Just that he had died. Not how he'd died.

Why wait for dinner? Maybe she should just go see him now and discuss it. Tell him what had happened with her dad and give him a chance to open up about his own time in the service. She'd sworn to herself she would never date anyone in the military. At least no one who could actually see combat. She snorted. Her dad had been on a peacekeeping mission. It hadn't even been a war zone. And he'd still died.

Unless the person in the picture was somehow miraculously not Zeke Vaughan, she was going to have a serious problem. Except, she knew in her heart of hearts exactly who it was. There was no nameplate on the picture, but all the rest of them had one, identifying the branch, dates served and their rank.

Before she could stop herself, she knelt down by the framed print and looked at it closer.

The guy stopped working and glanced at her for a second.

She pulled in a deep breath. "Is there a nameplate that goes with this one, too?"

He looked down and pointed at the box on the other side of him. "It's probably still in there. They all have one."

Feeling a sense of doom, she shifted until she could reach the flat box, teasing one of the flaps open. Yes, it was there. But it was upside down. Suddenly she didn't want to turn it over. Didn't want to know. But how did that saying go? With knowledge comes power. Or something like that.

Would it matter if he was no longer serving?

No. Of course it wouldn't. He'd gotten out. He had to have. And unless he was thinking of reenlisting, then it was all fine. They could still go forward with their plan for dating.

So why was she shaking so hard?

Because she'd just met a guy who had swept her

away. That had shown a depth of emotion and sensitivity that had eaten away the foundations of the walls surrounding her heart. Had taken away some of the fear of losing someone.

She flipped the nameplate over. It was indeed Zeke. Ezekiel Manning Vaughan, to be exact. She smiled at his middle name. It fit him.

She looked at the rest of the plaque. Field surgeon with a rank she didn't recognize. But when she reached the end of the nameplate, she froze. United States Army Reserves. There was a beginning date, but nothing but a hyphen after that. There was no ending date.

Because he was a *reservist*.

Her eyes closed. She knew what that meant. He could be called back to duty at any time. In fact, it almost certainly meant that he would be deployed from time to time and had to go in for periodic training.

Deployed. For missions?

She dropped the plate back into the box and looked into the face on that picture.

Why hadn't he told her at dinner? It would have made everything so much easier. She could have held up her hand and told him she'd heard enough. That they couldn't date. Casually or otherwise.

Really, Shanna? Would it really have been that easy?

No. Of course not. But the fear was still there, swimming around her insides like it was there to stay. The fear that she could wind up just like her mom, mourning a husband who had died. The fear that she would fall in love with him only to someday have two uniformed men knock on her door and tell her how sorry they were, but that her husband had sacrificed himself…had been a hero. And if they had a daughter, she would be just like Shanna, dragging down the stairs in her ridiculous too-big pajamas and overhearing everything.

A wall of emotion rose up within her.

She couldn't do it.

She stood up and straightened her clothes. She needed to go see him in his office, if he was there. Tell him about her father. And then explain why she couldn't be involved with him, unless he was looking to exit the reserves in the next little while.

Except they wouldn't have hung that plaque if his discharge was imminent, would they?

There was only one way to find out.

Shanna's text was terse, consisting of only three words. Can we talk?

He thought they'd already talked. At dinner last night. Unless she'd had second thoughts.

And that was going to be a problem, because he cared about her. Way more than he should, despite everything he'd said about wanting to take things slow. For the first time, he wanted to keep seeing a woman. What he'd said was true. He wanted to take things slow. But hell, if she suddenly didn't, it was going to be a blow. A big one.

Because whatever this was with Shanna was different. He loved her joie de vivre, her zest and passion for her work and for life in general. He wasn't sure what was happening between them, but knew he wasn't ready for it to end. For the first time since Kristen had walked out on him, he wanted to be in a relationship.

Did he love her?

Maybe, but what if he was wrong about everything?

What if he was making another huge mistake? What if they both were, and she ended up walking away without a backward glance? His insides curdled, turning what he'd eaten that morning rancid.

So what to do about her text? All he could do was answer it.

I'm free now, if you are.

His phone pinged a second later.

On my way.

He started counting, somehow thinking that the seriousness of whatever this was might be able to be measured by how long it took her to get to his office.

He got to twenty before the knock came at his door. It was serious.

Taking a bracing breath, he said, "Come in."

She slid into the room with a stillness that sent a chill through him. There was no sign of the woman who had joked about role-playing and who'd taken him to places he hadn't known existed. No sign of the woman who said if he didn't like Cuban food, they were finished.

No sign of the woman who had softly kissed him last night before she got into her car to leave.

Shanna sat.

He waited. And waited.

A minute later, she drew a deep breath. "You mentioned you'd lived in the Panhandle before moving to Tampa. Did you work at a hospital there?"

"At times."

"What does that mean exactly? *Where* did you work?"

Why was she asking about that? Whatever it was, he sensed this was not the time to beat around the bush or give her vague answers. Although he didn't see how any of it mattered unless her belief system somehow didn't allow for military service. He tried again. "I was a combat field surgeon, then when back in the States I worked at a military hospital."

She swallowed visibly. "Why didn't you tell me this last night?"

"It didn't seem relevant to our conversation. Is it?"

She slowly nodded. "Maybe not to you. But it is to me. I told you my dad died when I was a kid."

"Yes."

She bit her lip as if not sure exactly what she wanted to say or how to say it. "I can still picture where I was when I heard the news. I remember my mom crying. I came downstairs and saw men in uniforms standing in our living room. They were awkwardly patting her on the shoulder. And I knew then and there that something horrible had happened. To my dad. They mentioned sacrifice and how he'd saved other people." Her chin trembled. "He wasn't supposed to die. He was on a peacekeeping mission and instead ended up being blown up."

His insides twisted. He had a feeling he knew exactly where this was going. "I'm so sorry, Shanna. I can't imagine being a child and learning about my dad that way."

"I like you, Zeke. A lot. But…"

His brows went up. "But?"

"How long will you be in the reserves?"

Memories of his arguments with Kristen came roaring back. Arguments he never wanted to have again. He kept his voice very soft as he answered. "My contract is for four years."

"Four…" She stopped, her eyes closing for a few seconds before looking at him again. "And you can be called into active duty at any time during those four years?"

He eyed her. "It's a possibility, yes." He leaned across the desk. "Shanna, I'm sorry about what happened to your dad, and I understand what you must be—"

"I'm not sure you do. Can you guarantee that you won't die on some road on the other side of the world?"

She knew he couldn't. No one could.

"You know I can't promise that. But I was a field surgeon. That's different from being a soldier who goes into battle."

"That's just it. My dad wasn't supposed to be going into battle, either."

"I'm still trying to figure out exactly what this means. Are you saying you don't want to date me now that you know?"

If she was going to ask him to leave the reserves, he couldn't. Not without a valid reason, and he didn't think *my girlfriend doesn't want me to serve* qualified any more now than it had when Kristen had asked him to leave the military.

Wasn't this what he'd dealt with last time? And he and Shanna weren't even serious yet. But he'd wanted to get there.

And now? He was having some serious reservations.

"I don't know what I'm trying to say. I just feel like this came out of nowhere."

He took a deep breath. "Listen, I know it's scary. I know what you went through hurt, and I'm not trying to discount any of it. But my service means a lot to me. It means a lot to my dad, who can barely even recognize me now..." He drew a deep breath. "Even if I wanted to, I can't get out of my contract, Shanna. Can you somehow see past this and still give us a chance?"

Her eyes filled, a single tear coursing down her cheek that turned his insides to an agonizing fire he felt sure would consume him.

"I can't, Zeke. I'm so, so sorry, but I just can't." She stood and swiped at the moisture on her cheek.

He tried to reach out one last time. "Maybe talk to your mom about your dad and ask if she'd do it all over again, if she had the chance."

"None of that really matters now. Because it changes nothing. He died. And she suffered horribly."

She was right. They could talk about what-ifs all day long, but when it came down to it, if she wasn't willing to take the risk, then they might as well throw in the towel before they even got started.

"I'm sorry, Shanna."

"So am I. This isn't easy."

And yet it seemed like it was. At least for her. Maybe he could at least affirm her in her decision, so they could both move on.

"Since it seems there's nothing left to say, let's forget last night ever happened and go back to the lives we'd planned to live. Agreed?"

"Agreed." As she walked to the door, he murmured, "I'm sorry about your dad, Shanna. I truly am. I have a feeling a lot of his best traits show up in you."

As soon as she left the room, he sank back in his chair and pressed his fingers to his eyelids to keep his own emotions in check. And with that, he picked up the phone and dialed a familiar number.

When she answered, it took him a minute to respond in a voice he hoped passed as normal. "Hi, Mom. How's Dad?"

He listened as she talked for a few minutes, putting a positive spin on most of it. But then again, that was his mom. She'd always been a glass-half-full type of person. When she turned the conversation back toward him, asking how he was, he suddenly knew what he wanted to do. What he *needed* to do.

"Would it be okay if I came home for the weekend?"

"Of course it would be. Is everything okay?"

His teeth clenched for a second. "Things here are okay. I'm just homesick and want to see you both."

"Oh, honey. You know you can always come home. Always."

He needed to end this conversation before she realized everything around him was falling apart. "Okay. I'll see you tomorrow."

Shanna barely made it out of his office before she had to rush to the bathroom and lock herself in a stall as more tears silently dripped down her cheeks. How could something that had looked so promising end so badly? And yet he'd said he could see her dad in her without ever having known him.

If she'd known who he was from the very beginning would she have kissed him on the beach? Slept with him? *Fallen* for him?

Because she knew without a doubt she had. Fallen for him. Head over heels. Only to have everything derailed by one tiny omission. Two, really. Because if she had shared how her dad had died, he might have told her he was still in the service and things would have ended with a smile and handshake.

Except when she had stumbled on him in the waiting room, looking so defeated after Matthew Landrum's death, how could she say that the outcome wouldn't have been the same? That they wouldn't have slept with each other?

But at least then she would have known the score. Would have known it really was just a fling.

You can't help who you fall in love with.

Maybe not, but you sure as hell could decide whether or not you acted on it.

And to have to give his heart patients breathing treatments, knowing that at any moment Zeke could walk in and stir up feelings that were almost unbearable, made her cringe.

He might never be called to duty. Maybe she'd been stupid in talking to him before having all of her facts straight.

She should talk to someone about what being in the reserves actually entailed.

Making two phone calls only made her shoulders dip. Yes, they could be deployed. Sometimes overseas and sometimes they could be sent to national disaster areas within the United States. That she could have handled. But the possibility of losing him in either one of those scenarios?

He'd told her to talk to her mom. But she couldn't. Not right now. Maybe in a few weeks when the dust in her heart had settled a bit.

In the meantime, she wanted to talk to Dan Brian about an idea she'd had a while ago and see if he might be interested.

"So you would work some days at the hospital and some days out in the community, is that what you're saying?"

"Yes. As you know, I'm licensed as a home health

respiratory therapist as well as hospital work. Would there be any grant money that could go toward some kind of clinic? Even just in a rented building or a mobile unit that could act as a clinic? Kind of like the blood banks do?"

Dan twirled a pencil, stopping periodically to jot notes to himself. She sure hoped those notes were about what they were discussing. "This couldn't happen right away, you understand. I'll need to research it and see if there are precedents anywhere in Florida."

"So it could take how long, do you think?"

"I'm thinking a year or two." He frowned. "You're not thinking of quitting, are you, Shanna? We'd sure hate to lose you."

And she'd hate to leave the hospital. But right now, the options were stay and wait. Or stay...and stay.

"I'm not thinking about it. But I would sure like to get out into the community. The Halloween event is great, but I also want to do some practical stuff for people who can't afford treatments or medications."

"I get it. And we do have a safety net of sorts. It's just not as good as we'd like it to be, yet."

"I understand. If you can just check into it and let me know if there's hope, or if it's an impossible task. I know you'll give me an honest answer either way."

He nodded, eyes narrowing. "Is there something behind this? Something I can help with?"

Could he somehow change that plaque under Zeke's picture and give it an ending date that wasn't four years away?

Glinda certainly could have. But unfortunately, unlike the good witch, she didn't possess any magical powers. Other than to fall in love with the wrong man.

Only he wasn't the wrong man. He was just in a profession that had caused her and her mom such pain. Well, she'd just have to see how the next week or so went and see if there were ways to avoid working directly with him.

Zeke was gone.

When she got to work Monday morning and heard he wasn't there, she was sure he'd been called to duty.

Her heart squeezed. And if he was?

Oh, God. What if he was?

"Do you know when he'll be back?"

"I'm not sure," Maura said. "He's asked the hospital to reroute his cases to Dr. Bernard at County General."

"And you don't know where he went?"

Maura looked at her a little closer. "I don't know. I just know it was sudden."

Was it because of what she'd said to him in his office? Could he actually ask to be deployed? Was that even a thing?

The panic from seeing his picture in that hallway rose up in her again. "Okay, thanks. I just wasn't sure what to do with any of his cases."

"As far as I know, he has nothing pending. Maybe check with Pulmonology." Maura smiled. "I'm sure they have plenty to keep you busy."

She was sure they did. But they couldn't keep her

mind from running through some pretty horrific scenarios. Like what if he weren't even in the United States anymore? She had no idea how she'd even go about contacting him.

And why would she need to? Hadn't they said everything that needed saying?

She thought they had. Until now.

He'd told her to go and talk to her mom. Maybe that's exactly what she should do.

"Thanks, Maura. I'll check with them."

As soon as she could get away for the day, she headed for her mom's house. But the second she opened the door, the floodgates opened and, try as she might, she couldn't get them closed again.

Her mom dragged her into the house, folding her in her arms. "What is it?"

"I... It's Zeke." Her voice shook so hard, she could barely get the words out.

"Oh, honey. Is he okay?"

She shrugged, then realizing her mom might think the worst, she managed to get out, "As far as I know he is, but..."

"Tell me what's going on."

"I think I did something stupid. Really stupid."

Her mom eased her over to the couch and helped her down onto it. "I'm sure whatever it is can be undone."

"I don't think this can."

"Are you pregnant?"

Her eyes widened. "Of course not."

Leave it to her mom to pretty much know where things stood between her and the surgeon.

"Well… You care about him, don't you? And although he hasn't said anything, I'm pretty sure he cares about you."

"I don't see how that will make any difference at this point. I—I just can't be with him."

Her mom rolled her eyes. "That tells me exactly nothing. Unless he's been diagnosed with some horrible disease and only has a few months to live, then…"

He hadn't. But his dad had been diagnosed with one. The thought made her feel even worse.

"Mom, can you sit down for a minute?"

Her mom perched on a chair across from her and watched her. "Okay. I'm ready."

"Zeke is in the army reserves."

She blinked. "So?"

Her mom didn't see what the problem was.

As if hearing her thoughts, she went on. "Shanna, where is this going?"

She took a deep breath. "I have kind of a weird question to ask you. It's about Dad. We never really talked about what happened the day he died."

"I know. You were only ten. And you can't know how many times I tried to look at that day through your eyes, and it's just so terrible. To have found out that way. And then I had to get help…"

The thought of making her mom relive that time almost made her back out of asking the question Zeke had suggested she ask. But she had to know. She reached and grasped her mom's hand. "What advice would you have given Dad back then if you could foresee the future? Foresee what would happen to him?"

Her mom gripped her hand back. "I would have told him to be more careful. But he had an injured buddy in a truck nearby and was anxious to get him back to the base. Only the bomb went off and killed him. But his friend lived. And knowing that would have made him happy."

It wasn't quite what she was looking for. "If you knew ahead of time that Dad would die, would you have married him? Would you have asked him to leave the military?"

Her mom's head tilted. "Oh, honey. No. I would never have asked that. He loved his job more than anything except us. If you're asking if I have regrets over marrying him, no. Not one. Even after what happened. I had your father for twelve wonderful years. That's more than some people ever get."

For some reason that didn't help her. She didn't want Zeke for one year or four… But she also realized how wrong it was for her to even hint that he should try to get out of his contract. That's not what love was. Love meant sacrifice. Loving someone so much that you want the very best for them. Even if it meant their death.

How many firefighters had run into burning buildings only to never reemerge? How many people died every day during the course of doing their jobs or even just helping others?

She'd made this all about her and her fears and had thought very little of the whys behind what Zeke did. Zeke's patient had died, devastating him. But did that mean he wouldn't try to do the surgery that first time, just because of what *might* happen? Their world would probably be paralyzed if everyone thought like she did.

Zeke might die any number of ways. So might she. But did that mean they shouldn't try to grasp at happiness when it was within reach?

God. No. It didn't.

Why hadn't she seen that a week ago, when she'd freaked out over that plaque? Maybe because she'd never really dealt with the grief of her father's death. But what her mom had said really had helped her see it from a different perspective.

If she knew her father was going to die, would she have rather never known him at all? Or did those memories of all of those happy Halloweens supersede what had happened when she was ten?

Of course it did. She'd loved her dad with a fierce love that survived even his death.

"One more question, Mom. Do you mind if I head home? I need to find a way to get in contact with someone."

"Zeke?"

She nodded.

"Do you want his address? I have it on his mortgage paperwork."

"I don't think he's there."

Her mom frowned. "Where is he, then?"

"That's just the problem. I don't know. But I need to find him before it's too late."

"It's never too late."

"It might be this time, Mom, but I need to try." Shanna hesitated before adding, "I want to be more fearless, like you."

"Honey, I am not fearless. I just don't know where or when my road is going to end. So I want to do all the living I can right now. You daddy taught me that."

"See? That's exactly what I mean. I think maybe today is the day I need to take that leap."

"All I'm going to say is maybe try to call his cell phone."

His cell phone. Why hadn't she thought of that? "Mom, you are a genius. Thank you!"

She went over and gave her mom a big hug. "I love you."

"I love you, too."

As she headed to the door, her mom said, "Where are you going?"

She turned back and smiled. "I'm going home. To make a very important phone call."

Her mom held up crossed fingers. "Good luck. Just tell him how you feel, honey. Because if things are as bad as you say they are, that might be the only way to make things right."

"I will. And thank you."

She got to her house and leaped out of her car, making her way to the door. What if he was overseas already? Would his cell phone even work? Surely Everly Memorial would know if he was going to be gone for months on end, wouldn't they? Unless he'd quit. Unless he couldn't stand the sight of her.

She swallowed. Could she bear to hear the truth if it were that devastating?

Spending a minute trying to do some of the breathing exercises she gave her patients, she finally screwed up the courage to dial that number rather than just shoot off a text message. Like she'd told her mom, now was the time to be fearless. No matter what the cost.

The phone rang once, twice, three times. Just when she thought it might roll over to voice mail, he answered. "Give me a sec to get out of this."

Get out of what? Was he in danger?

"Wh-where are you, Zeke?"

There was no answer. In the background, she thought she could hear the sound of engines rumbling. Tanks? Military equipment?

"Zeke?"

The sounds faded to nothing. And still his voice hadn't come back on.

Her heart pounded in her chest as myriad thoughts careened across her brain, none of them making any sense.

"Okay, now I can talk. Unless you're going to tell me to go away."

"Go away?" She shook her head. Hadn't he already done that? "Zeke, I'm so sorry—"

Her doorbell rang.

God, not now!

She was just going to let it ring. This was way more important. "I'm so sorry for what I said in your office. You haven't been at work… Did you ask them to deploy you?"

"Deploy me? Why would you think that?"

"Maybe because if I were you I wouldn't be able to stand the sight of me."

Her doorbell rang again. Still she didn't move.

"Someone's at your door, Shanna."

"I don't care."

There was a pause. "I hope that's not true. Come see who it is."

Why did that sentence sound wonky? Shouldn't he have said, "*Go* see who it is"?

Come see.

Her hand went to her mouth as she stood with shaking legs and somehow made it over to the door. Opened it.

There stood Zeke. *Her* Zeke.

"But how…? Where were you?"

"I decided to take my own advice," he said. "Can I come in?"

"Of course." She stood aside and waited for him to get inside before closing the door behind him.

"What advice is that?"

"I went home to talk to Mom. About whether she would marry Dad all over again, even if she knew what was coming."

Shanna nodded. "And she said she would."

"How did you know that?"

She wrapped her arms around his neck and held him closer than she'd ever held anyone in her life. And then she stood on tiptoe to whisper in his ear, "Because my mom said the very same thing. And I realized she was right. And I was wrong."

His fingers tangled in her hair and held her there for several minutes. "Not wrong, Shanna. Just scared. As scared as I was of losing you, just as I'd realized I love you."

"Y-you love me?"

"Isn't it obvious?"

She leaned back and looked at him. "No. Is it obvious that I love you?"

This time he laughed. "No. But you do?"

She nodded. "I do."

"I should have done a better job of listening when you came to my office. But I'd had a relationship end over my refusal to leave the military, and it seemed like history might be repeating itself. I just couldn't see past that. Couldn't think of the right words to say."

"I get it. And I'm sorry I made you feel that way. I did think about resigning my position here at the hospital, though. I wasn't sure I'd be able to see you day in and day out without telling you how I felt."

Her eyes widened. "Wow. I talked to Dan about working out in the community for the same reason. He wouldn't give me the green light until he'd studied it more. So... Here I am, making a phone call to you instead and praying I'd get to tell you how I feel before it's too late."

He cupped her cheeks and kissed her. "Obviously, it's not too late. For either of us. Oh, wait, I almost forgot. I have something for you."

"What is it?"

"Stay here. I have to get it out of my car."

Puzzled, she let go of him and watched as he walked back through her door, closing it behind him. It sent a chill through her before she forced her heart to calm its pace. He'd be back. This was hello, not goodbye.

Her bell rang again, and she laughed. "Zeke, what in the world…?"

When she opened it, he stood on her step again, this time holding a pumpkin that was flickering with light. And on its surface he'd carved a heart. Only this time, it wasn't the complex heart of his medical profession. It was a simple cartoon-style heart that sat in the middle of two words.

She read it out loud. "*I heart you.*' Oh, Zeke…"

"I really do."

"I love you, too." To keep from weeping, she wrinkled her nose and tried to show him how happy she was instead. "But… You have to promise me you'll keep dressing up for Halloween. Because that pirate costume…" She kissed her fingertips and blew it away. "It was very, very sexy."

He went over and set the pumpkin on her coffee table and then swept her into his arms, settled them down onto the couch and kissed her shoulder. "I'm pretty sure your *Wizard of Oz* costume blew mine out of the water. But for now, how about we settle for you and me and a reality I never thought could happen."

"You and me. That is better than any costume I could imagine."

With that, he pulled her in for a long, sexy kiss whose magic promised to take them into the future. And beyond.

EPILOGUE

SHE HELD HIS hands to her lips and kissed his knuckles. "I'm so very proud of you, Zeke. Proud of your work at the hospital. Proud of the work you've done for the military."

Their relationship had survived his time in the reserves and had even survived a deployment. It hadn't been easy, and there had been bumps along the way, but she wouldn't change a thing. Not one single thing.

Zeke's dad had been able to come to their wedding three years ago, and watching her husband as he'd kissed his father's brow during the reception had been her undoing. She'd had to bury her face into his tux for several minutes as he'd stroked her hair and held her tight.

It was worth it. Every painful, wonderful minute of this thing called life.

As Zeke stood in his military uniform on his last day of service, holding their three-year-old little boy, while she cradled their infant daughter, she realized she could never imagine her life any other way.

It was true. She was proud of him. Proud of the life

they'd carved out for themselves. And most of all, she was proud that they'd both been fearless enough to risk everything. For each other.

For love.

* * * * *

COMING SOON!

We really hope you enjoyed reading this book. If you're looking for more romance be sure to head to the shops when new books are available on

Thursday 26th October

To see which titles are coming soon, please visit

millsandboon.co.uk/nextmonth

MILLS & BOON

MILLS & BOON®

Coming next month

THE NURSE'S HOLIDAY SWAP
Ann McIntosh

Those penetrating hazel eyes locked on hers, searching and sending heat cascading through her veins.

"If you're in pain, you could go home. No one would blame you."

"Don't be silly," she replied. Her breath wanted to catch in her chest. He was so close his warmth and delicious scent touched her, making her heart beat erratically. "I...I'm fine. Besides, we're short staffed."

She didn't think he moved, but suddenly the moment seemed incredibly intimate.

"Well, if you have to leave, just let them know I said you could."

It suddenly occurred to her that with the way they were positioned, if she lifted her chin just a little, she'd be perfectly positioned for his kiss, and her heart went from thumping to racing.

What are you thinking?

Totally flustered, she forced her gaze down to her lap and away from the temptation he offered. Had she really been about to make a fool of herself with her boss? Imagining the warmth in his gaze was more than friendly concern?

Gathering her composure and giving her head a mental shake, she straightened, making her face impassive.

"Don't fuss." She made her voice as firm as she could, adding a bit of a shooing gesture with her right hand in emphasis. "Go back to work and I'll be out in a minute."

Javi's gaze dropped to where her bare legs poked out from beneath the drape, and she immediately felt naked.

Exposed.

Funny how when he was bandaging her up that hadn't even crossed her mind!

"Right," he said, abruptly turning for the door. "See you on the ward."

And it was only when the door closed behind him that she could breathe again.

Continue reading
THE NURSE'S HOLIDAY SWAP
Ann McIntosh

Available next month
www.millsandboon.co.uk

LET'S TALK
Romance

For exclusive extracts, competitions
and special offers, find us online:

- MillsandBoon
- @MillsandBoon
- @MillsandBoonUK
- @MillsandBoonUK

Get in touch on 01413 063 232

For all the latest titles coming soon, visit
millsandboon.co.uk/nextmonth

GET YOUR ROMANCE FIX!

Get the latest romance news, exclusive author interviews, story extracts and much more!